• HERBAL HOMICIDE •

"The county medical examiner is going to do a post-mortem on Dr. Thornhill. He doesn't think the cause of death was a heart attack." Tracey paused, nervously twisting his cap in his hands, and then continued: "He thinks it was poison."

"I know," said Charlotte.

"You *know*!" Tracey stared at her.

"I figured it out. Look at this." She slid the herbal across the table, pointing to the passage on monkshood.

Tracey read the text, his finger leading his eye across the page. . . " 'Monkshood was imported by the colonials, who used it for relief of pain from rheumatism, pleurisy, peritonitis, and other ailments. . . . Its internal use has been discontinued because of its extreme toxicity.' "

Kitty sighed. "You know, I think I'll stop giving Stan that tincture of monkshood for his shoulder."

Charlotte Graham Mysteries by Stefanie Matteson

MURDER AT THE SPA
MURDER AT TEATIME

MURDER ON THE CLIFF
(*Coming in November*)

MURDER
AT
TEATIME

STEFANIE MATTESON

DIAMOND BOOKS, NEW YORK

MURDER AT TEATIME

A Diamond Book / published by arrangement with
the author

PRINTING HISTORY
Diamond edition / March 1991

ISBN: 1-55773-477-1

Diamond Books are published by The Berkley Publishing
Group, 200 Madison Avenue, New York, New York 10016.
The name "DIAMOND" and its logo are trademarks
belonging to Charter Communications, Inc.

PRINTED IN THE UNITED STATES OF AMERICA

10 9 8 7 6 5 4 3 2 1

For My Father

· I ·

CHARLOTTE GRAHAM STOOD on the landing and waved
goodbye to her friend Stan Saunders. At her back was the
base of a hillside on a spruce-covered island off the coast
of Maine. In front of her was the channel that separated the
island from the mainland, its swells crowned by whitecaps.
With her white skin, black hair, and tailored white blouse
and black suit, she looked as natural against the gray water
and rocky shore as an elegant, long-legged sea bird. Now in
her early sixties, she was still as regal as ever: the prominent
jaw with its wide, generous mouth, the broad-shouldered
figure that was so well-suited to the starkly tailored fashions that were her trademark—these were attributes that had
borne the years lightly. The glossy black hair, once worn in
a famous pageboy, was now pulled back in a tight chignon,
but no one could have mistaken the brisk, stylish stride that
was as much a part of her image as her clipped Yankee
accent. One of the most famous movie stars of her day, she
was revered by the American public not only for her talent
but also for her courage. In an age when studio makeup
men had turned starlets into look-alike glamor girls, she had
forbidden them to tamper with her heavy black eyebrows;
in an age when female stars could be either clotheshorses
or sexpots, she had fought bitterly for substantial roles, and
had gotten them; and in an age when a few wrinkles spelled
the end of a Hollywood career, she had gone on to triumph
on Broadway.

Which is what had brought her to this rugged island. For the first time in years she had nothing to do. As of Memorial Day she had been replaced in *The Trouble With Murder*. She had asked to leave: for two years the show had been her life and the Morosco Theatre her home. But the longer a show runs, the more difficult it is to keep fresh, and she had had enough. For the moment. The critics had hailed her performance "the triumphant conclusion of a brilliant career." Conclusion like hell. For the last twenty years the critics had been prophesying the twilight of her career. But she'd always proven them wrong. One had once cracked that her career had been recycled more times than a reusable soda bottle. The truth was, she needed to work. She didn't know anything else; she wasn't happy doing anything else. She would prove them wrong again. Meanwhile, she was treating herself to a much-needed vacation with her old friends Stan and Kitty Saunders.

It was a desolate spot to pick for a retirement home, she thought as she watched Stan guide his boat around the flank of the island. But it was ideal for Stan, who in his retirement was making a name for himself as a seascape painter. She had been friends with the Saunders for more than forty years. They had met on Cape Cod, where she and Kitty had been playing in summer stock, and Stan had been playing bohemian artist. Kitty and Stan had later married and had a family, forcing Stan to trade in his brushes for a more lucrative career in public relations. But he had never given up his dream of becoming a full-time painter. Now he was back in the same place he had been forty years ago. For that matter, so was Charlotte, though she had been there many times before: trying to find work—it was the chronic plight of the actor.

But she wasn't going to think about it now. Something would turn up—it always did. She looked up: all she had to think about now was getting to the top of the hill. Stan and Kitty's house was on the west end of the island, but Stan had dropped her off on the landing because she wanted to see the Ledges. The Ledges was the garden for which the island was famous. Not a garden exactly, but a network of winding stone-stepped paths and terraces sculpted out of the rocky hillside overlooking the channel. Rustic shelters and lookout benches were perched here and there for taking in the view of the harbor. Kitty had insisted that arriving via the Ledges was the only way to get the full flavor of the island. The Ledges was the life's work of a man named J. Franklin Thornhill, a professor of economic botany and an amateur landscape architect, who spent his summers in a cottage called Ledge House at the top of the hill.

From her vantage point Charlotte could see little more than the evergreen-studded hillside and the pink granite steps that marked the beginning of the path. Taking a deep breath of sweet sea air, pungent with the scent of rockweed, she set off toward the steps. After the pitch and roll of Stan's boat, the rocks under her feet felt very comforting. Manhattan suddenly seemed far, far away. Beyond the first few steps, the path took on the character of a wild rock garden. Lichens and mosses in various shades of green and gray clothed the rocks and tree trunks. Sheep laurel and low-bush blueberries, whose greenish fruits were already beginning to turn, nestled among the ledges. The woodsy scent of the blueberries, overlaid by the resiny scent of the balsam firs that blanketed the hillside, hung heavy in the warm afternoon air. Smell was said to be the most evocative of the senses, and surely no other sense could more keenly call to mind a time in which one was something else, maybe something better. For Charlotte, the smell of blueberries evoked memories of picking blueberries on Cape Cod with Stan and Kitty years ago. She remembered their innocence, but oddly enough had little recollection of her own.

Perhaps she'd always been cynical. Kitty's dream had always been to live with her family in a little white cottage surrounded by pink roses and a white picket fence, to greet her husband at the door at six with a martini in her hand and two charming children clinging to her skirts. If Charlotte had ever dreamed of a little white cottage, the dream had long ago been sacrificed to her career. Along with a few other things, like children. She had no regrets, but she sometimes envied Kitty the neatness of her life. Everything at the right time, in the right order. Smooth sailing all the way. How harmonious (if maybe a bit boring) to have had only one husband instead of four. Even though she'd had plenty of time to get used to it, the number—*four*—still offended her sense of order. She blamed her marital history on her Yankee heritage: her Yankee sense of propriety kept driving her back to the altar, and her Yankee sense of independence kept driving her away.

As the path ascended the hillside it became more shady. Ferns sprang from crevices in the granite slabs. Rustic cedar-log bridges crossed mossy rivulets that cascaded down the hillside. Pitch pines clung to weathered crags, their trunks dwarfed and gnarled like bonsai by the wind. Through the branches she occasionally caught a glimpse of the harbor. She could hear the rumble of engines as the boats came and went. Just as she was beginning to get winded, she saw a path leading off to the first of the shelters, a cedar pavilion built into the face of a huge granite bluff, like the shelter in a Japanese landscape painting. A few minutes later she was sitting in a wooden chair, her chest heaving. She was in good shape for a woman of her age, but she wasn't used to climbing cliffs. The view was every bit as spectacular as Kitty had led her to believe. The shelter seemed to be suspended in the air above the channel, the sides and roof forming a frame in which the harbor and the town of Bridge Harbor hovered between sea and sky in a nest of green hills. To the west lay the mansion-dotted shoreline that had once made Bridge Harbor the queen of summer resorts. To the east lay the bay, stretching away toward the horizon, its low-lying islands blending into a mass of soft, slate blue. Beyond the bay lay the mouth of the Bay of Fundy, and beyond that, the shores of Spain. She was reminded of the opening lines of a poem by Edna St. Vincent Millay: "All I could see from where I stood/Was three long mountains and a wood/I turned and looked the other way/And saw three islands in a bay."

After resting for a moment, she headed back to the main path. Stopping for a moment on a little bridge, she looked out at the streamlet that flowed between the walls of a fissure in a granite outcropping. At the foot of the outcropping, she could see the slipperlike sac of a pink lady-slipper growing under a huckleberry bush. Then she noticed another, and another. They were all over the place. They were now so rare it was unusual to see one, let alone dozens. She loved the sac with its delicate veins and its deep cleft. Stepping off the path for a closer look, she noticed a glint of blond out of the corner of her eye. She caught her breath. Pushing back the undergrowth, she felt her stomach contract. Hidden beneath the boughs of a juniper bush overhanging the streamlet lay the dead body of a golden retriever. The dog's head rested in a pool of vomit. The soft reddish-gold tendrils of fur were already beginning to dry into a stiff, brown mat. His lips were lined by white froth, and his protruding eyes were ringed by a circle of red. "The poor thing," she said to herself. Kneeling down, she felt the dog's stomach, which was already beginning to swell. He'd been dead for only fifteen, maybe twenty minutes, she guessed. Gently, she ran her hands over the body. No wounds. Maybe he had died of some disease, but she doubted it; it looked as if he'd suddenly been taken ill. Maybe he had come to the streamlet for water.

She had once had a dog who died like this. He had been poisoned. She never found out by what, or by whom. She preferred to think he had accidentally gotten into some rat poison.

But she had always wondered if it had been deliberate.

·2·

CHARLOTTE AWOKE THE next morning with a vague sense of disquietude. For a moment she wondered why, and then remembered the dog. His name was Jesse, and he had belonged to Dr. Thornhill. But he had been a friend of everyone on the island. He had made a habit of greeting everyone who landed at the Ledges landing, and had probably been on his way down to greet Charlotte when he got sick. Stan had broken the news to Dr. Thornhill shortly after Charlotte's arrival. On his pre-bedtime walk later that night, Stan had run into Maurice, the Ledge House handyman, who told him that he'd buried Jesse in the rose garden outside of Dr. Thornhill's library that afternoon. According to Maurice, Dr. Thornhill hadn't left the library since, and as far as he knew was still sitting there, staring out at Jesse's grave. Dr. Thornhill was a widower, and Jesse had been his constant companion. Last night. The back of her head ached, and the inside of her mouth felt like cotton batting. When was the last time she had stayed up until all hours reminiscing and drinking brandy? She couldn't remember. Probably the last time she saw Stan and Kitty.

She lay in bed surveying her room, which was in the former hayloft of the barn. The Saunders had converted it into a cozy guest apartment, which was connected by a flight of stairs to the farmhouse kitchen. Plants hung in the floor-to-ceiling window, through which she could see a flat gray sky. From downstairs came the clatter of breakfast dishes and the boom of Stan's voice summoning her to breakfast. She sat up on the edge of the bed, her brains sloshing around in her head. Once Stan had sounded his bugle, there was no quarter given to sluggards. Getting out of bed, she walked over to the window. Below her, a lawn led down to a gate in a white picket fence (Kitty's dream come true). Beyond the fence lay a mist-shrouded cove surrounded by wild roses. In the middle of the cove stood a tiny spruce-covered island that looked as if it had floated in on the tide during the night. The spruces were tipped with gold: the rising sun was already beginning to shine through the fog. The island was one of many called Sheep Island, Kitty had said. She had explained that the early settlers had grazed their sheep on these little islands, where they were safe from predators and didn't need to be fenced in. On the other side of the cove stood a farmhouse that could have been a "before" to Stan and Kitty's "after": unpainted, falling down, overlooking a ramshackle wharf. Lending the perfect note of rustic authenticity to the picturesque scene.

But picturesque wasn't everything. How could they stand it? Charlotte wondered. It wasn't as if they'd grown up in the country. They'd spent their entire lives in the Boston suburbs. Route 128 was the closest they'd ever come to country living. Perhaps it was the romance of living on an island: the idea of being master and mistress of a minute world of pure perfection. But they could have found a more populated one. As far as she could tell, there were only three other households on the island: Dr. Thornhill, who lived at Ledge House with his niece; his daughter, Marion Donahue, who lived with her husband and son in a cottage out on the east end; and a lobsterman named Wes Gilley who lived with his family in the ramshackle farmhouse. Of the three, the Gilleys were the only other year-round residents. Kitty liked to think their isolation was relieved by the gravel bar or "bridge" from which the town took its name, but since the bar was passable for only a few hours a day, Kitty's sense of connectedness struck Charlotte as illusionary. If you dallied in town more than a couple of hours after low tide, you had to wait eight hours until the bar was again exposed by the receding tide to cross the channel—or cross it in a boat.

Even the larger world to which the bar linked the island wasn't all that large. With a population of five thousand—tripling to fifteen thousand in the summer—Bridge Harbor wasn't exactly a metropolis.

As far as Charlotte was concerned, they could have it. She got nervous after more than a few days in any place that didn't have sidewalks. She dressed quickly. It was none too warm in her unheated hayloft. After pinning her hair into a chignon, she descended the stairs to the kitchen.

The kitchen was a large, cozy room in the ell that linked the farmhouse to the barn. It was dominated by an old cast-iron cookstove that Stan was feeding with sticks of wood from a basket at his feet. The warmth of the stove was welcome. It was the kind of morning that gave rise to the saying that Maine has two seasons: winter, and August.

"How are you this morning, Charlotte?" boomed Stan as he lifted a lid off a burner to add another stick of wood to the fire. The inside of the firebox glowed red, and the stove made a contented thumping sound as it digested its meal of seasoned maple.

Charlotte poured herself a mug of coffee from the pot on a back burner. "A little rough around the edges," she replied. Taking a seat at the long pine table in front of the sliding glass doors overlooking the cove, she found herself studying her host.

Stan had undergone a metamorphosis since moving to Maine to pursue his dream of becoming a full-time painter. The once cleanshaven face was covered by a bushy, reddish-gray beard, and the three-piece suit had been replaced by paint-spattered dungarees, an Irish sweater, and a Greek fisherman's cap. He even moved differently, with the athletic grace of a man twenty years his junior. He was playing the role of the colorful marine painter to the hilt, thought Charlotte. And good for him—he'd waited long enough for the part.

"Retirement must agree with you, Stan," she said. "You look terrific."

"Thank you," he replied, joining her at the table with

a mug of coffee. "I owe it all to that witch doctor of a wife of mine. She's had me on this health kick: no sugar, no alcohol, red meat only in moderation." He gave her a sheepish look. "I cheat a little on that second one, as you know."

"A little?" teased Charlotte.

"He doesn't exactly look like he's suffering, does he?" said Kitty, who had entered from the adjacent dining room.

"Not a bit," agreed Charlotte.

Kitty stood at the counter with her hands on her hips, the picture of the well-preserved suburban matron. Her ash-blond hair was perfectly coifed, and her tall, slim figure was clad in matching pink slacks and monogrammed crewneck sweater. Her face barely showed her age, which was not surprising in light of the fact that she'd treated herself to a face-lift on her last birthday (Charlotte was one of the few in whom she'd confided, most of her friends having been told that she was vacationing in the Caribbean).

"I complain about it," Stan continued, changing his tone. "But I do feel a hell of a lot better. The newest twist is that she's using me as a guinea pig for one of her herbal remedies." He looked over at his wife. "Probably trying to poison me off so that she can cash in my life insurance policy."

Charlotte was glad to see that the change in Stan's outward appearance hadn't affected his personality: he was as curmudgeonly as always.

"Now darling," said Kitty with a reproving look, "you *know* that herbal remedy has worked. The rheumatism in his shoulder was so bad he couldn't even play golf," she explained. "And that's serious."

"You're damned right it's serious," barked Stan.

"We made the rounds of the Boston rheumatologists, but none of them could do a thing for him," Kitty went on. "Then I read in one of Frank Thornhill's books about an herbal remedy for rheumatism, and he's been fine ever since."

"It's true," Stan agreed. "The pain in my shoulder was so bad I could hardly lift a club, much less swing it. My game had gone all to hell. Now I'm shooting in the eighties again. I just rub on a little of the witch doctor's secret remedy, and the pain disappears like that." He snapped his fingers.

Charlotte looked skeptical.

"Really," said Kitty, as she buttered a plate of English muffins, "herbs are very effective. Many of our most potent modern medicines were originally derived from herbs. Digitalis, from the foxglove; morphine, from the opium poppy; atropine, from the deadly nightshade . . . "

"I gather this is the latest enthusiasm?" asked Charlotte, arching an eyebrow at Stan.

Stan nodded. "At least she's not on a redecorating kick," he said. "For a while there I couldn't keep the furniture down."

"Fran Thornhill, Frank's niece, has an absolutely glorious herb garden up at Ledge House," continued Kitty, joining them at the table with the English muffins. "She has her own mail-order herb business, 'Ledge House Herbs'—I've been working up there with her, helping her out."

She spoke as if there were an exclamation point after every other word. Charlotte was amused by the fact that her affectedly stagy speech had become more pronounced with time, like the British expatriates whose Mayfair accents become more clipped the longer they spend on American soil.

"The locals call her a witch," said Stan, reaching for a jar of marmalade. "Next thing you know they'll be calling you a witch, too."

"A white witch. Like Glenda, the good witch of the east."

Charlotte smiled as Stan slathered a muffin with a quarter-inch of marmalade while Kitty looked on in mute disapproval. It looked as if Kitty's prohibition against sugar, like that against alcohol, was honored more in the breach than in the observance.

"Does she sell herbal remedies too?" asked Charlotte. "I should think that would be against the law."

"It is. Practicing medicine without a license. Besides, it's dangerous—a lot of herbs are poisons. In small doses, they have therapeutic effects, but in large doses they can be deadly. 'What can kill, can cure,' goes the saying. For instance, the herb I'm using for Stan's rheumatism . . . "

"See what I told you?" interrupted Stan. "Watch out, or she'll be experimenting on you next."

"Oh hush," continued Kitty, unfazed. "I've learned a lot from Frank. He wrote the classic reference book on herbal remedies, *The Living Pharmacy*. He teaches economic botany at Harvard, or used to. He's cut back on his course load a lot in recent years because of his health."

"Pompous old fart if you ask me," commented Stan.

"We didn't ask you," chided Kitty. She turned to Charlotte. "He's dying to meet you. He says he's a fan."

"He sits all day in his library gloating over his rare books," continued Stan. "Wears white gloves so he won't get fingerprints on the pages."

"For your information, Stanton Saunders, he has one of the finest collections of rare botanical books in the country. He's very charming," Kitty went on, ignoring her husband. "Fran would like to meet you too. They've invited us over for cocktails this evening. Fran and I have planned something special. I hope you'll want to go."

"Of course," replied Charlotte. She didn't want to disappoint Kitty. Besides, she could hardly pick and choose among the social activities on this little island. She was about to ask Kitty more about the Thornhills, when there was a knock on the kitchen door.

The visitor was Howard Tracey, the Bridge Harbor chief of police. Because the tide was up he'd taken the police launch over from town, and docked it at the Saunders' wharf.

As a police chief, Charlotte thought, he wasn't very convincing, but then Bridge Harbor wasn't East Harlem. He had a round, boyish face that was shaded by the visor of a baseball cap. A badge was pinned to his windbreaker.

Although Stan didn't introduce her—he had long ago learned that she preferred anonymity—she found Tracey studying her intently.

"Pardon me, ma'am," he said tentatively, "I hope you won't think me out of place if I say you're the spitting image of the movie star Charlotte Graham."

Charlotte smiled. She was used to being mistaken for herself by fans who couldn't quite believe she was for real. She was about to explain, when she caught the twinkle in his mild blue eyes.

She threw back her head and laughed. "You're putting me on," she said delightedly in her famous voice, which was at once both soft and husky.

"We've been expecting you," said Tracey. He removed his hat, and crossed the room to shake Charlotte's hand. "The *Bridge Harbor Light* ran an item that you'd be staying with the Saunders." He extended his hand and smiled broadly.

Leave it to Kitty to blab. But no harm done. She returned his handshake, smiling at him warmly with her large, pale gray eyes.

"Would you like a cup of coffee, Chief?" asked Stan, inviting him to join them at the kitchen table. "We also have some of my wife's herb tea," he added with an expression of distaste.

"Coffee's fine, thanks," replied Tracey, taking a seat.

"What brings you over here?" asked Stan as he poured out another mug. "I don't imagine you crossed the channel just for a cup of coffee."

"Can't say that I did," replied Tracey. "It's Jesse, Dr. Thornhill's dog." He looked over at Charlotte. "I heard about how you found him on the Ledges."

Charlotte nodded.

"Dr. Thornhill called me about him last night," Tracey continued. "He thinks he was poisoned."

"Charlotte thought the same thing," said Kitty. "Do you think it might have to do with the development?"

"What development?" asked Charlotte.

"The Chartwell Corporation's planning to build a big resort out here," explained Tracey. "Biggest on the New England coast. The Bridge Harbor Resort Hotel—hotel, condos, golf course, conference center, nightclub—you name it." He spoke with a thick Maine accent in which "harbor" came out *haba*.

Charlotte was familiar with the name—the biggest builder of resort complexes and theme parks in the country. "Where?" she asked.

"The hotel would go on the site of Ledge House," explained Stan. "The condos and golf course would go out on the east end, near the Donahues' place."

What would happen to the Ledges? Charlotte wondered. The image passed through her mind of armies of camera-toting tourists littering its beautiful terraces with cigarette butts and soda cans.

"They're planning to build a causeway where the bar is," added Kitty. She turned to Tracey. "About Jesse, poor thing. Do you think those dreadful CCC people have been causing trouble again?"

Tracey frowned. "Maybe."

Charlotte was baffled. "CCC?" she asked.

"Citizens for the Chartwell Corporation," explained Stan. "They'd like to see the town get the jobs. The county's got the highest unemployment rate in the State. Chartwell says the hotel alone will create four hundred jobs."

"They've been causing trouble up at Ledge House, or at least someone has," Tracey said. "Last week somebody put a bullet through one of the library windows, and let the air out of the tires of the Ledge House jeep. Poison-pen letters too, some of them pretty vicious . . . "

"Dr. Thornhill's against the development?" interjected Charlotte.

"Dead against it," said Tracey.

"I don't get it," said Charlotte. "If he owns the site that's been proposed for the development, why is it even being considered?"

"It's a long story," said Stan. "The development scheme was cooked up by Frank's son-in-law, Chuck Donahue. An insurance broker from Boston. He's got some connection with the Chartwell Corporation. He's got about a hundred acres or so out on the east end that he's anxious to unload.

He's in the deal with our neighbor, Wes Gilley, who's also got a hundred acres or so."

"They've been putting the pressure on Frank to go along with them, but so far it hasn't worked," said Kitty.

"They're hoping he'll croak," said Stan.

"What do you mean?"

"Well, the professor's getting up there," explained Tracey. "He's still pretty vigorous, but he's got a bad heart, and the odds are he's not going to be around much longer. They're figuring he'll leave the place to Marion, Chuck's wife. She'll be able to do what she wants with it."

"Like sell out to Chartwell."

"Or some other developer," said Tracey. "The island's a choice piece of real estate. Chartwell's not the only one with their eye on it."

Stan got up to refill their coffee mugs. Charlotte wondered where he and Kitty stood on the issue. On Thornhill's side, no doubt.

"The trouble is, it's hard for me to keep an eye on things out here," Tracey continued. "I haven't got the staff to put a man out here full time. Of course, if there was someone responsible staying out here who would be willing to keep an eye on things for me . . . "

Charlotte smiled, amused at the New England way of doing business. The subject at hand was always dealt with indirectly, as if it would be bad manners to actually come to the point. There was a charming formality to it that harked back to the courtliness of an earlier era.

She looked over Tracey, only to find him looking right back at her—much to her surprise. She thought he had been appealing to Stan and Kitty.

"I know you've had some experience at police work," he continued, a twinkle in his eye. "I've read *Murder at the Morosco*. I'm a bit of a crime buff, you see. I'll read anything that has to do with detection."

Two years before, Charlotte had helped solve the sensational murder of her co-star in *The Trouble With Murder*. A young reporter for a New York magazine had done an article on the case, which he had later expanded into a book. Called *Murder at the Morosco*, it had been a best seller.

"That was a little different," she said with a rueful smile. "I was directly involved." She had shot Geoffrey on opening night during the murder scene, with a bullet that the murderer had planted in a stage prop.

"It must have been a surprise," said Tracey with Yankee understatement.

"It was," she replied, remembering her astonishment at seeing real blood oozing from the wound. She'd suspected all along that it was Geoffrey's lover who'd tampered with the gun, but it had taken her weeks to gather the evidence that had cleared her of suspicion, and put him behind bars.

"One question," said Charlotte. "Do Wes Gilley and Chuck Donahue have anything to do with the CCC?"

Tracey nodded.

"They founded it," said Stan.

It was an ugly situation, Thornhill's son-in-law and his neighbor inciting the community against him. She made a mental note to find out more about Gilley from Stan and Kitty.

"How are relations between Donahue and Dr. Thornhill?"

"Not as bad as you might think," replied Tracey, taking a sip of coffee. "The Professor thinks the world of Marion. He didn't approve when she decided to marry Chuck. She had a promising career as a concert pianist, just like her mother. I guess he figured an early marriage would put an end to it."

"Did it?"

"Ayuh. Though she still gives piano lessons, I think. He still doesn't approve of Chuck, especially since the Chartwell business. But he tries to keep relations cordial, on the face of it anyways. For the sake of Marion and the boy, Kevin. The other boy died in an accident a couple of years ago."

"I'd be happy to do anything I can," said Charlotte. For a Mainer, Tracey had actually been quite direct, she thought. He hadn't even prefaced his request with a commentary on the weather.

"Thanks," replied Tracey. He withdrew a business card from his wallet and passed it across the table to her. "It won't be much of a bother—just a matter of calling the station to report anything out of the ordinary."

Charlotte nodded.

Tracey drank the rest of his coffee, and rose to leave. "We're mighty pleased to have someone of your stature visiting Bridge Harbor, Miss Graham," he said, tipping his baseball cap. "Kind of puts the town on the map."

Charlotte smiled. It isn't difficult for one actor to recognize another, and in Tracey she spotted an amateur who took as much delight in his role of country police chief as she did in hers as movie queen.

But she knew he wasn't the least bit starstruck by her fame. She also knew he was a lot shrewder than he made himself out to be.

Once the fog had burned off, it turned out to be a beautiful day—cool, crisp, and clear, with puffy white clouds floating in a sky of lapis blue. While Kitty puttered around the house and Stan worked in his studio—he had a show coming up in Boston—Charlotte explored the neighborhood, if that's what you'd call it. Her first destination was the cove, where she sat on a driftwood log on the shingle beach, watching the sailboats slide across the pale blue water and inhaling the fragrance of wild roses and rockweed, which mingled deliciously with that of the wood smoke from the cook-stove. Now that the fog had lifted, she could see the sprawling mansions on the opposite shore, whose owners, the great industrial and banking figures of the Gilded Age, had referred to in mock humility as "cottages." Although the stretch of shoreline was still known as Millionaires Row, most of the larger houses were no longer in private hands. Too costly to maintain, they had been donated to charity or converted into hotels or rest homes. But Bridge Harbor still maintained its reputation as the unpretentious summer hideaway of the country's oldest, wealthiest, and most influential families, and it was no doubt this cachet that the

developers of the Bridge Harbor Resort Hotel were hoping
to cash in on for their honeymoon-and-golf resort. Which
was how she thought of it, like the honeymoon-and-golf islands off the coast of Scotland.

From the cove, she followed a marshy path lined by
buttercups and elderberry bushes back to the road. Once
it passed the Gilley homestead—or rather junkyard, since
the area where a yard might have been was littered with
rusted-out junk—the road petered out into a wooded track
that ran along the north shore of the island, high above the
water. For a while she sat on a mossy promontory, chewing
on the leaves of the wintergreen plants that grew under the
firs, and watching a fat raccoon on the rocks below placidly
gorge himself on mussels, deftly washing and opening each
shell. She returned for a lobster-roll lunch with Stan and
Kitty on the patio. Then she took a nap.

A minute world of pure perfection.

Late that afternoon Charlotte and Kitty headed up to
Ledge House for cocktails. Charlotte was already familiar
with the route, having followed it from the top of the Ledges
the day before. The Gilley Road, as the road leading to the
Saunders' house was called, crossed open fields, now grown
up to wild roses and scrub. Just past the Saunders' house was
an old family cemetery, neatly demarcated by an iron fence
and studded with the weathered gravestones of the island's
settlers. Beyond the fields lay the sea, now a deep turquoise
in the late afternoon light. As they walked Kitty stopped to
fill a pillowcase with wild rose petals. The rose petals were
an ingredient in the Ledge House potpourri, one of the most
popular of the mail-order herb products. Leave it to Kitty to
find an outlet for her boundless energy even on this sparsely
populated island, thought Charlotte as she watched Kitty
shake rose petals into the pillowcase. For forty years Charlotte had looked on as Kitty flitted from project to project
with all the fickleness of a child at an amusement park.
Rarely did she stick with a new enthusiasm long enough
to accomplish anything. How different the story of her life
might have been if all the enthusiasm she had frittered away

on her various projects could have been channeled in one direction. Over the years Charlotte had often wondered why she and Kitty had remained friends; they were so different. She had concluded it was because Kitty reminded her of her mother, a gushing lover of ruffles and costume jewelry, whose childlike enthusiasm for the stage had propelled Charlotte into her career.

At the end of the Gilley Road they turned onto the island's main road. Facetiously named Broadway, it ran from the point where the bar joined the island uphill along the south shore to Ledge House and out to the Donahues' on the east end. Looking out over the blanket of roses, Charlotte could see the bar, which had emerged from the receding waters of the channel like the spine of a giant sea monster. As they turned onto Broadway her thoughts were interrupted by the chugging of a motorboat hidden behind the cliffs of the south shore. The sound was followed momentarily by the appearance of the boat itself, a battered old lobster boat skippered by a beer-bellied lobsterman who lifted his hand from the helm in a solemn greeting. He was accompanied by a young brown-haired girl, who waved at Kitty with a big smile.

"Wes Gilley and Tammy," said Kitty, waving back as the boat drew up to one of the buoys that marked the underwater location of the lobster pots.

Seeing Gilley reminded Charlotte that she had meant to ask Kitty about her neighbor. From the looks of his house, the money that he stood to make from the development would come in handy. But looks could be deceiving. The Maine lobsterman had a reputation for being as eager to exaggerate his poverty as the Texan is to exaggerate his wealth. If he worked at it, the lobsterman could make a good living. The question was whether Gilley worked at it.

"Were the Gilleys the original settlers of the island?" she asked, adopting the local practice of taking the indirect approach.

"Yes," Kitty replied. "A Gilley settled the island in the late seventeenth century. He was an Englishman, a naval officer I think. The story goes that he bought the island from the Indians for two quarts of rum."

"Cheaper than Manhattan Island," observed Charlotte.

Kitty smiled. "The old Gilley place used to stand on the site of Ledge House. It burned down years ago. Now all the Gilley Island Gilleys live in town, except for Wes and Virgie. It's hard for them, but they make ends meet."

"Do you think Gilley had anything to do with the trouble at Ledge House?" she asked, finally getting around to the subject.

"That's what Stan thinks," Kitty replied, adjusting the flowered headband that was color-coordinated with her pink sweater. "But I don't believe it."

"Why not?"

"I know he looks like a derelict, but he's really a dear. He's always bringing us something: lobsters, firewood, homemade jelly. Generous as the day is long. His family's lovely, too. Virgie's just as sweet as can be, and the children are adorable. Tammy and Kim are over at our house all the time."

Spotting another rosebush, Kitty ran off to collect more petals, leaving Charlotte to picture Wes without the benefit of her friend's rose-colored glasses. Had what she said meant that Wes really was Mr. Niceguy? or only that she wanted him to be? With Kitty, it was often hard to tell the difference.

"Charlotte, you should see the way they live," Kitty continued, rejoining her. "They don't even have indoor plumbing, much less television. That's why the girls come over, to watch TV. You should have seen what they got for Christmas last year. It was pathetic. I wanted to give them some presents, but Stan said it would be showing up their parents. I suppose he was right, but I gave them a little something anyway."

"But if the development goes through, their financial worries will be over," observed Charlotte. "I bet Chartwell's going to pay more than two quarts of rum for their land. What do they have? A hundred acres?"

"About that. But I don't think the development will go through. The way people in this town talk, you'd think it was a *fait accompli*. They don't realize how hard it is to get projects like this off the ground. Not to mention the fact that Frank wants nothing to do with it."

Past the rise, the open fields gave way to woods of tall pines. A stone fence ran along one side of the road, indicating that what was now woods had once been pasture.

They walked in silence, inhaling the bracing, resiny scent. Red squirrels chattered in the trees, and a sparrow whistled. Charlotte threw back her head and studied the pattern made by the pine branches against the sky. Maybe a place without sidewalks wasn't so bad after all.

Ahead, the Ledge House barn came into view, a beautiful old structure that seemed to antedate the house. It had probably been part of the original Gilley homestead. Beyond it lay the herb garden.

"If you don't think Gilley is responsible," said Charlotte, picking up the thread of their conversation, "then who do you think is?"

"I don't know. Maybe one of the other CCC people," Kitty replied. "Charlotte, you can't imagine how worked up they are. They're already talking about how they're going to spend all the money they'll make. Some of them have been really nasty to Frank. To us too, for that matter."

"Why you?"

"They know we're against Chartwell's coming in. Stan's spoken at several of the meetings. And you know Stan— he doesn't mince words."

Charlotte smiled. He was also an outsider. The Saunders had recently been elevated from the rank of mere tourists to that of "year-round summer people," but they would never have the same status as natives. In New England anyone who couldn't trace their ancestry back to the Revolution was a newcomer.

"I know one thing for sure," said Kitty as they approached the gap in the stone fence that marked the entrance to the herb garden.

Ahead they could hear the low murmur of conversation punctuated by occasional laughter.

"What's that?" asked Charlotte as Kitty turned to open the gate.

"Wes didn't poison Jesse. He loved that dog like he loves his own children."

·3·

THEY ENTERED THE herb garden via a path of crushed pink granite that led to an open area in front of the barn. Two men were seated in lawn chairs in the open area facing the garden. One of them rose to approach them. He was a tall, impressive-looking man with wire-rimmed glasses, a thick red mustache, and a stiff military bearing. He was casually dressed in a golf sweater.

"Frank Thornhill," he said, introducing himself. He turned to Kitty: "Kitty, we're delighted that you and Stan are willing to share your famous guest with us for the evening. We're sorry he couldn't be here."

Kitty explained about Stan's show.

"I've been an admirer of yours ever since I first saw you on the screen," continued Thornhill, turning back to Charlotte. "It was in 1942. I waited in the cold for hours. Rumor had it that you'd be making a personal appearance, but you never showed up. Now I'm finally meeting you in person."

"I hope you're not disappointed," she said, flashing him the coquettish smile that she reserved for gentlemen admirers of a certain age.

"On the contrary, you are even more beautiful in person than you are on the screen—if that's possible."

Charlotte smiled again.

Taking her commandingly by the elbow, he led her toward the cluster of chairs. "I was twenty-five, as I recall, and, I confess, smitten," he went on, puffing on the pipe he held in one hand. "I can even remember the name of the picture— it was *The Scarlet Lady*."

Charlotte groaned. "That's one I've tried to forget. It was one of those ghastly costume dramas," she explained to Kitty. "People only went to it to see what I wore—it was my clotheshorse period."

"That may be," said Thornhill with a little nod. "But if I may be impertinent, what a horse!"

Charlotte laughed the deep, husky laugh for which she was famous. "I'll have to keep that in mind for my epitaph," she said. "Now it's my turn to compliment you. I had the pleasure of climbing the Ledges yesterday."

A shadow crossed Thornhill's face. *Of course*, Charlotte thought. He would have been told that it was she who'd discovered Jesse.

"They are very beautiful," she told him.

He beamed, displaying a mouth full of large teeth yellowed to the shade of old ivory. "Thank you. My grandfather was a banker who was devoted to two things: his bank and his wildflowers, especially his trailing arbutus. I spent a lot of time with him as a boy and I decided then that some day I'd have a wildflower garden, too, although I still don't have any trailing arbutus."

"The mayflower," said Charlotte.

"Yes. The sweetest fragrance of all. They're on the protected list now, you know. I'm afraid I'm at least partly to blame. I've picked far too many in my day, including more than a few from my grandfather's garden."

They had reached the chairs, where a fat man was seated facing away from them, puffing on a big cigar.

"This is my dear friend Felix Mayer," said Thornhill, thumping him soundly on the shoulder. "Felix has been my book dealer and general book factotum for nearly thirty years. The greatest book dealer in the country."

Felix turned around. "The *world*, my dear Herr Professor," he corrected in a thick German accent. "The world."

"I beg your pardon, Felix. The world, by all means." Thornhill thumped his shoulder again. "Three hundred pounds of pure culture."

"I beg to correct you again, my dear Herr Professor,"

said Felix, raising a perfectly manicured forefinger. "Two hundred and eighty-nine pounds, but"—he chuckled—"I agree that it is all culture."

He was a fat, pink, roly-poly man with a shiny bald forehead and steeply arched eyebrows that were suspended high above his lively hazel eyes. He wore a white suit, a black and white striped tie, and black and white wing tip shoes. A gold-tipped Malacca cane leaned against the arm of his chair.

Thornhill introduced him to Charlotte, whereupon he rose and bowed elegantly from the waist, clasping his hands behind his back like a Prussian officer. "May I kiss the lady's hand?" he asked.

"By all means," replied Charlotte, extending her wrist in her grandest dowager empress manner.

"I am most pleased to make the acquaintance of the First Lady of the American cinema," he said, bowing again as he kissed her hand. He repeated the performance for Kitty, whom Thornhill also introduced.

Charlotte wondered briefly if he would click his heels, but much to her disappointment, he didn't.

"Felix will be staying with us through the Fourth," said Thornhill, who had watched the performance with great amusement.

"*Ja*," said Felix as he pulled out their chairs. "Book dealers are a form of parasite. We grow fat on the business of our wealthy clients. I am taking advantage of our dear host's hospitality to make some contacts. Many very rich book collectors spend their summers on the coast of Maine."

"Make hay while the sun shines, eh Felix?" said Thornhill sententiously. "Now, what can I get everyone to drink? Gin, Scotch, vodka . . . "

Charlotte asked for a gin and tonic, as did Kitty.

"Are you a book collector as well, Mr. Mayer?" asked Charlotte as he helped himself to the hors d'oeuvres on a cocktail table.

"No," he answered, wolfing down a caviar-topped cracker. "I enjoy the pleasure of handling books, but I have no desire to own them."

She was surprised. "Why is that?"

"For the dealer, books do not represent permanence and security the way they do for the collector. In fact, for the dealer, books are a sort of *memento mori*. They are continually passing from one set of hands to another as the result of a divorce, a loss of money, a death . . . The occupation of book dealer," he continued, raising his forefinger again, "is an occupation with a lesson to teach in the price of misfortune and the fragility of human life."

"This is a man," said Thornhill as he mixed the drinks at a bar tray, "for whom the obituaries are as important as the stock quotations are for a stockbroker. He makes a daily practice of scanning the obituary columns of the newspapers on two continents for possible sources of consignment material."

Felix chuckled. "You know what they say about the great Felix Mayer?"

"What?" asked Charlotte.

"That he can hear the death rattle before the doctor is called in."

"What a gruesome thought!" Kitty exclaimed.

"Well, my dear friend," said Thornhill as he passed around the drinks, "if that's why you're here, you had better reevaluate your powers of prognostication. I assure you that although my ticker may not be in the best of shape, I'm not planning to give up the ghost until I'm good and ready."

Felix continued munching, his hazel eyes sparkling with amusement. "That is not why I'm here, as you know," he said. "However, should you decide to, as you put it, give up the ghost . . . "

"You, my dear friend," interrupted Thornhill, "will have the pleasure of selling my collection. As you well know."

"Thank you, my dear Herr Professor."

"Always on the lookout for a commission, eh Felix?" teased Thornhill.

Felix set down his plate, wiped his mouth, and belched quietly. "Please," he said. "We are in the book-collecting business, are we not? In our business, there is an old saying: 'Collectors thrive among the dead.' If the great collections of the past had not been broken up, where would you have acquired your books? The noblest function of the collector is to hand down the achievements of civilization from one generation to the next. *Les morts aident les vivants*. The dead help the living, *nicht wahr*?"

Thornhill raised his glass to Felix. "Well-said, my good man. Well-said."

"Would you gentlemen mind terribly if we excused ourselves for a moment," asked Kitty after they had toasted Felix's observation. "I'd like to give Charlotte a tour of the herb garden before the other guests arrive."

"By all means," said Thornhill. "Speaking of herbs, my niece Frances, who will be along shortly, has asked me to invite you, Miss Graham, to an herb luncheon tomorrow. Our cook, Grace Harris, likes to experiment with herb recipes. She'll be trying out some new dishes on us."

"I'd be delighted," said Charlotte. "Thank you."

"Meanwhile Frances is planning a little celebration for us this evening. Some of her pagan rites. I'm sure you know all about it, Kitty."

"Yes," said Kitty, her eyes sparkling. "In observation of the summer solstice. It's today, you know. We celebrate six festivals a season." She counted them off: "May Day; Midsummer, to celebrate the longest day of the year; Lammas Day—that's on August first, to celebrate the beginning of the harvest; St. Fiacre's Day on August thirtieth, to celebrate the patron saint of gardeners; Michaelmas on September twenty-ninth, to celebrate the end of the harvest; and All Saints' Eve which is the same as Halloween."

So the Midsummer Festival was Kitty's "something special," thought Charlotte. She wondered what she was letting herself in for.

Leaving the men to their book talk, Charlotte and Kitty entered the garden, which was set in a protected area between the barn and the house, on the site of an old apple orchard. The gnarled trunks of the old apple trees studded the herb beds, creating the impression of a fairy tale garden.

Ledge House was a popular stop on the garden club tour circuit, Kitty explained. During the season, groups came out a couple of times a week, combining a climb up the Ledges with a visit to the herb garden.

"We'll begin with the colonial gardens, and work our way back," she continued eagerly, leading Charlotte down a gravel path that ran through the center of the garden. "I'll give you the same spiel I give the other visitors. Fran lets me give the garden tour when she's busy."

Charlotte nodded. Kitty was never more vivacious than when she was in the grip of a new enthusiasm, and the herb bug seemed to have bitten her especially hard.

"We have a total of thirteen gardens, each with its own theme," Kitty said. "We also have fields across the road where we grow herbs in larger quantities, and we have several growers in the area who supply us with herbs. We ship our seeds, plants, and herb products all over the country."

They were approaching a garden laid out in the form of a wheel, with brick paths forming the spokes. In the center stood a tall cross—twenty feet or more in height. The crosspiece was gaily decorated with a wreath of dried herbs and colored streamers that waved in the breeze.

"The maypole," explained Kitty, in answer to Charlotte's mystified stare. "It's a pagan fertility symbol, celebrating the renewed fertility of nature. The custom comes from the phallic festivals of ancient Egypt and India. Did you know that *phallos* means pole?"

Charlotte raised an eyebrow.

"Fran's is a standing maypole," she continued. "It stays up all year, to symbolize immortality."

Kitty led her through the gardens, each of which bore a signpost giving the garden's theme. Each garden also had an ornament that provided the focal point for the plantings: a wooden shrine, a birdbath, a sundial. Charlotte leaned over to smell the herb that surrounded a straw bee skep.

"Horehound," explained Kitty. "Used by the colonials to relieve coughs."

Leaving the colonial garden, they headed back toward the long garden paralleling the barn, where Kitty led her through the Shakespeare garden, ornamented with a bust of the bard; and the saints' garden, ornamented with a statue of St. Francis. At the third garden, she paused near an iron cauldron.

"This garden is our biggest attraction," she said. "The witches' garden. It contains the herbs the witches used in their magic, both black and white. On this side are the poisons and drugs used by the black witches, and on that side, the medicines and tonics used by the white witches."

Taking a seat on a garden bench of weathered teak, Charlotte studied the bed before her, which was dominated by a clump of violet-blue flowers on five-foot stalks. The flowers were oddly shaped: the lower petals were protected by a darker top petal that flopped over them like a hood. Some of the plants looked as if they'd been dug up: the turnip-shaped roots were scattered on top of the ground and the flower stalks lay wilting in the sun. Picking up one of the toppled stalks to right it, Charlotte watched in fascination as a bee reached its long tongue into the little hooded shelter.

She was about to ask the flower's name, but Kitty was already onto the next garden. "This way," she said. "The centerpiece of this series of gardens."

"The Elizabethan knot garden," interjected a woman who had just emerged from the barn. Walking past Felix and Thornhill, who were still deeply engaged in conversation, she joined Charlotte and Kitty by the cauldron.

She was tall, with a long face framed by gray hair in a Prince Valiant cut. Her eyes were obscured by thick eyeglasses. She was dressed entirely in green: green slacks, a green turtleneck, and a short cape of green wool. The only non-green items in her ensemble were a long strand of amber beads, several bangle bracelets, and a ring with a huge yellow stone.

"Fran, I'd like you to meet my good friend Charlotte Graham," said Kitty. "Charlotte will be staying with us for a week or two. Charlotte, this is Frances Thornhill. My employer," she added with a smile.

As Charlotte shook Fran's hand, she felt a peculiar numb sensation in her fingers, and wondered if it was from the plant she had just touched. *How extraordinary*! she thought. She would have to ask Kitty the plant's name.

"Nice to meet you. It's a replica of a sixteenth-century design," said Fran, nodding at the knot garden. "The idea is to create a knot effect by using herbs in an interlacing pattern. We use germander, hyssop, wormwood, box . . . "

She was interrupted by a greeting from a young couple who had just entered through the garden gate.

"Oh good, Daria and John are here," said Kitty.

Led by Fran, the three women rejoined Thornhill and Felix, where they were introduced to the new arrivals. The young woman was Daria Henderson, a bookbinder who was repairing some of Thornhill's books, and who Thornhill described as the conservator of his collection.

"Getting all the books in tiptop shape, right, Daria?" said Thornhill.

"Yes, sir," she replied amiably, with a dazzling smile.

She wasn't conventionally beautiful—her features were too bold and angular—but with her thick, curly black hair, her perfect white teeth, and her nut-brown complexion, she was very striking.

The young man was John Lewis, a botanist on the faculty of a Midwestern university. He was the Ledge House scholar-in-residence, one of a series of young scholars whom Thornhill invited each summer to use his library. He was staying in the gardener's cottage across the road.

"John is compiling a computer-generated index of the contents of my collection of early printed herbals," explained Thornhill.

John nodded in acknowledgment.

In contrast to Daria, John was tall, blond, and thin, with

wire-rimmed eyeglasses, a protruding Adam's apple, and a goofy, lopsided grin.

"I'm glad we're all here," said Fran once the introductions were over. "We can begin. If you'll excuse me a minute, I just have to get some things out of the barn. We're going to have an herb-scrying session."

"Scrying?" said Charlotte.

"You'll see," said Fran, striding off toward the barn.

The new arrivals took their seats, and Thornhill took their drink orders. While Thornhill mixed the drinks, Charlotte asked John about his work.

He explained that he was creating a database of herbs and their therapeutic uses. "Scientists in search of a drug for a disease will be able to consult it to find out what herbs have been used to treat the symptoms. Then, instead of playing molecular roulette with synthetic substances, they can start by isolating the active chemical principle of the herb."

"But I thought scientists at the pharmaceutical companies did that as a matter of course," said Charlotte.

"They used to," he replied. "In fact, one in four of the drugs prescribed today contains constituents that were originally derived from plants. But the profit-making pressures are such today that it's easier and more profitable to recycle old drugs in new guises than to develop new ones."

"I see," said Charlotte.

Fran returned from the barn, carrying a canvas bag from which she removed four garlands woven of herbs and flowers, one for herself and one for each of the women guests. In her hand she carried a magic wand, which was actually a wire sphere woven with herbs and flowers and fastened to a rod.

"Have I stumbled onto a production of *A Midsummer-Night's Dream*?" asked Charlotte, placing the fragrant garland on her head.

"Sort of," said Fran with a big smile. "A midsummer night's festival. To celebrate the turning of the year from waxing to waning. We're supposed to have a midnight revel, but since everyone around here is in bed by nine, we're having cocktails instead. I guess that means we'll all die in our beds."

"What are you talking about, Fran?" asked Kitty.

"The soul leaves the body at midnight on Midsummer Night and travels to the place where death will eventually separate it from the body," she explained. "That's the reason for the midnight revel. If you fall asleep during the vigil, it means that you'll die within the year."

Charlotte noticed that Fran wore no shoes. She had big, misshapen feet, with unsightly bunions.

"Midsummer is also when the witches and evil spirits walk abroad," she continued. "The herbs in the chaplets are to break their power." She pointed them out: "St. Johnswort, vervain, and mugwort. I picked them all at the stroke of noon today. That's when they're at their most powerful."

"What's to protect the men?" asked Thornhill. "I need special protection. Living with a witch is a dangerous position to be in."

"No need to fear," said Fran. "I'm a white witch. The basic principle of the white witch's canon is 'harm none.' The white witches say that whatever magic one performs will be returned to them threefold: 'three times ill or three times good.' So it pays to perform good magic." Reaching into her bag, she pulled out three boutonnieres, and passed them out to each of the men. "But just in case there are some black witches around, here's a boutonniere of mugwort. Mugwort is the magic plant of midsummer." She chanted an incantation: "Eldest of worts/Thou hast mighty for three/And against thirty/For venom availest/For flying vile things/That through the land rove . . ."

"*Artemesia vulgaris*," said Thornhill, pinning on his boutonniere. "Called mugwort after 'mug,' the drinking vessel, because it was used to flavor beer before the introduction of hops in the seventeenth century."

"Also an old-fashioned remedy for Parkinson's disease," added John, not to be outdone when it came to herbal lore.

"It helps in astral projection, too," Fran chimed in. "You

put a vase of it on your bed stand at night. You'll have to let me know where you go."

"How about Paris?" joked Daria.

"These are also for the ladies," Fran continued. Reaching into her bag again, she produced three handkerchiefs, which she passed out to the women. "I put a drop of dogwood sap on each of these this afternoon. If you put a drop of dogwood sap on a handkerchief on midsummer, your wish will be granted."

"Wonderful," said Kitty. Gripping the handkerchief tightly in her hand, she closed her eyes and made a wish.

"But," added Fran, "you must carry the handkerchief with you at all times until your wish comes true."

Charlotte followed suit, wishing for a good film script or a good play. It had been her steady wish for the last forty years.

"Now I'm going to light the midsummer fire. To keep the evil spirits away. It's a symbol of the conquest of the darkness by the light." She went over to the cauldron and lit the fire that had been laid inside, with the incantation: "Fire! Blaze and burn the witches." Once the fire had caught, she returned to the barn and emerged a few minutes later with three masks, which she affixed to posts that had been set into the ground on three sides of the witches' garden. At the base of each, she set a candle in a glass jar and a small earthenware cup. "Midsummer is also an auspicious time for divining the future," she explained as she worked. "I'm going to use a divination ritual from ancient Greece. The masks symbolize the triple face of the all-seeing goddess: the maiden, the mother, and the crone."

"Where does she get this stuff from?" Felix whispered as she worked.

"She says they're Greco-Roman and Druidic rituals that she gets from my herbals, but I think she makes them up," replied Thornhill. "If she doesn't watch out, she's going to be burned at the stake one of these days."

"But first I'm going to use a ritual to improve my eyesight," Fran continued. From her bag, she withdrew a bunch of herbs, which she held up to the fire. Removing her glasses, she stared into the fire through the herbs. "If you look at a midsummer fire through a bunch of larkspur, your eyesight will be protected for the next year," she explained. "Anyone else want to try?"

"Sure," said John, jumping up to join her by the fire.

As he removed his glasses Charlotte noticed how handsome he really was. He had an Englishman's good looks, a bit washed-out by American standards. With a tan and a few extra pounds, he would be very handsome indeed.

After John had finished, Fran proceeded with her ritual. At the mask of the maiden, she raised her wand—which, she explained, protected her while she invoked the spirits— and uttered an unintelligible incantation. Then she held up the earthenware cup to the mask. Finally she emptied the contents of the cup onto the fire. She repeated the ritual for the other two masks.

As Charlotte watched all she could think of was the words from *Macbeth*: "Eye of newt, and toe of frog/Wool of bat, and tongue of dog/Adder's fork, and blind-worm's sting/Lizard's leg and howlet's wing—"

Lastly Fran circled the cauldron three times and returned to her seat, still gripping her magic wand.

"Now what?" asked Thornhill. He addressed the other guests: "Never a dull moment around here."

He made it sound as if he was barely tolerating Fran's self-conscious rituals, but Charlotte suspected he rather enjoyed the bizarre note in his otherwise stuffy routine.

"Now we wait for the fire to die down," Fran replied. "Then we do the scrying: looking into the future. You look for the pattern in the coals. I can do it for you or you can do it yourselves."

As they waited the conversation turned to Charlotte's film career. John turned out to be an old-movie buff. As he talked about her films, she was astounded by his knowledge. He could list the credits of her major films, which she would expect of a movie buff, but he could do the same for her dogs. She was a bit baffled by the attention the younger generation paid to movie trivia. She didn't see the appeal of knowing who had won the Oscar for best supporting actress in 1952. She would rather have memorized some poetry. She was always caught off guard by these younger fans. She had a tendency to think of her fans as blue-haired old ladies, but many of them hadn't even been born when she had won her second Oscar, to say nothing of her third and fourth.

But if her career was of interest to the other guests, it certainly wasn't to her, and she was relieved when Fran got up to check on the fire.

"Okay, I think it's ready," Fran said, pulling the bench up to the cauldron. "Who wants to go first?"

"I will," said Daria.

"Do you want to scry yourself, or do you want me to do it for you?"

"Oh, please, you do it for me."

Fran sat down, waved her magic wand, and peered into the coals. "The fire is hotter on one side," she said after a minute. "That means love is in the air." Setting down her wand, she picked up a poker and stirred the coals, sending sparks into the still air. "I see a young man coming into your life."

"What does he look like?" asked Daria.

"Tall, thin, good-looking, blond hair . . . " Fran looked up at John, who smiled his lopsided grin and looked over at Daria. "Wait, I see two men," Fran continued, peering back into the cauldron. "Two good-looking men."

"Looks like you have some competition, young man," said Felix.

"The other is stocky, brown hair." She leaned closer to the fire, the glow of the coals reflected in her glasses, and then looked up. "He's the one you should stick with. He's your lucky guy."

John curled down the corners of his lips in an expression of mock dismay.

Kitty was next. Again, Fran waved her magic wand and peered into the coals. Kitty was not to move: her present house brought her good luck. After Kitty came Felix, who was told that a big consignment he was anticipating would come through, earning him a big commission.

Next came John. As he asked whether he would be granted tenure at his university, he looked over at Thornhill.

"Good luck, young man," said Thornhill.

A bit sarcastically, Charlotte thought.

Fran replied that he would receive tenure.

Good news for all.

When Charlotte's turn came, she decided to take a stab at it herself. As she approached the cauldron, Fran instructed her to relax before peering in. "Don't look for symbols," she said. "Wait for them to appear." Taking a seat on the bench, Charlotte waved the wand over the fire and then stared into the glowing reddish-white mass of charred wood. The heat felt good on her face. Breathing deeply, she let her eyes unfocus. Suddenly she saw the body of a yellow dog take shape amid the glowing coals. Jesse! It was a little unnerving to have his death dredged up from her subconscious like this. Not that she didn't realize how it must have been lurking at the back of her mind.

"What do you see?" asked Kitty.

"Nothing," said Charlotte, rising from the bench. She didn't want to discuss it. She shrugged. "I guess I just don't have the gift."

"I'm next," said Thornhill. Taking a seat on the bench, he waved the magic wand and stared dramatically into the cauldron. "A picture is emerging very clearly. I see an old man with a red mustache. He's wearing a tuxedo . . . "

Fran sat grinning, pleased that her parlor game was going so well.

"He's standing at a table. The table is covered by a white tablecloth. No, it's not a table, it's an altar. He's in a church. Yes, there's the minister." Picking up the poker, Thornhill made a show of stirring the coals, and then peered back into the cauldron. "A woman is standing next to him. She's wearing a white dress. It looks like some sort of ceremony. Yes, a wedding. It's a summer day. I think it's August. Yes. August twenty-second, to be precise."

"Frank!" exclaimed Kitty. "Are you getting married?"

Thornhill looked up, grinning. "That's what the coals say."

"Oh, Frank, that's wonderful," she gushed.

"Congratulations, old man," said Felix, raising his glass. "I propose a toast to our dear host and his bride-to-be."

The group drank the toast.

"Tell us all about her," commanded Kitty. "Where did you meet her? How long have you known her? Where does she live? We want *all* the details."

"We met on the tour of the gardens of Spain and Mallorca that I conducted last April," he said. "She lives in Connecticut. She's president of her local garden club. She has a big show coming up, which is why we can't be married sooner. Frances has met her. She was up here over Memorial Day weekend."

Charlotte looked over at Fran, whose expression was sour. She clearly wasn't pleased with Frank's announcement. Marching back up to the cauldron, she again waved the magic wand over the fire and recited the words: "This rite of midsummer is ended. Merry meet and merry part." She then closed her eyes and stood silently for a few minutes. But merry she wasn't. Without a word, she padded off in her bare feet down the gravel path to the house, a chorus of the guests' thank yous ringing behind her.

"Well," said Kitty, breaking the awkward silence. "I think Charlotte and I will get back to Stan." She stood up. "We don't want to be caught wandering around after the sun goes down."

"That's right," said Thornhill. "Remember to stay awake for the witching hour. Forestall death for at least another year. As for me, I'm risking all by going to bed at my usual hour of ten o'clock."

Charlotte and Kitty bade goodbye to Thornhill and the other guests, and took their leave. As Charlotte looked back,

she could see the twisted limbs of an old apple tree silhouetted by the glow from the fire in the cauldron.

Tracey had asked her to keep an eye out for anything
unusual. She wondered if Fran's Midsummer Night festival
would qualify.

·4·

THOUGH THORNHILL MIGHT have chosen to go to bed, Charlotte, Kitty, and Stan had kept their midnight vigil, assuring their survival for yet another year. On the way home from Ledge House, Kitty had kept up a steady chatter about the witches: on Midsummer Night the air was filled with them flying to and from their sabbat with the devil. After that, they hadn't dared to go to bed. Actually, Kitty told them, modern science believed the witches' rides to have been hallucinations induced by a mysterious herbal ointment. But you could never rule out the possibility that the witches *had* actually left their bodies, she added. After all, hadn't one scientific law after another been thrown out as knowledge had become more advanced? Perhaps astral projection existed on a plane that modern science was not yet able to comprehend. All of which had provoked not a little caustic commentary from Stan. Happily, they'd all survived to greet another beautiful day.

At midday, Charlotte headed up Broadway to the luncheon at Ledge House. For someone who had just left Broadway, she was spending a lot of time there, she observed. Turning in at the garden gate, she headed down the gravel path. As she neared the barn a clump of plants came sailing past her nose. Looking over at the knot garden, from which direction the clump had come, she saw what was happening: Fran was on her knees, ripping up the knot garden, her pride and joy. Plants were flying in every direction. The intricate pattern of the design was now interrupted by gaping holes, and torn-up plants lay scattered about in heaps.

"What are you doing?" Charlotte cried.

Startled, Fran stopped her frenzied pulling and turned around. Removing her glasses, she wiped the tears from her eyes with a muddy hand that left her face streaked with dirt. "She's not going to have it," she said.

"Have what?" Charlotte asked, kneeling down beside her.

"Have the garden, that's what," Fran said, pushing her gray bangs out of her eyes and taking a deep breath.

Once again she was dressed entirely in green, this time a pale gray-green. But instead of the chaplet of herbs, she was wearing a peculiar green skull cap. On her feet she wore bulky tan orthopedic shoes.

"Who's not going to have the garden?" asked Charlotte. She waited patiently while Fran struggled to regain her composure.

"That woman," she said finally, laying down her trowel. She looked up at Charlotte. "He's going to be sorry he did this to me." Rising from her knees, she waved an arm at the garden. "I created this herb garden: every plant, every sign."

"Would he make you leave?"

"Yes, he would."

"But how long have you lived here?"

"Eighteen years. He owns it, but I consider it my home as much as his. Oh, I have an apartment in Massachusetts where I live during the winter—I don't live here year-round—but . . . " Her voice trailed off. "You know what he said to me? He said that he and Eleanor would do everything in their power to make me welcome. Now, isn't that generous of them. Me! Welcome!" she said, pointing at her chest. "In my own home. Some strange woman making me welcome in my own home." She sat back down on her knees and reached out to pick up an uprooted plant. "Besides," she added, toying with the plant, "he's too old to get married. He'll be sixty on Tuesday."

"That's not too old," protested Charlotte. She hadn't been much younger herself when she'd been married for the fourth time. And who knew? Maybe there would be a fifth. "Besides, maybe she's really very nice."

"Oh, no," said Fran, shaking her head. "I've met her. One of those spoiled garden-club types. The mink coat brigade, I call them. She'll want to take over. She's already acting like she owns the place. You know what she said to Frank? 'Frank honey,' " she mimicked in a high, flirtatious voice, " 'herbs are nice, but they just don't have the *display* that annuals do. Couldn't we replace some of the herbs with something more showy, like zinnias?' "

"Zinnias!" Even to Charlotte's untutored eye, replacing the herbs with zinnias seemed like sacrilege.

"Do you believe it? 'More color,' she said." Fran continued: "I'm sorry about running off. It's just that it was such a shock. He had hinted around, but I didn't think he would actually go through with it, not after all these years. But do you know what? I cast a protective spell just before I left."

Charlotte remembered her waving her wand over the fire.

"Magic shouldn't be used for negative purposes, but it's okay to use it to protect yourself. Which is what I did. I used it to protect myself from the machinations of that greedy bitch."

"I'm sorry, Miss Thornhill," said Charlotte. "But I'm sure things will work out all right."

"Fran. Please call me Fran," she said. "I'd like to think that, too, but I'm not so sure. Not sure at all."

Leaving Fran, who had already begun to reset the plants she had dug up in her fury, Charlotte continued on through the herb garden to the house, which stood at the far end of the garden. It was a rambling old Victorian structure with porches jutting off in every direction. They were furnished with a variety of rocking chairs, gliders, and porch swings designed for nothing other than being idle. It was a house built in the brief era when all was possible—the confident, optimistic era before resources and time were scarce, the era in which there was leisure for pleasant conversation, for reading a book on a breezy veranda, or for watching the sun sparkle on the distant bay.

Before the millionaires had made Bridge Harbor fashionable it had been the quiet summer retreat of artists, intellectuals, and writers who were attracted by its natural beauty. They had built modest cottages like Ledge House, where they pursued the simple pleasures of sketching, canoeing, and hiking. The natives had nicknamed them rusticators. No doubt Thornhill was a relic of this genteel tradition, Charlotte thought. If so, the idea of a hotel and nightclub on Gilley Island must be as distasteful to him as the thought of girlie magazines on display at Widener Library.

Following a path leading around the side of the house, she emerged at a terrace at the rear. From a balustrade topped with urns of pink geraniums she could see a carefully manicured lawn bordered by tall spruces. At the foot of the lawn stood the gazebo at the summit of the Ledges. Beyond the gazebo lay the channel and the town of Bridge Harbor. On a warm and sunny June afternoon, the feeling was heavenly, like being on a cloud two hundred feet or more above the water.

A table shaded by a yellow umbrella and elegantly set with blue and white Chinese export porcelain stood in the center of the terrace. Around the table sat the guests. With the exception of Fran, it was the same group as the previous evening. Charlotte greeted Thornhill and the other guests, and took a seat.

"Felix and I were just talking about the psychology of book collecting," said Thornhill as he mixed Charlotte's drink. "Felix was saying that the drive to collect begins with bibliophilia—the love of books—and progresses to bibliomania, which is an incurable disease."

"Why incurable?" asked Daria.

"Because the bibliomaniac is never satisfied," replied Felix. "There is always another book that he must add to his collection. And—fortunately for the dealer—the more unique or unattainable a book is, the more he wants it."

"Then the real motivation is greed," observed John.

"*Ja*. Sometimes uncontrollable greed."

"Now wait a minute," protested Thornhill. "I must take issue with you there, Felix. Surely the collector is also motivated by the desire to take a part—however small—in the cultural heritage of mankind. The book collector is, after all, on a higher plane than the beer can collector."

"*Ja*, this is true. The interest of the book collector is in culture, just as the interest of the philatelist is in geography or the interest of the numismatist is in currencies. Or the interest of the beer can collector is in breweries. But the basic instinct—the drive to possess—is the same."

"Then, what produces the instinct?" asked Daria.

"Aha," said Felix, raising a manicured forefinger. "That is a question for the psychiatrist, not for the book dealer."

"The Freudians would say it's an expression of the need to control," said John. "A manifestation of the anal retentive personality."

"I daresay you know more about it than I do," Felix replied. "But in that case, *Homo sapiens* is not the only species to exhibit the anal retentive personality. Why do magpies carry off trinkets, or dogs bury bones? No, the collecting instinct is very basic." He paused to refill his glass and then proceeded to empty half of it in a single swallow. "And very potent. The lengths to which a collector will go to acquire a book are legendary."

Thornhill handed Charlotte her drink, and seated himself at the head of the table. "I sense one of Felix's biblio-anecdotes coming on," he said, adding, "My good friend here is the greatest book raconteur in the world."

Felix smiled smugly. "I am glad you say the world, my dear Herr Professor." He turned back to the others. "*Ja*, there have been many cases of book collectors—how do you say in English?—going off the rails. Murder has even been committed for a book."

Thornhill nodded. "The story of Don Vincente."

Felix proceeded to tell the tale with great skill. It involved a Spanish monk named Don Vincente who coveted a book that was said to be the only one of its kind. When the book came up for sale at auction, he staked his life's savings on it, but was outbid by a rival. Shortly afterward, the rival died in a fire and the collection was destroyed. The prize volume, however, mysteriously found its way into Don Vincente's collection. When the authorities learned of this, he was tried for murder. In a heroic effort to save him, his lawyer tracked down another copy of the volume in a Paris library. The lawyer argued that since more than one copy of the book existed, it was impossible to prove that Don Vincente's book was the one in question.

"But on hearing this," Felix concluded, "Don Vincente broke down. 'Alas,' he cried. 'My copy is not unique.' You see, he didn't care about the consequences, he only cared about possessing the one book that no one else could ever hope to own."

For a moment there was silence as they contemplated the fate of Don Vincente, who, Felix added, was hanged for murder.

"But," said Charlotte, "doesn't it take more than this drive to possess to build an outstanding book collection? I should think it would take a great deal of intelligence and taste. After all, anyone can accumulate books, but not everyone can build a great collection."

Felix looked at her, his eyebrows raised like circumflexes above his lively hazel eyes. "This is true, *meine gnädige Frau*," he said. "May I compliment you on your perspicacity. The act of collecting is a game. In the words of one of the great collectors: 'After love, the most exhilarating game of all.' *Nicht wahr*, Herr Professor?"

Thornhill, who was lighting his pipe, chuckled at the reference to his impending marriage.

"Like any game, it requires attributes such as skill, cunning, perseverance, patience, and boldness."

"Then, skill is more important than money," said Daria.

"Absolutely. Our dear host is a case in point. From his youth, he has been a collector of—how shall I put it?—uncommon daring. He has assembled one of the finest privately owned botanical collections in the country. A remarkable achievement for a man who, although wealthy, to be sure, has never possessed the vast wealth of the other great collectors of his generation."

"Thank you, my good man," said Thornhill, basking in the compliment. "But I never could have done it without your guidance."

"Not true," said Felix. "Our dear host possesses all the skills of the great book collector. I will give you an example. For years, our host was known in the book-collecting world as the arch-rival of another of this century's greatest collectors, Charles W. MacMillan."

The name rang a bell with Charlotte—MacMillan was the reclusive heir to a New England brass and copper fortune.

"Mr. MacMillan was a man of tremendous wealth, and yet our dear host has assembled a collection that is every bit the equal of his. The MacMillan collection today forms the foundation of the world-renowned botanical library of the New York Botanical Society."

"My collection is a damn sight more than the equal of his," interjected Thornhill testily. "It surpasses his any day."

"My apologies, my dear Herr Professor," said Felix. "I will correct myself: the Thornhill collection as it stands today surpasses the MacMillan collection as it stood at the time of Mr. MacMillan's death."

Charlotte sensed a sardonic edge to Felix's voice, but she could have been wrong. She had a tendency to read meanings into words that weren't there, a product of the actor's eye for detail combined with her own overactive imagination.

"Picking nits, aren't you Felix?" said Thornhill. He continued: "I'll never forget the look on old Mac's face when I bought that nurseryman's catalogue out from under him." He chuckled to himself. "Tell them that story."

"One of the legendary moments in book-collecting annals," said Felix.

He proceeded to tell another tale involving a rare seed catalogue that MacMillan needed to complete a collection of early American nurseryman's catalogues, a special interest of his. Thornhill was the victor in an auction room duel for the catalogue, but he paid a price many times more than what it was worth. "In the huddle following the sale, our dear host was asked why he paid so much," Felix wound up. "He replied, 'Because MacMillan wanted it.' "•

"Ha," said Thornhill, slapping his thigh with delight at the conclusion of the story. "I got him, didn't I?"

Thornhill was a man for whom revenge was sweet, thought Charlotte.

"But my dear Herr Professor, he got the better of you later on, didn't he?" said Felix. "With *Der Gart*."

"What's the story of *Der Gart*?" asked John eagerly.

"You tell it, Felix. You do it so much better than I," said Thornhill, who was obviously enjoying himself.

"The book was *Der Gart der Gesundheit*, or *The Garden of Health*, an herbal printed in Mainz in 1485 by Peter Schoeffer, Gutenberg's son-in-law," said Felix. "A book of extraordinary beauty and rarity, indisputably the most important of the herbal incunabula."

"Incunabula?" said Charlotte.

"It refers to the earliest printed books—those books printed before 1500," explained Thornhill.

She nodded.

"It was to go on the block at a London auction house," Felix continued. "It was the kind of book that comes on the market perhaps only once in a decade." He suddenly brought his fist down on the table like a gavel, rattling the silverware. "Within seconds of opening, the bidding was up to five thousand pounds. Which was all well and good except for one thing: two people had bid the same amount simultaneously and neither of them would yield."

"MacMillan and Dr. Thornhill?" asked Daria.

"Exactly. Mr. MacMillan held tight because he thought a break in the deadlock would run the price up, and our dear host held tight because he had promised himself he wouldn't pay any more than that. The auctioneer bullied, he wheedled, he told stories—nothing worked."

Thornhill was sitting with his forehead cradled in his

palms as if the mere memory of the event were painful.

"What happened?" asked Daria.

"First I'll tell you where each of them was sitting. Mr. MacMillan was sitting at the front of the room and our dear host was sitting at the back. What happened was this: the auctioneer invoked an obscure rule which holds that the lot goes to the bidder who is sitting *nearest* the platform."

"And MacMillan got the book," said Daria.

"*Ja.* But what was so galling to our dear host was that he was outsmarted. You see, Mr. MacMillan knew about the rule."

"I vowed that from that day forward I'd never lose my nerve again when it came to a book I wanted," said Thornhill. "And I never have."

" 'It is not the yielding to temptation that oppresses me, but oh, the remorse for the times I yielded not,' eh Herr Professor?" said Felix with a chuckle.

Thornhill nodded.

"The upshot of the story is that this precious book is now a part of our dear host's collection, along with four other prize herbals from the MacMillan collection," continued Felix. "They are worth at least five times as much today. They are the *crème de la crème* of the early herbals."

"How did they come to be part of your collection?" asked John.

"That's another story," replied Thornhill as he refilled his pipe with tobacco from a leather pouch. "I had offered many times to buy MacMillan's early herbals, but he had always turned me down. Until he astonished me one day by calling me up and offering to sell them to me."

"Why?" asked Daria.

"He was dying, but I didn't know that at the time. He had no descendants to leave his collection to. So he sold me the herbals, and left the rest of his collection to the botanical society."

"It has always puzzled me, this decision to sell his prizes," said Felix. "Especially to his rival. The real collector would rather give his collection away intact than sell it piecemeal. Many of our greatest libraries owe their existence to a collector's reluctance to break up a lifetime's work."

"Yes," agreed John. "It seems out of character."

"He thought they'd be going to someone who'd appreciate them," explained Thornhill. "I'll never forget him sitting in his wheelchair in his library in that big old barn of a mansion in Worcester. 'Frank,' I remember him saying to me, 'Take care of them. They are my children.' "

"My children," harrumphed Felix. He continued: "A great collector. The irony is that he had begun work on a catalogue of his collection shortly before he learned of his illness. In fact, I think it was about to go to the printer's when he died. Christmas Eve, 1959, as I recall."

"What's ironical about that?" asked John.

"That he began work on it when he did. You see, the decision to publish a catalogue often signals the end of a collecting career. It stamps a collection with the imprimatur of completeness. Alas, in his case, this was sadly true."

Thornhill looked up. "Aha, here comes Mrs. Harris with our lunch."

The entire length of the rear of the house was taken up by a screened veranda whose columns of native stone supported a series of second-story porches. A gray-haired woman with a bouffant hairdo was unsteadily trying to maneuver a tea wagon through one of the veranda doors.

Thornhill jumped up to help her. "Let me give you a hand, Grace," he said, taking charge of the wagon.

"Why, thank you, Frank," she replied in a deep Southern drawl. Removing her rhinestone-studded glasses, she fluttered her eyelashes at Thornhill.

Charlotte pegged her as the type of Southern woman for whom flirting is as natural as breathing, whatever the age or social position.

Replacing her glasses, Grace turned back to the wagon. She wore a blue pants suit and a flowered blouse with a pert bow at the throat. Clearly she considered herself a cut above the ordinary domestic servant.

"Mrs. Harris, I'd like you to meet Miss Charlotte Graham," said Thornhill as they reached the table.

"Pleased to meet you, I'm sure," she said with a shaky half-curtsy. She smiled blankly at Charlotte.

Also the kind of cook for whom sampling the sauce is as much a part of the job as salting the stew, thought Charlotte as she returned the greeting.

"Well, Grace," said Thornhill, resuming his seat. "What's it to be today?"

Reaching into her pocket, Grace withdrew a slip of paper and read in a high, quavering voice: "Rosemary and sorrel soup, chicken fricassee with tarragon, herb pilaf, mint puff biscuits, and strawberry-rhubarb pie."

"Everyone is in for a big treat," said Thornhill as Grace served the dishes. "Mrs. Harris is one of the finest cooks north of the Mason-Dixon line." He went on to explain that she had run a small restaurant in town that was famous for its home cooking. When the restaurant became too much for her (Charlotte translated this to: *when the booze became too much for her*), she'd gone to work at Ledge House, where she had taken an interest in cooking with herbs. She had published several pamphlets of herb recipes.

"Upon my word, Frank, you do go on so," said Grace after he had finished praising her talents. Then she addressed the guests: "Now, you all enjoy your dinner." With that, she pivoted on her heel and headed into the house, as if exhausted by the strain of social intercourse.

"I think you'll find it delicious," said Thornhill. "Even up to your gourmet standards, Felix."

"What is the most expensive book you've ever handled, Mr. Mayer?" asked Daria as the guests turned to their meal, which was as delicious as promised.

"That's easy. The Gutenberg Bible—the most coveted of all books. I consider it the high point of my career. There are only forty-seven copies extant, all of which are now in institutions."

"May I ask how much you sold it for?" asked Charlotte.

"Ach, that's a sensitive point, Miss Graham."

"Why is that?"

"I sold it to a German museum for two point two million."

"That seems like a substantial enough sum to me."

"But you see, I had purchased it for the same price." He sighed. "The economy turned sour after I bought it, and I was unable to sell at a profit. I held onto it for as long as I could, but I finally had to say to myself: 'Felix, you are a bookseller, not a book collector.' So I sold." He washed down a mouthful of chicken with a swallow of Scotch. "But meanwhile, I had the pleasure of being the owner of the most beautiful book ever printed."

"I agree that it's the most beautiful book ever printed," said Thornhill. "But I am proud to say that I am the owner of the second most beautiful book ever printed: *Der Gart*, printed by Gutenberg's son-in-law. The herbals were the first books to be printed after the Bibles," he explained. "But unlike the Bibles, they didn't survive in large numbers. They were used so heavily that they fell apart. Those that did survive are often in poor condition."

"*Ja*," said Felix. "The Thornhill collection not only includes some of the greatest prizes among the herbal incunabula, it also includes copies in unusually fine condition. Unfortunately," he continued between bites, "good copies are disappearing from the market. The day is rapidly approaching when all the early herbals will be in institutions as well."

"In my opinion, that's where they should be," interjected John. "With all due respect to Frank, I think it's a shame these books are still in private hands. Some are the only copies in the country."

"Ach, my dear young man," said Felix, wagging his finger under John's nose. "You are being most ungracious. Scholars such as yourself owe a debt of gratitude to collectors such as our dear host. Private collections have formed the foundations of the world's greatest libraries."

"It's true," said Daria.

"If it weren't for collectors," continued Felix, "books

such as these would be scattered all over the world, of little use to anyone."

"Of what use are they here?" asked John with a lopsided grin. "Stuck away in an unlocked vault. In addition to being inaccessible, they are vulnerable to deterioration and theft. There are no climate controls here, no security precautions. In my opinion, they'd be much better off in a library."

"In a library," snorted Thornhill. "That's where they'd be vulnerable. If they weren't stolen, they'd be defaced by some juvenile delinquent. I know what you think, John," he continued as he passed around the serving dishes for seconds. "But you forget that my collection is not inaccessible."

John looked skeptical.

"You, young man, are a case in point. Anyone—scholar or not—is welcome to apply to use my collection."

"Apply. That's just my point," said John. He leaned his gangly frame back in his chair and crossed a lean, pale leg over a knobby knee. "Besides, you can hardly say that your collection is accessible in such a remote location."

"First, young man," said Thornhill patronizingly, "I have never denied anyone access to my collection. Second, geographic inaccessibility is a relative concept. My collection is more accessible to someone from New England than a collection in California. And third, by granting you the liberty"—he stressed the word *liberty*—"of computerizing the contents of my herbals, I am making them more accessible than they would be in a public institution."

With the exception of Felix, who looked as if he could go on forever, the guests had finished eating. Charlotte leaned back: she was unusually relaxed amid the interesting conversation, good food, and delightful surroundings.

Thornhill collected the empty plates, along with congratulations for the cook, and took orders for pie and coffee, which were waiting on a serving tray.

The debate continued over dessert, with Thornhill and John tilting at each other with the academic's dispassionate enjoyment in argument for argument's sake. Taking advantage of a lull in the verbal jousting, Felix asked John about his work.

"Before my esteemed colleague launches into his self-serving paean to the computer age," interjected Thornhill, "may I ask who would like more coffee?"

Receiving answers in the affirmative, he poured the coffee and cut another slice of pie for Felix—his third.

"It's very simple," replied John finally. "My esteemed colleague, while acknowledging that these herbals have provided us with some of the most potent drugs in our pharmacological armory, views them as historical curiosities: quaint repositories of superstition, magic, and folklore, whose usefulness to mankind has long been exhausted. I, on the other hand, see them as guides to the wealth of therapeutic possibilities that still lie hidden in nature."

"I'm afraid I still don't understand," said Felix. "Do you mean these herbals are important in helping science to find new drugs?"

"Don't worry," said Daria. "He speaks academicese. If you stick with it long enough, you'll get a translation."

"Sorry," said John. "Yes. And in helping to test the old ones. Most of the world still relies on herbs to treat disease. Western medicine is simply too expensive to meet the world's health needs. Instead of dismissing herbs as hocus-pocus, Western scientists have to face the fact that herbal medicine constitutes a health-care system and that, as such, it deserves to be scientifically analyzed for safety and effectiveness."

"Very interesting," said Felix, who was still eating.

"Much more progress along these lines is being made in the Communist countries, where the development of new drugs isn't dependent on the profit-making motive," John continued. "The Communist governments are backing a concerted effort to search the plant kingdom for new therapeutic agents, particularly those with anti-viral and anti-cancer properties."

He cast a sidelong look at Thornhill, who was puffing pensively on his pipe. Charlotte bet that praising the Communists would be equivalent to waving the red flag in front of the bull in more than just one sense. Thornhill was a diehard old Yankee conservative if ever there was one.

"Tommyrot," muttered Thornhill, rising to the bait.

"I'm sorry," said John. "I don't hold with your view of American pharmaceutical companies as shining examples of capitalistic achievement."

Thornhill laid down his pipe. "Look, young man. Maybe we should just nationalize the drug companies," he said, his face reddening. "I bet that would keep all you pinkos happy."

"I didn't say that," protested John.

"After the revolution, the country would be in need of scholars of your caliber. Let's see. You could computerize the contents of the *Physicians Desk Reference*. Now, that would be a real piece of scholarship. For a piece of work like that, you might even be granted tenure. Maybe someone would even be willing to publish it. That would be a change, wouldn't it?"

Wherever the line of propriety was, Thornhill had crossed it. Not only had he made it clear that he didn't think much of John's politics, he had also made it clear that he didn't think much of his scholarship.

But John took it good-naturedly. "But after the revolution, we wouldn't have old fossils like you in charge who don't understand the first thing about computers, either," he said with a smile. He rose to pour himself more coffee, but remained silent. After a few minutes, he excused himself.

"Pardon my manners," said Thornhill after he had gone. "But these parlor pinks get my goat. He sits there eating my food, drinking my liquor, to say nothing of using my library, and has the nerve to criticize me for not donating my books to the public. John L. Lewis—he certainly lives up to his name."

"The idealism of the young," said Felix, who was picking the crumbs out of the bottom of the pie plate.

"The arrogance of the young is more like it. Not that he's all that young. Of course," Thornhill continued, changing his tone, "I'm all for putting my collection on computers if it will help someone, but to want academic recognition for it? That's not scholarship—it's secretarial work."

"I think there's a lot more to it than that," said Daria, coming to John's defense. "Not that I understand it myself. But I know he has to develop the computer programs and all that."

"Well, maybe I'm a bit behind the times," said Thornhill conciliatingly. "Bit of an old fossil, I guess, just like John said." He turned to Charlotte. "Would you like more coffee, Miss Graham?"

"No thank you. I have to get back to the Saunders' while the tide is still out. I promised Kitty I'd go shopping in town with her. Besides," she added, "I wouldn't want to keep two devoted bibliophiles—or is it bibliomaniacs— from their work."

"For bibliomaniacs, books are not work, they are pleasure," said Felix. He turned back the lapel of his jacket to reveal a series of half a dozen pockets, each containing a catalogue. He pulled several out. "You see, Miss Graham, I am a bookseller who is always ready to do business."

"So I see."

"In addition to bibliomania, bibliophiles are subject to another addiction, catalogue-mania," he continued. "For us, there is no greater pleasure in life than to spend hours poring over book catalogues. My tailor has allowed me the maximum indulgence in this vice."

"And in another vice as well," said Thornhill.

"*Ja*," replied Felix. Turning back the other lapel, he revealed another series of pockets. He withdrew two cigars from one of the pockets and handed one to Thornhill. "Cuban. Aged a full year. You can't buy them legally in the United States. But"—he raised a forefinger—"I have a connection."

"I've had a wonderful time," Charlotte said as she rose to leave. "I'd like very much to see some of the books in your collection some day."

"I'd be delighted," replied Thornhill, who also rose.

"How about tomorrow? There's no time like the present, as they say."

"Yes, thank you."

"I'd be happy to give you a tour of the bindery too," said Daria. After setting a time, Charlotte and Daria thanked Thornhill for the meal and went through the hand-kissing routine with Felix once again.

As they left, the two men were hunched over their catalogues, cigars in hand. Looking back, Charlotte thought they looked more like bettors consulting tout sheets than bibliophiles deciding what rare books to buy.

·5·

CHARLOTTE WAS STRUCK by the smell the minute she entered the Ledge House parlor the next day. It might have been called eau de summer house: a combination of must from years of being closed up during the winters, rubber from the boots and slickers stored in the hall closet, and lemon oil from the freshly polished furniture—all overlaid by the sweet, salty smell of the sea breeze and the resiny smell of the balsam firs. It reminded her of the many happy summers she'd spent at her second husband's summer house in Connecticut. Had he lived—he had died suddenly of a heart attack when he was only forty-two—she would probably still be happily married. Her first marriage had been the product of a teenage romance—a common enough mistake and one for which she felt no remorse—but her third and fourth marriages had been ill-fated attempts to recapture the happiness of her second. But maybe she was deceiving herself. Maybe she would have tired of Will in time, or he of her. It had been a marriage of shared ideals and mutual respect, which many contend is the best kind, but it had never been a marriage of passion.

She had been attracted to Will and his family by their sober Yankee values, values that had given her the sense of order and security that she needed to offset the craziness of Hollywood. They belonged to a disappearing breed of New England aristocrat that invests its faith in honesty, brains, and good manners. She had once heard a pundit remark, in a paraphrase of Plato, that for the affluent Wasp, the unexamined life *is* worth living. It was true—introspection wasn't their strong point. Nor was there much uncertainty in their secure little world: they were shielded from unpleasantness by a cocoon of money and tradition. But their lack of doubt made them confident and fearless; they wore a patina of grace and simplicity that it took others a lifetime of achievement to acquire. If that grace sometimes carried an element of smugness, it was easily overlooked in favor of their loyalty and generosity. And if they were sometimes a bit stuffy, they were also unfailingly kind, unassuming, and cultured. In general, as nice a bunch as you could find anywhere.

Judging from Ledge House, Thornhill was cut from the same mold.

The parlor was furnished with the comfortable elegance that is the mark of old wealth. Thornhill's Boston antecedents had been in the China trade, and the room was decorated with the precious cargo of the great clipper ships. A round table with a quartet of wicker chairs cushioned in faded chintz stood in the center of the room. On it rested a large *famille rose* bowl heaped to overflowing with Fran's potpourri, which added a spicy note to the room's other smells. An antique mahogany sideboard topped by a pair of ginger jars decorated with a blue and white dragon design stood against one wall, and a pair of tall Chinese coromandel screens flanked the door on the other wall. At the rear, a stretch of French doors opened onto the screened veranda, where a somnolent Felix reclined on a chaise longue, his head slumped over the book in his hands. Beyond the veranda, the blue sky was cloudless.

Once again Charlotte had walked up Broadway to Ledge House, this time for a tour of the bindery and library. The door had been answered by Grace, who had gone off to announce Charlotte's arrival. As Charlotte awaited her return, a silver Mercedes Benz with a license plate reading CHUCK D pulled into the driveway and parked just beyond the front door. Charlotte assumed the driver was Chuck Donahue. As he got out of the car she noticed that he bore a strong resemblance to his father-in-law, supporting the popular wisdom that women tend to marry men who look like their fathers. His hair was more blond than red and he was much beefier, but he had the same cold blue-gray eyes and the same bushy mustache. Unlike Thornhill, however, Chuck was a flashy dresser. He wore a double-breasted navy blue blazer and gray flannel slacks, accented by white patent leather loafers and a red silk handkerchief. His clothes made him look more like a racetrack habitué than an insurance broker. "An overdressed jerk" was how Stan had described him, with his usual caustic accuracy.

He strode briskly up the front steps and through the door, only to be brought up short by the presence of a stranger in the parlor.

"Mr. Donahue?" said Charlotte. She stood up and extended her hand. "Charlotte Graham. I'm staying with Stan and Kitty Saunders."

Spreading his lips in what she presumed was meant to be a smile, he strode across the room to greet her. "Pleasure," he muttered. He spoke out of the side of his mouth, as if a cigar was clenched between his teeth. Glancing at the door to the adjacent room, he asked: "Are you here to see Thornhill?"

"Yes, but not at the moment," she replied. "Daria Henderson's going to give me a tour of the bindery in a moment. Then Dr. Thornhill's going to show me some of the books in his collection."

"Oh," he answered, looking relieved. He pushed oily strands of blond hair away from his forehead with a nervous gesture. "Well," he said, turning away, "nice to have met you." He entered the library, closing the door behind him.

Charlotte turned back to find Daria descending one of the twin staircases that flanked the front door. They exchanged greetings, and Daria escorted her upstairs to the bindery, which had been set up in a sunny, spacious bedroom at the back of the house. In the center stood a long counter, at which John sat on a stool, hunched over a book. He was wearing a black turtleneck that made him look like a bohemian poet. The strong odor of his French cigarette filled the air. As they entered, Charlotte noticed him eyeing Daria admiringly. She was dressed in blue jeans and a V-neck sweater that showed off her perfect figure.

"Welcome to the Ledge House bindery," said Daria. "You remember John."

Charlotte said hello, and took a seat opposite him at the counter.

"I've been trying to remember the title of one of your pictures," he said. "You played a vamp who lures a rich man away from his wife."

The Bitter Wife," said Charlotte. It was one picture in which she thought she got what she deserved at the end. In a sense, she had. She had married her leading man, which had been punishment enough indeed.

"It's one of my favorites," John continued. "You were the epitome of the scheming gold digger. Why is it that we always remember the heroes, and never the villains? It seems to me that the villains are short-changed."

"Because the Hollywood villains aren't memorable. Hollywood would never take the risk of offering the public a villain whose motives stemmed from anything more complicated than material gain; it would be bad for the box office."

The thinking was that villains with grandeur and imagination like Lady Macbeth or Iago were too complex for the movie-going public to understand. Which was one reason Charlotte preferred the stage.

"I guess you're right," said John. "But you didn't come here to discuss films," he added. "I'll shut up so that Daria can talk to you about bookbinding." With that, he picked up his book and began to read.

Charlotte looked around the room. "I feel like I'm in a medieval torture chamber," she said. The large presses with iron-toothed wheels looked more like devices for stretching limbs on a rack than devices for restoring old books.

Daria smiled, her brown eyes flecked with specks of gold. "They're medieval instruments, but only for torturing bindings into shape. The tools we use today are almost identical to the tools used five centuries ago."

Leading Charlotte around the room, she explained the function of each of the tools: a frame for stitching the bindings; a miniature oven for heating the stamping tools; a paper cutter for cutting the boards, or covers. The earliest books, she explained, were luxury items, affordable only to the very rich. Unlike modern books, they were purchased unbound and unillustrated. The binding and illustration often took a year or more and cost more than the book itself.

Charlotte was impressed by her professionalism. She was only in her twenties, but she was already running her own business. She had never been led to assume, as had so many women of Charlotte's generation, that someone else would be responsible for her economic security. It was an assumption that often failed, and when it did, its victims played a game of self-deceit that Charlotte thought of as *Until*: they would work *until* they got married, *until* the baby came, *until* they had saved enough for the down payment on a house, *until* the kids got through college. Until the *untils* had added up to a lifetime of temporary work with nothing to show for it.

"How did you get into this business?" asked Charlotte as they resumed their seats. "Does one aspire to become a bookbinder?"

"No. I think it's something most people get into by accident. Suffice it to say that once I got into it, I was hooked."

She had learned her trade from a New York bookbinder named Carolyn Freeman who had since retired, designating Daria the unofficial heir to her business, she explained. Besides restoration work for museums and libraries, she also did private work—doctoral dissertations, family Bibles, and, as she put it, "Great Aunt Fannie's recipe book sort of stuff." She had gotten her present job through Mrs. Freeman, who was a friend of Dr. Thornhill's. Mrs. Freeman had worked with him on the MacMillan collection.

Charlotte was confused. Why would Daria's mentor have been working with Thornhill on the Macmillan collection? "Would you say that again, please?"

John, who had been engrossed in his book, perked up his ears at the mention of the famous botanical collection.

Daria smiled. "Dr. Thornhill was a trustee of the botanical society. He still is, for that matter. When MacMillan left his collection to the society, Dr. Thornhill was asked to oversee the transfer. He was the only trustee who knew anything about botanical books. Some of the books needed repair, so he called in Mrs. Freeman. She'd done some work for MacMillan before he died. On *Der Gart*, for instance. Felix talked about its being in immaculate condition, which is true, but when a book is five centuries old, it's bound to experience some wear and tear. I have a bit more work to do on it myself."

"How long will your work here take you?" asked Charlotte.

"Until the end of the summer," Daria said. Gathering up a stack of cardboard rectangles, she carried them over to the counter, where she began matching each to a piece of linen book cloth. "It's not standard practice for the binder to come to the collector. But Dr. Thornhill was willing to foot the bill for moving my equipment up here. Besides," she added, "the prospect of getting out of the city for the summer sounded pretty good."

"I should think it would," said Charlotte.

"Most of the work I'm doing here isn't as complicated as *Der Gart*, though," Daria continued. "John, let me see that Grenville," she said, reaching for the book in his hands. "For instance, a book like this—an eighteenth-century herbal—is in very good condition." She handed it to Charlotte. "All I have to do is clean it up, oil the binding, and make a box for it."

"Is that what you're doing now?"

"Yes," she said, as she glued the cardboard and linen together with deft, sure strokes. "It used to take me days, but now I can make one in a few hours."

Charlotte donned her glasses—Ben Franklin-style spectacles that gave her a professorial air—and picked up the book. The pages opened to a beautiful hand-colored engraving of the same violet-blue flower she'd seen in the witches' garden, the one that had made her fingers numb. The name, written at the foot of the page, was monkshood, or *Aconitum napellus*.

"What about you?" asked Daria. "What brings you to Bridge Harbor?"

Charlotte laid the book down. "I guess you could say I'm here for a rest cure. I finished in *The Trouble with Murder* last month, and since I don't have any other immediate offers, I'm taking some time off."

"I'm sure there's no shortage of offers for an actress of your caliber," said John, who was fiddling with a 35mm camera on the counter. He picked it up and focused it on Charlotte.

"Not a shortage, but not a steady flow either." She scowled at the lens. "If you click that thing, I'll be very upset." She spoke jokingly, but there was an edge to her voice. Generally she was indulgent of her fans, but candid photographers irked her beyond reason, the result of having spent a good part of her life eluding overzealous paparazzi.

John laid down the camera.

"Thank you."

"I would like to photograph you some time."

"Maybe," answered Charlotte, with a little smile. "I'd like to hear some more about your work," she said, changing the subject. She smiled. "It seems that our conversation yesterday was interrupted."

"It does seem that way, doesn't it?" he said sardonically. "I'm sorry I walked out." He shook his head. "As you could see, Frank doesn't miss a chance to give me a hard time about what I'm doing."

"I sensed that he disapproved," said Charlotte, observing that she was picking up some of the local talent for understatement.

"He thinks of his herbals—not these," John said, dismissing the herbal in front of her—"but the incunabula, as sacrosanct, and my efforts to make them more accessible as some sort of sacrilege. Don't ask me why." He paused. "I do know why. It diminishes their uniqueness. The tragedy is that he doesn't even realize the incredible wealth of historical information they contain."

"Such as?"

"Science, medicine, folklore. You name it. Language, for instance. Before *Der Gart*, all books were printed in Latin. It was the first book ever printed in the vernacular. In this case, a medieval German dialect."

"Can Dr. Thornhill read medieval German?"

"No." He paused to light one of his French cigarettes, and offered one to Charlotte, which she accepted. "I don't even think he realizes that *Der Gart* represents the birth of the modern science of botany."

"Why is that?" she asked.

"The illustrations in the herbals preceding *Der Gart* were copied from manuscripts handed down from the Greeks and Romans. They were copied and recopied so many times that few of them bore any relationship to real plants. *Der Gart* was the first to contain illustrations drawn from nature. The artists actually *looked* around them for the first time." He flicked his ashes in an ashtray. "Frank says the public wouldn't appreciate his herbals. But he's the one who doesn't appreciate them." He stopped suddenly, and gave Charlotte a contrite look. "Sorry if I'm being a bore."

"Not at all." She had the self-educated person's respect for erudition. She'd spent her high school years at a posh Connecticut finishing school, her absent father's only contribution to an upbringing that was otherwise lacking in the amenities. As a result, her education was long on deportment but short on knowledge. She'd often said she'd been educated on Hollywood's sound stages: she could always be found between shots with her nose in a book. But there were gaps in the scope of her knowledge that regularly cropped up to annoy her.

"I'd take you down to see *Der Gart* and the other early herbals now," said Daria, "but I think Dr. Thornhill's got someone in the library with him. If he's still busy later on," she continued, "I'll get *Der Gart* out of the vault and show it to you up here."

Charlotte thanked her. In fact, she could hear Thornhill talking with another person—probably Chuck Donahue—in the library below.

"I wouldn't let Dr. Thornhill bother me if I were you," said Daria, turning her attention back to John. "You know why he picks on you, don't you? He's jealous. He doesn't understand what you're doing. He'd never admit it to you, of course, but you make him feel out-of-date."

"Exactly." John smiled in appreciation. "The universities are full of dinosaurs like him who look down their noses at the scholarship of their younger colleagues, especially if it has to do with computers. It's nothing new: the words and numbers people have been at loggerheads for centuries."

"They feel threatened," said Daria.

"Yes. Which would be okay if the job market weren't so tight. But in a tight job market, it stifles creativity."

"Why?" asked Charlotte.

"Because it's the old scholars—the ones who've quit thinking, quit writing, quit innovating—who control the future of the young scholars. In an open market, the young scholar who deviates from the academic orthodoxy of his elders can always find a niche. But today the young scholar who doesn't stick to the straight and narrow runs the risk of being denied tenure."

"Which means what? Being denied the security of a life-time job?"

"More than that. It means being condemned to servitude. Tenure is a class system. The tenured professors—or should I say parasites—get the lightest class loads and the highest salaries, and the untenured professors have to take up the slack. We're the ones who get the heaviest class loads, the most boring subjects, the most inconvenient times. . . . "

"All for peanuts," chimed in Daria.

"Peanuts is right." He rocked back on the edge of his stool, gripping the edge of the counter. "It's a question of power: the old men have it, and they're not about to relinquish it to the young, especially to a young scholar whose politics are too left-wing, whose interests don't fit neatly into one discipline, and who's contemptuous of their hidebound ideas."

"And you are all of the above," said Charlotte.

He rocked forward, landing with a thud. "I guess I am." He smiled, a warm smile that erased the bitterness of his words.

The three of them sat quietly for a moment, the sounds of the house magnified by the lull in their conversation. The drone of a soap opera was overlaid by the sharp tones of voices raised in argument from below. Then the doorbell rang, bringing the echo of Grace's footsteps in the parlor. They heard her speak briefly to the visitor, and then start up the stairs.

John glanced at his watch. "Well," he said, breaking the silence. "I know you came here to talk to Daria about books, not to listen to me spout off, so I'll be off." He slid hastily off his stool, picked up his camera, and strode out of the room, nearly colliding at the door with Grace, who entered holding a twenty-dollar bill in her outstretched hand.

From below, the sound of arguing became louder, and then, as the door to the library opened, very loud. They heard Chuck shout, "You'd better leave it to me, you understand?" and then the sound of the screen door slamming.

"Oh me, oh my," said Grace, shaking her head in disapproval. "Those two fight like cats and dogs."

A minute later they heard the sound of Chuck's car starting up, followed by the sound of flying gravel as he took off down the driveway.

"Pardon me, girls," Grace said. "Would either of you have change for a twenty? Wes Gilley's at the door with the lobsters I ordered for tonight's dinner. It's Frank's— I mean Dr. Thornhill's sixtieth birthday—but all I have is a twenty, and he doesn't have any change."

"I think I do," said Daria, reaching for her pocketbook. As Daria looked for the change Charlotte wandered over to the window. The view was spectacular: sailboats skipping across the sun-spangled bay, the forest of masts in the harbor, the waves lapping against the banks of the emerging bar.

Daria handed Grace the change.

"Thank you, dear," she said, with a pert wobble of her head. "We're having lobster thermidor. Marion and Chuck are coming over—I think." She turned to leave. "Would you girls like some tea? I'm just getting tea ready for Dr. Thornhill. I always take it to him at four, just before *The Edge of Night*."

Charlotte declined the invitation, having eaten a late lunch at the Saunders'. Daria did too, much to Grace's disappointment.

"She's sweet," said Daria, after Grace had left.

Charlotte agreed that Grace did have her own peculiar brand of charm, but her thoughts were on John. If he harbored a grudge against Thornhill, he might be responsible for the trouble at Ledge House, although she couldn't imagine him writing poison-pen letters or letting the air out of the jeep's tires.

"I gather John and Thornhill don't get along," she said, priming the pump.

"No. It's really a shame. I think John blames Dr. Thornhill for the fact that his career isn't going anywhere."

"But they're at different universities, aren't they? How could Dr. Thornhill influence John's career?"

"All it takes is one person with clout, and Dr. Thornhill has plenty—the grand old man of economic botany and all that."

"Do you think that's what he's doing?" Charlotte remembered the sarcastic edge she'd sensed in Thornhill's voice at the scrying session, when he'd wished John good luck in his tenure ambitions.

"I doubt it. John has a bit of a chip on his shoulder."

"Why's that?"

"His background, I guess. He comes from a coal mining family. He's named after John L. Lewis, the union leader. He resents the fact that success seems to come so easily to people like Dr. Thornhill. Resents it and aspires to it at the same time, if you know what I mean."

Charlotte nodded. "But if Dr. Thornhill isn't blackballing his career, why hasn't he been granted tenure?"

"Supply and demand. It's not lack of talent. He's brilliant. He can actually read the early herbals like *Der Gart*. No, I think he's just blaming Dr. Thornhill for a situation that's not anyone's fault."

"It sounds as if you admire him."

"I do. When one of these early herbals came on the market recently, the prospective buyer asked John to check it out. He found major flaws: a page was missing, there were transpositions in the text. No one else had noticed. The point I'm making is this, I guess: everyone wants these herbals to enhance the prestige of their collections, but nobody actually ly reads them. Except for John, that is." Leaning forward on the counter, she smiled her dazzling smile. "But we're not lovers, if that's what you mean."

Charlotte threw her head back and laughed. "Yes, I guess that's what I was wondering—at the back of my mind."

"I suspected as much," Daria said. "No, we're not lovers. Not yet, anyway. It's not that I'm not attracted to him. It's just that . . . I don't know. These things always seem to get so complicated, and I'm not sure I want complications in my life right now. I guess I'm not ready for a love affair."

Charlotte looked at Daria sympathetically over the tops of her glasses. "I know the feeling."

From below, they heard Thornhill calling for Grace.

"That's right," replied Daria, smiling. "I guess you would. I thought you'd finally met your match in your last husband. At least, it seemed that way from what I read in the gossip columns."

"I thought so too." After separating from her third husband, Charlotte had decided she'd be best off with someone whose achievements matched hers, but in another field—a writer, a politician, a businessman—someone who wouldn't be threatened by being Mr. Charlotte Graham. Jack had seemed just right: he'd built a small family-owned mining company into one of the country's biggest conglomerates. But it hadn't worked. They had both come to realize that he didn't like living with a competitor for the limelight. "We're still good friends," she said. "But we finally had to face the fact that he wanted someone who would massage his ego and take his suits to the cleaners. I guess I didn't fill the bill."

"I should say not," said Daria.

From below, they heard a thud, followed by a low moan. Charlotte caught Daria's eye—it suddenly dawned on them that Thornhill's call to Grace a few seconds earlier had carried a note of urgency.

A moment later they were downstairs. They found Thornhill kneeling on one knee next to a wicker chair that had toppled over—it was the chair they had heard hit the floor. One arm was draped around Grace's waist and the other was clenched to his chest. His appearance was alarming. His complexion was gray, and beads of sweat stood out on his freckled temples, despite the cool breeze blowing through the doors to the veranda. He was gasping for breath.

"It's his heart," explained Grace, who seemed untowardly calm. "He gets these spells. He'll be all right in a few minutes. Won't you, sugar?" She patted his head, and wiped his face with the washcloth she held in one hand.

"My legs feel so heavy," he complained.

"Have you called a doctor?" asked Charlotte.

"No. I gave him a nitro, though. He'll be all right," she repeated, as if trying to convince herself. "If you girls could just help me get him to his room . . . "

"I'll help you in a minute," said Charlotte. "First I'm going to call an ambulance." She didn't think he looked all right at all. She remembered seeing the bar from the window. The tide was out: an ambulance could make it across.

The nearest hospital was in Bridge Harbor; a regional hospital with an excellent reputation. The availability of good medical care was one reason why the Saunders had chosen Bridge Harbor for their retirement.

"Do you really think that's necessary, honey?" protested

Grace. "He's always pulled out of these spells before."

"We'll let the ambulance crew decide that," replied Charlotte curtly. "Is there a phone in the library?"

Grace nodded.

With the ambulance on its way, Charlotte returned to the parlor to help Daria and Grace carry Thornhill to his room. He wasn't especially heavy, but his inability to move his legs made their job difficult. At last they arrived at his spare, cell-like bedroom, its stark appearance relieved only by an engraved portrait of a bewigged Carl Linnaeus, the Swedish botanist.

As they laid him on his narrow bed Charlotte had an uneasy feeling. For some reason she was reminded of the image of the yellow dog that had appeared in the coals of the fire in the witches' cauldron.

·6·

WHAT DO YOU think of this?" asked Stan, sliding the local weekly across the table to Charlotte, who was sipping her morning coffee. "In the box," he added.

The item was an editorial entitled "The Man Who Would Be King"; it was prominently displayed in a box on the front page next to a story on the proposal to grant a tax abatement to the Chartwell Corporation.

"Once upon a time," read Charlotte, "there was a beautiful republic by the sea whose people were very poor. Among the republic's territories was a beautiful island, which was owned by an old hermit. Many pilgrims wanted to visit the island, but there was no bridge. So the people said to the hermit, 'Let us build a bridge so the pilgrims can visit our island.' The hermit said, 'But where will the pilgrims stay?' The people replied, 'Let us build an inn where the pilgrims will stay.' 'But who will tend the inn?' asked the hermit. 'We will tend the inn,' replied the people. 'The inn will give us work and make us prosperous again.' The hermit considered the people's petition, and then said: 'I will not allow it. I am now king of all I survey. If I allow the pilgrims to visit my island, I will no longer be king, for they will not obey me.' And so the people suffered. But the hermit lived happily every after."

"Kipling, it's not," Charlotte said drily as she finished reading. "Isn't *pilgrim* the Maine expression for a summer tourist?"

Stan nodded. "As if the meaning weren't clear enough. What they left out of their little fable is how the inn would help the local newspaper: *And when the inn was built, the local bellyache grew fat with revenues from ads designed to separate the pilgrims from their hard-earned cash.*"

"Chamber of Commerce journalism," commented Charlotte as she gazed out at the sparkling cove, where Gilley's lobster boat was making its way around Sheep Island from lobster buoy to lobster buoy.

"You can say that again. Well, their nasty little fable may backfire on them when people find out that Frank's in the coronary care unit. But maybe not. I'm not sure I'd trust the town's good will to extend that far."

"I wonder how he's doing?"

She was answered by a knock on the door. It was Tracey. He had again walked over from the Saunders' wharf. Charlotte still couldn't get used to the idea of a place that sometimes was an island and sometimes wasn't.

"How's Frank?" asked Stan as they greeted Tracey at the door.

"Not too well," he replied solemnly. "He's still in the coronary care unit."

"Sorry to hear it," replied Stan. "Would you like to come in?"

"Thank you, no," said Tracey. "I have to be getting on up to Ledge House. I wonder if you'd like to come along, Miss Graham? Something's come up that I think you might be interested in."

A few minutes later they were hiking up the road toward Ledge House, chatting easily about lobster traps and the other arcana of Maine life. It seemed to be becoming a regular commute for Charlotte—one that she was becoming fond of. As she was of her companion. She and Tracey couldn't have come from more dissimilar worlds—he had spent his entire life in the same little corner of Maine—but they had much in common, chiefly their devotion to their work. She also sensed behind his round red cheeks and mild blue eyes that familiar strain of Yankee grit, the ballast of the soul that keeps the ship steady in the roughest of waters. For her, it was like coming home again. After a while, they walked in comfortable silence. But if they were silent, nothing else was: birds sang, katydids buzzed, the waves lapped against the bar, the boats in the harbor rumbled, and—a motorcycle engine roared. As they reached the top of the rise, they could see the offender: a long-haired teenager on a trail bike, mindlessly tracing figure eights over and over and over again in a grassy field. So much for the pleasures of nature.

"Who's that?" asked Charlotte, as the teenager came around again, sending the dirt flying. He was wearing a studded leather jacket and a knapsack emblazoned with the name of a rock group.

"Kevin Donahue, Chuck and Marion's boy," explained Tracey. "Another one of those obnoxious teenagers."

"Well," she said, turning to Tracey, "what's up?" Enough with the small talk, already, she thought. (Four decades in Hollywood and New York had coarsened whatever New England courtliness she might have once possessed).

"Daria Henderson just called the station," he replied. "She went to the vault this morning to get out one of Dr. Thornhill's rare books. Said something about showing it to you, in fact." He paused. "But it wasn't there. All the rare books that were supposed to be in the vault were missing."

"Missing!" exclaimed Charlotte. "How long have they been gone?"

"She doesn't know. They weren't there when she looked for them two weeks ago. She thought Dr. Thornhill had put them somewhere else, which is what she thought at first this time too. But they're nowhere to be found."

Ahead, they could see the gardener's cottage where John lived. "How about John Lewis, the scholar-in-residence?" said Charlotte. "Maybe he was using them over at the gardener's cottage."

"She checked with him right off," said Tracey.

"Does that mean someone's stolen them?" How ironic that they had just been talking about their vulnerability to theft, she thought.

"Evidently," he replied in his thick Maine accent.

For such a small place, Gilley Island certainly had its
share of trouble, Charlotte mused. She was reminded of the
editorial in the newspaper: it did seem that an island was a
little kingdom, a symbol of independence and individuality,
a minute world of pure perfection. But it was also sinister
somehow in its detachment from the strictures of mainland
society. When something went awry, it seemed to go more
awry on an island. She was reminded of stories she'd heard
about the islands off the coast of the Canadian Maritimes:
one island inhabited by thrifty, hard-working, God-fearing
folk, and its neighbor by utter degenerates, with only a rotten gene or two down the centuries to account for the difference.

The question was, who was responsible for the rotten gene
on Gilley Island? Someone with a grudge against Thornhill
might commit malicious mischief, but why steal his books?
She wondered about reselling them, and concluded it might
be very difficult. "What's the procedure for reporting stol-
en books?" she asked. "There must be a way of alerting
dealers."

"There is," Tracey replied as they walked up the driveway
to the front door. "Mr. Mayer is going to tell us about it.
He's taking care of it."

The door was answered by Grace. She said nothing, as
if recent events had robbed her of the energy required for
her syrupy sweetness. Charlotte and Tracey followed her
into the library, a spacious room that ran the full depth of
the house. Unlike the parlor, which had a feminine quality, the library was a man's room, filled with dark wood
and capacious club chairs of the kind found in grand old
hotels that care more about comfort than image. Despite
the brightness of the day, the atmosphere was dusky. Heavy
green drapes were drawn over the windows. The books were
housed in polished walnut bookshelves marked with brass
plates. From the shelves hung engraved portraits of gentlemen in seventeenth- and eighteenth-century dress, presumably the authors of some of the books in the collection.
One portrait—of a man in an Elizabethan ruff—had been

tilted aside to reveal the rectangular vault concealed behind it. The gleaming stainless steel door stood open, exposing the empty interior.

In the center of the room stood an old English refectory table, at which Daria sat in one of four ornately carved arm-chairs. She rose to greet them, as did Felix, who had just hung up the telephone.

Tracey introduced himself to Daria and Felix. He then explained Charlotte's presence: he didn't expect that they would mind the assistance of someone who had helped solve the famous "murder at the Morosco" case.

"Not at all," said Felix, lowering his ponderous torso into a large armchair by the fireplace. "The more heads the bet-ter. A very interesting case. There was a book written about it, was there not?"

"Yes," replied Charlotte. "*Murder at the Morosco.*"

"A likely title," he said with a smile. After lighting his cigar with a great deal of licking, puffing, and lip-smacking, he proceeded with his remarks: "I presume Chief Tracey has filled you in on what's happened. At his direction, I have notified the proper authorities of the theft."

"Who are the proper authorities?" asked Charlotte. She sat at the table in one of the ornate armchairs, facing a tile-ornamented fireplace.

"The FBI, when the loss is over five thousand dollars and when it is presumed the books have left the state. And, of course, the local law enforcement authorities," he added, with a nod to Tracey.

Nodding in return, Tracey made some jottings in a note-book. He also sat at the table, looking distinctly out of place in a dark blue uniform shirt with his name embroidered in gold thread above the breast pocket.

"How are the dealers notified?" he asked.

"A computer bulletin board alerts dealers around the world within hours," replied Felix. "Dealers with computers have immediate access to a list of missing books. Dealers without computers can call a special number or consult a list that is mailed out monthly."

"It sounds like an efficient system," said Tracey.

"Very efficient," interjected John, who had entered and was standing by the door. "The tragedy is that it's needed at all. Such a sophisticated system was never necessary in the past. But as rare books have become increasingly fashionable, theft has become a greater problem."

Daria introduced him to Tracey.

"Excuse me for interrupting," said John, crossing the room to shake Tracey's hand. "I just wanted to offer my services. I'm sure Mr. Mayer is doing everything in his power to help, but if there's anything I can do, please let me know. Obviously, I have an interest in seeing that the books are recovered."

"When did you last see the missing books, Mr. Lewis?" asked Tracey.

"A couple of weeks ago," he replied. "It was a Tuesday. I remember because I'd just returned from a long weekend in Boston." He walked over to a calendar that was hanging on a wall. "June twelfth, I guess it was."

"The day before I looked for them and discovered that they weren't there," added Daria.

"Will there be anything else?" asked John.

"Not at the moment," replied Tracey.

"I'm sorry this had to happen, but maybe it will be a lesson to Frank," he said, heading back toward the door. "Keeping books as valuable as these lying around is an open invitation to theft."

"I am afraid our young friend is right," said Felix after John had gone. "Let's hope our dear host will have a chance to put the lesson into practice once the books are recovered."

"A question about this notification system, Mr. Mayer," said Tracey, pencil in hand. "Would a dealer who is offered a book for sale automatically consult the computer bulletin board, or would he have to be tipped off first that a book might have been stolen?"

"A very good question, sir," replied Felix, with a little nod. "Usually a dealer would suspect theft before consulting the list, the tip-off, as you say, being that the seller cannot supply a verifiable provenance."

"Provenance?" asked Tracey.

"Origin. But in the case of extremely rare books such as these, the dealer would immediately suspect theft. If a seller should tell me, for instance, that he bought the books at a yard sale or found them in his grandfather's attic, I would immediately—what is the expression in English?—smell a fish."

"A rat," corrected Charlotte.

"Ah, *ja*," replied Felix good-naturedly. "*Smell* a rat or *suspect* something fishy, *nicht wahr*?"

Charlotte nodded. She noticed with repugnance the lack of concern with which he flicked the ashes of his cigar on the fine Chinese carpet.

"Does that mean the books are likely to be recovered?" asked Tracey.

"*Ja*—if they enter the market place," replied Felix. "But material gain isn't the only motive for theft. In fact, the thief who steals for material gain is usually quite easy to catch. It's the thief who steals out of some other motive who's hard to catch."

"Such as?" prompted Daria.

Felix settled back in his chair self-importantly, delighting in his role as resident expert. "One motive is the drive to possess, which we were talking about the other day. The thief who is motivated to steal for this reason doesn't try to sell the book, which makes it very difficult to catch him. This type of thief thinks he has a *right* to a book. Usually he keeps the book in a place that is directly under his control, such as a vault."

The group's attention shifted to the vault, whose gaping emptiness lent a jarring note to the otherwise tranquil atmosphere of the room.

"Then there's the casual thief, who steals because the opportunity arises. The janitor who accidentally comes across a valuable document, the visitor who is left alone in a room with an unlocked vault full of early printed herbals.

This kind of thief is easy to catch. He usually tries to sell the book, but goes about it so ineptly that he gives himself away."

"The vault wasn't locked?" asked Tracey, turning to Daria.

"Well, that's the thing," she replied. "It wasn't. Not when Dr. Thornhill was here, and he was here most of the time. He only locked it when he went down to Boston. He put the books in the vault more to protect them from light and dust than to protect them from theft."

"So anyone could have taken them," observed Tracey.

"I suppose so," said Daria in a tone of puzzlement. "But he's here most of the time, and even when he's not, there's usually someone around."

Charlotte remembered Stan's comment that Thornhill was in the habit of spending long hours in his library huddled over his books like a miser over his gold. The room was almost a separate apartment: there was a cot, an adjoining bathroom, and a kitchen corner with a small refrigerator and a microwave. French doors opened onto a terrace over-looking the rose garden, where a crude cross marked Jesse's grave. Beyond the rose garden was an arbor, and beyond that, the herb garden. A light breeze carried the spicy scent of herbs.

"What about last night?" asked Tracey. "Could someone have entered the library while you were at the hospital? I see that it's not very secure," he said, nodding at the open doors to the terrace.

"Yes, that's a possibility," said Daria. "The doors are never locked. Fran and Grace and I were all at the hospital."

Tracey made a notation in his notebook.

"Shall I continue?" asked Felix.

"By all means," said Charlotte.

"Finally there's the thief who steals out of anger. He harbors a grudge against an institution, or, in the case at hand, an individual. Usually he destroys a book rather than selling it. He is rarely caught, but we can take some solace from the fact that he rarely repeats his act."

"Then it's possible that the books were taken by someone with a grudge against Dr. Thornhill," said Charlotte. "For instance, a member of the Citizens for the Chartwell Corporation."

"Very possible indeed," said Felix, taking another puff of his cigar.

Or, Charlotte thought, *a disaffected colleague*. John certainly qualified in the grudge category. But she couldn't imagine him destroying books that he believed to be among civilization's greatest treasures.

"What kind of thief do you think is involved, Mr. Mayer?" asked Tracey.

"I doubt it's the thief who steals for gain," replied Felix. "This kind of thief is usually very professional: he knows which books are the easiest to sell. And the rarer the book, the more difficult it is to dispose of."

"But wouldn't it be possible to sell the books to an unscrupulous dealer?" asked Daria. "I'm sure there are dealers who wouldn't hesitate to pass a stolen book off on an unsuspecting customer."

"*Ja*," replied Felix. "I am afraid there are as many unscrupulous people in the bookselling business as in any other. I doubt, however, that such a dealer would sell the books to an unsuspecting customer. It is more likely that he would have a particular customer in mind, a bibliomaniac, perhaps, for whom the pride of possession would outweigh any moral scruples he might have about accepting stolen merchandise."

Pulling a monogrammed linen handkerchief out of one of his many pockets, he wiped his shiny forehead. Charlotte noticed that the toe of his foot, clad in white doeskin, tapped a nervous tattoo. Was he nervous because Daria's question challenged the integrity of his profession? Or was he nervous because he had stolen the books? He had access to them, and he knew the market. She looked down with a shudder at the little gray heaps of cigar ashes at the side of his chair. She could imagine what his apartment looked like. She knew it was ridiculous of her to think so, but to her his sloppiness alone made him worthy of suspicion. She had always had a passion for order. Even as a child she had been tormented by something as trivial as a wrinkle in her blouse or a grass stain on her skirt. But although she recognized that her fastidiousness was excessive, experience had nevertheless confirmed her opinion that sloppiness can sometimes be a manifestation of weakness of character. Besides, Felix's sloppiness wasn't all that made her uneasy about him. He also seemed to be playing a role: he was almost a caricature of himself—a shade too unctuous, too jovial, too much the *bon vivant*.

She made a mental note to ask her friend Tom Plummer to check Felix out through his contacts in the New York book world. Tom was the journalist who had written *Murder at the Morosco*. He had connections everywhere, or could make them. If Felix had stolen the books, he must have needed the money, in which case Tom's snooping would turn up some evidence of financial trouble.

"Now for the big question," said Tracey. "How much are the books worth?"

"It's hard to say," replied Felix, still puffing on his cigar. "In the book business, we say that a rare book is worth what someone will pay for it. There are no hard and fast prices. For instance, it's very difficult to estimate the value of a rare book if no one will take it off your hands."

"I shouldn't think that would be the case with these books," said Charlotte impatiently.

"This is true. In fact, it's difficult to estimate the value of these books for precisely the opposite reason: they are so desirable. Usually, one studies dealers' prices and auction house records to get an idea of a book's value, but some of these books haven't been on the market in decades."

"Mr. Mayer," said Charlotte with a polite smile, "can you give us a rough estimate of their value, please?" He was obviously milking his opportunity to show off to the last drop.

"Of course," he said, unperturbed. "I'm only explaining the difficulties involved so that you'll understand that my estimates may not reflect the true market value of the books."

Charlotte nodded.

Leaning his head back against the chair, he stared at the ceiling, his liver-colored lips moving in silent calculation.

"The earliest is the *Herbal of Apuleius*, printed in Rome in 1481. The first illustrated herbal ever printed. A copy in poor condition sold in London last year for twenty thousand pounds. Franklin's copy could expect to bring seventy thousand dollars."

Tracey let out a low whistle. "How do you spell that?" he asked as he made a notation in his notebook. Charlotte, too, was stunned at the amount. Felix had talked about *Der Gart's* being very valuable, but she had thought it unique in being worth so much.

"Next is the *Herbarius Latinus*, printed in Mainz in 1484 by Peter Schoeffer, Gutenberg's son-in-law," he continued. "This is a *very* rare book. There haven't been any copies on the market since the fifties. I'd have to say seventy thousand dollars as well."

"Were any of these books insured?" asked Tracey.

"I doubt it. The cost of the premiums would have been prohibitive."

Tracey nodded and made another notation in his notebook.

"*Der Gart der Gesundheit*," continued Felix. Turning to Charlotte, he said: "This is the book we were talking about the other day. The first book printed in any language other than Latin. Very rare and *very* valuable. A minimum of a hundred and twenty thousand dollars."

He really did have a prodigious memory for books, thought Charlotte as he again tilted his head toward the ceiling.

"Next: *Hortas Sanitatis*, printed in Mainz in 1491," he went on, spelling the title for Tracey. "Not as beautiful as *Der Gart*, but unusual because of the large number of illustrations—more than one thousand. I'd have to say eighty thousand dollars."

He paused to allow Tracey time to catch up.

"The last book, *Gerard's Herbal*, isn't an incunabulum—it was printed in 1597," Felix continued. "But it was the first great herbal printed in the English language."

"What's an incunabulum?" asked Tracey.

Charlotte explained, amusing Felix and Daria with her newfound expertise.

"That's Gerard," continued Felix, nodding at the portrait that had concealed the vault. "He was a friend of Drake and Raleigh. They brought him plant specimens from the New World, including the potato. That's a potato plant he's holding in his hand—he was the first to describe it."

"How much is *Gerard's Herbal* worth?" asked Tracey.

"Six thousand or so, ordinarily. But Franklin's copy was what we call an association copy, which means that it came from the library of a distinguished owner. In this case the owner was the herbalist John Parkinson, who published his own herbal in 1640. That's Parkinson there," he said, nodding at a portrait of a man wearing an Elizabethan skullcap and holding a flower. "Franklin's copy was annotated with Parkinson's notes, which makes it valuable indeed. Say, ten times it's usual value, or sixty thousand dollars."

Tracey added up the figures in his notebook. "According to my calculations, the books are worth about four hundred thousand dollars."

"That sounds about right," replied Felix.

Charlotte was astounded at the total. "Then this must be one of the largest book thefts in history," she said.

"Certainly among the top ten," replied Felix matter-of-factly. "Now," he continued, turning to Daria, "the authorities will require detailed descriptions of the missing books to help potential buyers identify the stolen material. Will you be able to see to that, Miss Henderson?"

"I think so," she replied.

"*Gut*. Title, author, date, publisher, number of pages, condition, binding description, illustrations, and so on."

Daria nodded. "I'll look through the files," she said. "I'm sure I can find that information somewhere."

Charlotte glanced over at the bank of half a dozen filing cabinets in the corner, each of them heaped with stacks of papers, and concluded it wouldn't be an easy job. Apparently Thornhill's acquisitive streak extended to papers as well as to books: it looked as if he never threw anything out.

"They will also want copies of any documents pertaining to the books," Felix continued. "Bills of sale, binder's reports—that sort of thing."

Daria nodded.

"I think that's all we can do for the time being," Felix said. He turned to Tracey. "I turn the case over to you, my good sir."

Tracey put his notebook away. Then he rose and crossed the room to shake Felix's hand. "I'm much obliged for your help, Mr. Mayer."

"My pleasure."

"What we have then," said Charlotte as she also rose to leave, "is a situation in which the books could have been stolen at any time over the past couple of weeks by anyone, from a professional thief to a bibliomaniac to a casual visitor to someone with a grudge against Thornhill."

"*Ja*, this is true, my dear Miss Graham," said Felix. "Book thieves cannot be narrowed down to a specific type. They come in all forms—male and female, young and old, rich and poor."

Charlotte and Tracey thanked Felix and Daria for their help, and headed back to the Saunders'.

Turning onto the Gilley Road a few minutes later, they ran into Wes Gilley, who was coming from the opposite direction. He was driving a battered old pickup filled with new lobster traps.

"Fine day for the race," he said as he pulled up alongside them. Leaning out the window, he spit a brown stream of tobacco juice over the side.

"What race is that, Wes?" asked Tracey. He looked perplexed, as if there was a race in town he should know about but didn't.

"The human race," replied Wes. He smiled broadly at his joke, revealing handsome teeth that were stained brown from chewing tobacco.

"Couldn't argue with you there," said Tracey, grinning.

Seeing Wes at close range, Charlotte was struck by the fact that he was a good-looking man, if you could get beyond his red-ringed eyes, three days' growth of beard, and the wad of chewing tobacco that bulged beneath his lower lip. The broad, unlined face under his navy watch cap was tanned to a deep bronze by the wind and sun, and his large eyes were a pale, delicate shade of blue, as if they'd been bleached by ocean salt and foam.

"They crawling good?" asked Tracey, inquiring about the catch.

Wes uttered an emphatic growl that sounded something like "daow," and which, Charlotte presumed, answered the question in the negative.

"Got six hundred jeezly traps out," he said disgustedly. "First time in my life I've had that many out. And I still ain't haulin' much."

"Ayuh," nodded Tracey sympathetically. "And when everybody's got so many traps out, you can't really put them where you want to."

"Jeezum, ain't it the truth," said Wes. "Alls you can do is put 'em where somebody else ain't and hope your guess is better than theirs." He spat another stream of tobacco juice over the side. "Ayuh," he continued, staring pensively out over the steering wheel. "Years ago I used to think that anyone who expected to make a livin' by settin' a trap in the water and expectin' a lobster to crawl into it was a damn fool." He turned to face them with a big smile. "I expect as I was right."

He spoke in a thick nasal accent. If you didn't listen closely to the words, you could be carried away by the antique cadence, with its broad a's, dropped g's, and lost r's. Until the fifties, Kitty had told Charlotte, the inhabitants of many of Maine's outer islands still spoke a little-corrupted form of Elizabethan English, but television had brought the beginnings of cultural homogeneity to even the most remote backwaters. In another generation or two, Gilley's accent would probably be indistinguishable from that of the evening news anchorman.

Wes put his truck into gear and said goodbye. Tracey had not introduced her, but Charlotte knew that Wes knew who she was. She had sensed him subtly sizing her up. She wondered if he was responsible for the vandalism. Kitty had pooh-poohed her suggestion that he might be the culprit, but Stan had quite another story. On one of his late-night walks—the night the air had been let out of the tires of the Ledge House jeep—he had seen Wes sitting up against the side of the barn where the jeep was garaged, drunk.

Wes drove a few feet down the road, and stopped. "Hey Howard," he shouted, looking back out the window. "When's that meetin'?"

"Sunday night, eight o'clock," replied Tracey. "Town Hall."

Gilley waved goodbye and drove off.

Tracey explained that the Board of Selectmen would be holding a public hearing on the proposal to grant the Chartwell Corporation a tax abatement for the Gilley Island development. The town would vote on the issue at a special town meeting the following week.

Tracey was saying goodbye to Charlotte outside of the Saunders' house when he was hailed by Kitty. "The police station called," she said. "They want you to call back right away."

A minute later he was calling the station from the Saunders' telephone. After listening for a few minutes, he hung up the phone with a worried frown.

"Dr. Thornhill's passed away," he said.

·7·

THORNHILL'S DEATH WAS a shock, but not a sudden one. Both Fran and Marion had been at his bedside. In the end, death had come as a relief. He had not gone gently into that good night. His final hours had been accompanied by convulsions, hallucinations, and finally coma.

The funeral arrangements were still uncertain, although a memorial service had been tentatively scheduled for Saturday. Fran and Marion were awaiting the arrival of Thornhill's brother, a Boston banker, to make the final plans. The body would be cremated as Thornhill had requested, and a modest memorial, which was Marion's idea, constructed on his beloved Ledges. Kitty had spent the previous evening helping Fran and Marion notify friends, relatives, and colleagues of the death, and was now helping Grace prepare food for the gathering that would be held at Ledge House following the service.

Charlotte sat on a stool in Stan's studio, looking out at the cove, which shone a pale green in the morning sun, the waves lapping against the shingled beach. Her thoughts dwelled vaguely on Thornhill's death: it was hard to believe he was gone, she mused as she watched the gulls wheel and turn and dive for crabs and periwinkles with raucous, excited cries. He had seemed so full of vitality despite his heart condition. How many of her friends and acquaintances had slipped away just as quickly? The older she got, the more tenuous the thread of life seemed to become.

By contrast with the peacefulness of the cove outside, the sea in the large canvas to which Stan was applying the finishing touches was roiled and angry. The painting depicted a big gray-green wave about to break on a cluster of jagged rocks surrounded by a swirl of white foam.

"I've never understood how you paint a wave," Charlotte said. "It's not as if a wave will stand still for you like a landscape."

"Exactly," replied Stan, adding a dab of brown to the tip of a gull's wing. "Trying to copy a small detail of a wave is the biggest failing of beginners. Before they can get it down, it's moved. The trick is to think of the detail as part of a bigger body of water."

"Yes, but how do you teach that?" she asked, referring to the classes Stan taught in seascape painting.

"Actually, I have a new technique. John Lewis, Daria's boyfriend, is taking photographs for me of waves breaking at different stages. The students sketch from the photographs until they they have a sense of the action. Then I try them out on the real thing."

He handed her a stack of student sketches, which showed the stages of a breaking wave outlined in blue pigment. Charlotte leafed through them, stopping at an unusual sketch of a bizarrely shaped rock.

"Crap," growled Stan, who was hanging over her shoulder.

"Why?"

"The whole point of a marine painting is to show the drama of the conflict between land and sea, not to show an unusual rock formation or a scenic shoreline. The viewer should have the idea that the painting could be anywhere, anytime. Universal, not specific."

"But Stan," she protested, "isn't that a matter of opinion? Perhaps some people *like* paintings of scenic shorelines."

"Now you sound just like Daria," he complained.

"What does she say?"

"It's not what she says, it's what she does," he replied, sorting through a stack of canvases leaning against a wall. "Here I am, trying to teach her how to capture the elemental battle between land and sea, and she insists on painting the sea barse-ackwards, to use the local expression."

"What do you mean?"

"Just that," he said. "Instead of painting the land in the foreground and the sea in the background, she wants to go out in a boat and paint the sea in the foreground and the land in the background. There," he announced, lifting a large canvas onto the easel.

It was an oil painting of the channel with the path of the Ledges, crowned by the gazebo, rising in the distance. Unlike Stan's dark, somber paintings, Daria's was light and airy, with subtle, abstract shapes that captured the magical enchantment Charlotte had felt upon first seeing the Ledges.

"Oh, Stan, I love it," she said quietly.

"You women are all alike," he groused. He stepped away from the easel. "Actually, it's not bad," he said, which coming from him was a compliment. "But as far as I'm concerned, it's not marine painting, that's all."

Removing the painting from the easel, he carried it back to its place. "Now she wants to paint the same scene by moonlight. The next thing you know, she'll be putting a goddam gondola in the foreground." Returning to the easel, he paused to rotate his shoulder.

"I doubt that," said Charlotte. "What's wrong with your shoulder? Is your rheumatism bothering you again?"

"It's lifting these canvases—it's a hard angle for me. I'll have to get Kitty to give me another dose of that monkshood."

"What did you say?"

"I said, 'I'll have to get Kitty to give me another dose of that monkshood,' " replied Stan with a puzzled look. "Why?"

"I'll tell you later," she said, sliding off her stool. "I've got to go up to Ledge House. You just gave me an idea."

The door at Ledge House was answered by Marion. Charlotte remembered that Thornhill's wife had been French, and concluded that Marion must take after her. Tall and slim, she had the long-necked elegance of a Nefertiti, with a high forehead, graceful brow, and large, Gallic nose. The prominent nose, which might have marred a face whose features were less well-proportioned, endowed Marion with an air of intelligence and authority. Her thick, wavy dark hair was cut very short and brushed stylishly away from her face. She might have been beautiful, but even allowing for the circumstances, her pale, drawn face lacked the animation that her generous features seemed to call for.

Introducing herself, Charlotte offered her condolences and her help, to which Marion responded graciously that Fran, Grace, and Kitty were providing all the help she needed. She spoke in a deep voice, made husky, Charlotte suspected, by too many cigarettes.

But Charlotte's wasn't purely a condolence call, as she tactfully explained. She wanted to use the library, she said, for a purpose that she would rather not take the time to explain at the moment.

Her mind too preoccupied with other matters to be curious, Marion showed her to the library and retired to the kitchen.

As Charlotte entered the library her mind was whirling. *What can kill, can cure*, Kitty had said. Stan's comment had reminded her of the engraving of the violet-blue flower in the herbal she had looked at in the bindery. Monkshood: the plant Kitty was using to treat Stan's rheumatism was the same plant she had seen growing in the black witches' section of the witches' garden. The same plant whose roots had been dug up. The same plant that had made her fingers numb.

She didn't know what she was looking for. It was only a hunch. And an image: the body of a yellow dog floating above the glowing coals at the bottom of an iron cauldron.

She scanned the brass markers—agriculture, horticulture, landscape architecture, plant exploration, history of gardening, systematic botany, trees and fruits—until she found what she was looking for: herbs and herbals. There it was—the linen-covered box Daria had made with the title, *A Complete Herbal by Thomas Grenville*, stamped in gold on the spine. Removing it from the shelf, she leafed through the pages. The book fell open to the page with the hand-colored engraving of the tall plant with the violet-blue flowers.

She started reading: "Monkshood—also known as friar's cap, helmet flower, grannie's nightcap, and wolfsbane—is a native of the mountains and woods of Germany, France, and Switzerland, but since the time of Gerard, it has been cultivated for ornament." She skipped ahead. "Many cases have been cited in which rheumatism that could not be helped by any other medication was cured with monkshood." Which would explain Kitty's success in treating Stan's shoulder. She read on. And there it was—the words seeming to leap off the page: *Monkshood is the most virulent of all plant poisons*.

She sank into a chair, stunned. Laying the book down on the table, she lit a cigarette with shaking hands. After a minute, she picked it up again, her eyes skipping over the text: *The variety that is the most poisonous is the common garden variety*, Aconitum napellus. . . . *The chief active ingredient is the alkaloid, aconitine*. . . . *The root is the most poisonous part*. She remembered some lines from *Henry IV*: "Venom . . . as pure as aconitum," the king says to the Duke of Clarence. As if there was none purer. Leaning her head back,, she stared out at Jesse's grave in the rose garden.

So her hunch had a basis in fact. Jesse might have been poisoned. Maybe by accident, maybe not. The same went for Thornhill. But by whom? Kitty immediately popped to mind, but suspecting her was absurd. She sighed. In life, one never knew what to expect: treasured friends become suspect, if only for a second, as murderers; cultured, well-mannered gentlemen (except for the cigar ashes) become suspect as thieves. It was different in the theatre: there everything was ordered, logical, continuous. Which was why she was an actress. Then again, maybe she was imagining it all. What to do now? she wondered. Talk to

Kitty. Kitty could tell her more about monkshood. So could Fran, but the fewer people who knew about her suspicions, the better. Putting out her cigarette, she headed out to the kitchen.

A few minutes later, Kitty was sitting with her in the library, her eager face overflowing with curiosity.

"Kitty, do you remember telling me about treating Stan's rheumatism with an herbal preparation? The herb was monkshood, right?"

Kitty nodded. "A tincture of the dried root."

"Where did you get it?"

"From Fran. She keeps a stock of dried herbs on hand. Why?"

Charlotte explained about seeing the roots lying around on the ground when Kitty gave her the tour of the herb garden.

"That's right. They were, weren't they?"

"Do you have any idea why?"

Kitty shook her head.

"Kitty, I think Jesse might have been poisoned with monkshood." She showed Kitty the herbal. "It says here that it's the most virulent of plant poisons. Maybe it was an accident, maybe not."

A frown creased Kitty's perfect brow.

"There's something else. Maybe I'm way off base, but I'm beginning to wonder about Thornhill. He experienced hallucinations and convulsions. I don't think hallucinations and convulsions are normal in a death from heart disease. Maybe they are." She shrugged. "I don't know."

Kitty's eyes widened. She leaned forward and gripped Charlotte's arm. "Charlotte, Fran said he had the sensation of flying."

"What does that mean?"

"Monkshood is the chief ingredient in the flying ointment I was telling you about. Fran talks about it in her witch lecture. The ointment causes an irregular heart rhythm; it also has hallucinatory properties. Scientists say it's the combination of the two that produces the sensation of flying."

"It sounds as if someone's actually tried it," said Charlotte.

"They have. One of the first scientists to experiment with it died of poisoning. He didn't have the proportions right. None of the recipes in the old herbals gives instructions on proportions. The exact composition was a secret that the witches passed on from one to another."

Charlotte sighed. This was all getting very strange. "Maybe we should find out more about monkshood poisoning," she said. She looked up at the bookshelves. "Some of these books must have information on it."

"I know just the one," said Kitty. She got up and went over to the bookshelf. Picking out a thick volume, she returned with it to the table. "It's a reference book on plant poisons," she explained. She looked up monkshood, and began to read: " 'One of the outstanding symptoms of aconite poisoning is a feeling of severe oppression in the chest. The blood pressure is low; the respiration is slow and labored; the pulse is slow, feeble, and irregular; and extreme irregularities of the heart rhythm may be observed.' "

"That would explain why the doctors thought Thornhill was having a heart attack," said Charlotte.

They were interrupted by a knock. Tracey peeked around the corner of the door, his baseball cap in his hand.

"Stan said I'd find you here," he said, closing the door behind him. "Do you have a minute?"

"Of course," said Charlotte, gesturing to a chair on the opposite side of the table. "New developments?"

Tracey said hello to Kitty and sat down. "I'd say so," he said. "The county medical examiner is going to do a post-mortem on Dr. Thornhill. He doesn't think the cause of death was a heart attack." He paused, nervously twisting his cap in his hands, and then continued: "He thinks it was poison."

"I know," said Charlotte.

"You *know*!" Tracey stared at her.

Charlotte nodded.

"By Godfrey, news travels like greased lightning around here," he said indignantly. He slapped his thigh with his cap, as angry as a state department official who's been informed of a news leak. "Would you mind telling me how you found out so jeezly dad-blamed fast?"

"I didn't find out," said Charlotte, repressing a smile.

"Now what in the name of Sam Hill do you mean by that?"

"I figured it out. Look at this." She slid the herbal across the table, pointing to the passage on monkshood.

Tracey read the text, his finger leading his eye across the page. Now and then he emitted a low whistle.

"What made the medical examiner suspect poison?" asked Charlotte.

"He didn't, not at first. He thought it was a heart attack. He was helping Dr. Thornhill's doctor on the case. The other symptoms were what made him suspicious—diarrhea, vomiting, convulsions."

Tracey looked up from the book. "I don't get it," he said finally. "How do you know this is the stuff that killed Dr. Thornhill?"

"I don't—not for sure," she replied, looking at him over the tops of her glasses. "But I have a pretty good idea."

She explained about Kitty's treating Stan's rheumatism with an herb that was poisonous in larger doses, about how she'd seen the roots of what she later learned was the same plant lying on top of the ground, and about Thornhill's deathbed hallucinations. She didn't tell him about the body of the yellow dog floating above the glowing coals.

"Is there any way to test for monkshood poisoning?" asked Kitty.

"Could be," replied Tracey. "I was just talking to the people over to the State lab. They say they can't test for an unknown poison: they have to have an idea of what they're looking for. Index of suspicion, they called it. They asked us to look into what Dr. Thornhill ate, but if we told them we suspected monkshood, that would give them something to go on."

"We were just looking at this book," said Charlotte, passing it across the table to him. "It's a reference book on plant poisons."

Tracey started to read in his thick Maine accent: " 'Monkshood was imported by the colonials, who used it for relief of pain from rheumatism, pleurisy, peritonitis, and other ailments. It is still used externally for rheumatism in Europe and elsewhere, but its internal use has been discontinued because of its extreme toxicity.' The next part is in italics: *'Clinical poisoning is fairly common. For this reason, monkshood is not recommended for internal use. Effective doses are practically toxic and toxic doses are practically ineffective.'* " He looked up. "Jeezum," he exclaimed, sucking in his breath.

Kitty sighed. "You know, I think I'll stop giving Stan that tincture of monkshood for his shoulder."

"Sounds like a good idea," agreed Tracey. "Here's the part on symptoms," he said as he continued to read to himself. "Ayuh," he said after a minute. "With his history of heart trouble, you can see why his doctors thought it was heart disease." He looked at Charlotte. "If you hadn't put two and two together and if the county medical examiner hadn't been on the ball, the poisoner might have gotten away with it. That is, if there is a poisoner."

"What do you mean *if*?" asked Charlotte.

"Well, I suppose it could have been an accident, or suicide."

"Accident, unlikely; suicide, definitely not," said Charlotte, who had been reading the Grenville. "Listen to this: 'In later stages, vomiting becomes violent and convulsive. Other symptoms are diarrhea, headache, giddiness, vertigo, and the sensation of choking. Tingling begins at an early stage: there is a sensation of ants crawling all over the body.' "

Kitty nodded. "Fran said he kept rubbing his legs as if something were crawling on them."

Charlotte shuddered. " 'Later the limbs become paralyzed,' " she continued, remembering his complaint about heavy legs. " 'The eyes protrude, and there is impairment of vision, speech, and hearing. There may be hallucinations, but the victim remains conscious. There is a great fear of death, and some victims become maniacal. Death is caused by cardiac or respiratory failure.' "

"Whew," said Tracey. "Not a very nice way to go."

"I wonder if he knew he'd been poisoned," said Charlotte. "If he did, he wouldn't have been able to say anything."

"How horrible," said Kitty with a tremble in her voice.

"How do you think the poison was administered?" asked Tracey.

From the kitchen came the muffled drone of a soap opera. With the sound helping to nudge her memory, Charlotte tried to picture the library as it had been when she'd called the ambulance. "His tea," she said. "It might have been in his tea. The tea tray was sitting right here on the table when I called the ambulance. Grace took it to him around four. He fell ill shortly afterwards." She remembered how impressed she had been at how neat it all was—the japanned tray with the embroidered linen tea towel, the hand-painted bone china tea service, the silver tea strainer, the plate of thinly sliced lemons, the silver lemon fork, the little vase of old-fashioned roses.

"By now, the dishes would be washed up," said Tracey. "But would the small amount of poison in a cup of tea be enough to kill a man?"

"Yes," said Kitty. "There have been lots of cases. There was a famous case in Belgium. Fran talks about it in her witch lecture. The people made a tea out of the root of monkshood. They thought it was another herb. Lovage, I think. Three out of the five people who drank the tea died within a couple of hours."

Tracey shook his head.

Picking up the Grenville again, Charlotte continued reading aloud: " 'The lethal dose is one teaspoonful of the fresh root. Symptoms may appear almost immediately and are rarely delayed beyond an hour. Death may occur from a few minutes to four days after ingestion.' " *What if she and Daria had taken Grace up on her offer of tea*? she wondered. She continued reading, raising her voice for emphasis: " 'If a small but fatal dose of the poison were to be given, the chances of detection in the body after death would not be great.' "

"Well, I'll be darned," said Tracey. "Looks as if somebody darn near got clean away with it."

"The question is who," said Charlotte.

"Who was here that afternoon?" asked Tracey.

"Okay," said Charlotte, starting to enumerate the possibilities. "Grace served the tea, but that doesn't mean anything—the tea could have been tampered with at an earlier time. Daria and John were upstairs in the bindery with me. Donahue was in the library with Thornhill. They were arguing, by the way. Oh, and Felix was out on the veranda, reading."

"That's five," he said. "Six, counting you." He had pulled a notebook out of his breast pocket and was taking notes. "This isn't going to be easy. I guess I'll have to take statements from everybody."

"Seven," said Charlotte. "I forgot Wes Gilley. He was dropping off some lobsters for dinner that night."

"Seven," sighed Tracey. This would be his first murder, and the first in town since the thirties, he said. He would have to call in the State police. But even with their help, he would have his work cut out for him.

"Here's something else that's very interesting," said Charlotte, who was still leafing through the Grenville. "This section is entitled 'An experiment on the action of *Aconitum napellus* on the animal economy.' "

Tracey gave her a puzzled look.

She read: " 'Two drams of a watery extract of monkshood were administered by syringe to a medium-sized dog. The extract was prepared by expressing the fluid of the fresh aconite root. Fifteen minutes later, the dog became drowsy, shut its eyes, and hung down its head. Four hours later, it experienced convulsions and died.' "

"Jesse," said Tracey. "Do you think the murderer might have experimented on Jesse to get an idea of what the lethal dose for a man would be?"

"Maybe," said Charlotte. "But his death could have been an accident. The roots looked as if they might have been dug up by a dog." She gazed out at the fresh mound of earth in the rose garden that was Jesse's grave. "We could exhume the body and have it tested."

Tracey made another notation, and then stood to leave. "Well, I'd better get going. I've got a lot to do."

As Charlotte rose to see him out her eye was caught by a book in a cardboard box filled with copies of the same book. The book was *The Living Pharmacy*; the author was J. Franklin Thornhill. "Wait a minute," she said, taking out one of the brand-new copies. "Here's Dr. Thornhill's book. Maybe he says something about monkshood." She checked the index.

"Is it in there?" asked Kitty.

"Yes," said Charlotte, returning to her seat. She turned to the page and began reading: " 'The drug was well-known to the ancients. It was believed to be the invention of Hecate, the queen of Hades, and was used to destroy criminals condemned to death or to dispose of unwanted relatives.' "

"I can think of at least one relative who might have wanted to get rid of Dr. Thornhill," said Tracey. "Chuck Donahue."

"Two," said Charlotte. "Fran is another. Dr. Thornhill was planning to remarry. She thought his new wife would make life so unpleasant for her that she'd be forced to leave." She continued reading: " 'Monkshood was used by the ancient Greek inhabitants of the isle of Ios for the elimination of the aged and infirm. Citizens who were considered to be no longer of use to society were condemned to drink a cup of the poison, called the farewell cup.' "

"Euthanasia," said Kitty.

Charlotte continued: " 'The cup was administered on the victim's sixtieth birthday.' *Oh God*," she said, dropping the book into her lap.

"What is it?" asked Tracey.

"Tuesday was Thornhill's sixtieth birthday. That's why Grace had ordered the lobsters—for a birthday celebration."

"It couldn't have been a coincidence?" asked Kitty, who could always be depended on to look on the bright side.

Charlotte shook her head.

"Maybe it *was* suicide," said Tracey. "Maybe Dr. Thornhill was depressed about getting old—that's not all that uncommon. Maybe he thought he had outlived his usefulness to society."

Charlotte cocked a skeptical eyebrow. "I think it's far more likely that someone else thought that."

Tracey shrugged. They sat in silence for a minute in the dim light. The room was silent except for the rustle of the breeze in the leaves of the hydrangeas planted around the veranda. On the mantel, an old steeple clock ticked away the minutes, and the refrigerator in the corner hummed.

Before, the idea that Thornhill had been murdered had given Charlotte an uneasy feeling, like being alone at night in an unsafe neighborhood. But now it scared her. She had suddenly come up against the homicidal mind, and it was a mind that was frightening in its complexity, a mind that was precise and cunning, a mind that delighted in the subtle irony of the fact that its victim had described his own mode of death.

Her gaze drifted out to the herb garden. The streamers of the maypole fluttered eerily in the breeze, like a flag after the parade is over. She remembered Kitty saying that it symbolized immortality.

"Oh, I almost forgot," said Tracey. He withdrew a piece of brown paper from his pocket and passed it across the table. "It was sent to the *Bridge Harbor Light*. It's the same as the other poison-pen letters that were sent to Dr. Thornhill. Same paper, same writing, same color crayon."

Printed in red crayon in a large, childlike hand, was the message: "THE KING IS DEAD. LONG LIVE THE PEOPLE."

·8·

THE SUSPICION THAT Thornhill had been poisoned touched off a flurry of activity. The State police arrived that afternoon and took statements from everyone who had been anywhere near the tea. The list included Grace, Felix, John, Wes, Chuck—and Fran, who, it turned out, had been in the kitchen. For the time being, Charlotte and Daria had been excluded from the formal list of suspects on account of their being upstairs at the time the tea was prepared. The suspects had been asked to remain in the vicinity, which meant that Felix would be extending his visit and that Chuck would not be returning to Boston as planned. Tissue samples from Thornhill's body had been sent to the state toxicology lab in Augusta to be tested for aconitine, along with samples from the package of tea and several of the cookies left over from the batch Grace had baked that morning. Tissue samples from Jesse's body had also been sent to the State lab. Thornhill's body would be quietly buried at some future date. The medical examiner had turned down Marion's request for cremation on the ground that the body might have to be exhumed for further testing. The memorial service had been canceled in favor of a small family service.

For Kitty and Stan, the suspicion that Thornhill had been poisoned with the same herb Kitty was using to treat Stan's rheumatism generated a lot of discussion—and not a little hostility. With his righteous indignation fueled by the better part of a shakerful of martinis, Stan accused Kitty of harboring a desire to do him in. Hadn't she always

displayed an inordinate interest in seeing to it that his life
insurance premiums were paid up? He had had enough of
her home remedies, thank you. What were a few points on
his golf handicap next to the possibility of being poisoned
by one of the most potent plant poisons known to mankind?
Kitty racked her memory for clues. Had she talked about
monkshood's poisonous properties with anyone? Had she
noticed anyone reading up on monkshood in the library?
Had she seen anyone digging in the monkshood bed? She
came up with nothing on all counts. One interesting fact that
had come to light courtesy of Maurice, the Ledge House
handyman, was that the monkshood bed had been dug up
a couple of weeks before Thornhill's death. But he had no
idea who had done it, or why.

After a shish kebab barbecue, Charlotte and the Saunders
had lingered on the patio discussing the case. The people
with the most to gain from Thornhill's death, they concluded, were Chuck and Wes. But a lot of others also
stood to gain, people whose feelings had been inflamed by
the editorial in the *Bridge Harbor Light*. Was the murder
related to the other incidents? they wondered—the bullet through the library window, the poison pen letters. If
so, Wes was a prime suspect because of his connection
with the tire incident. If Jesse had been poisoned, the
poisoning could have been an escalation of the threats,
a you-may-be-next reminder. Then again, the vandalism
might have been committed out of some other motive. It
wasn't an entirely farfetched notion that it was the work of
some local fundamentalist who was offended by Fran's pagan rituals. As for Fran, with both motive and means, she
was the other strong suspect. The prospect of being forced
out of one's home was enough to induce resentment in
even the most mild-mannered of people, and Fran was far
from that, as her temper tantrum had demonstrated. She
had vowed that Thornhill would be sorry he had decided
to get married. She had also cast a spell to protect herself
against "that greedy bitch." Had she also seen to it that the
spell was effective? Besides being forced out of her home,

she had an investment to protect: she had built the herb business from scratch, and having given up a job years before to keep house for her uncle, was hardly likely to go back to work now. Still another count against her was her relationship with Thornhill. Despite their blood ties (she was named after him) and their shared interest in gardening, they were not especially close, according to Kitty. In fact they were more competitors than colleagues.

But when it came to means, there were plenty of people with knowledge of herbal poisons. Fran was the obvious one, but what about John, Grace, or even Daria? None of the other three suspects on the State police's list exhibited a strong motive, although that could change: you never knew what you might uncover when you started turning over rocks in a murder investigation, Charlotte pointed out. John harbored a grudge against Thornhill, but that didn't seem motive enough for murder, on the surface at any rate. And Grace and Felix had no obvious motives at all.

The moon was high over the tips of the spruces on Sheep Island when they finally decided to call it a night. Charlotte eagerly climbed the stairs to her room in the former hayloft and collapsed onto the antique spool bed with its colorful antique patchwork quilt. But sleep eluded her. Her thoughts kept returning to the books. The fact that they were missing blinked irritatingly at the back of her mind like the idiot light on a dashboard. How in the name of Sam Hill, to use one of Tracey's favorite expressions, did they fit in with the suspicion that Thornhill had been poisoned?

The next day was a Friday. Only a week ago, Charlotte had been back at her town house on the East Side, packing her suitcase in anticipation of a restful vacation in Maine. How much had happened since then, she thought as she awoke to another beautiful day. She couldn't complain about the weather. Every day had been perfect: clear and cool, with an electricity in the air that charged her with energy. She hoped it would remain as good for Tom's stay. She had heard on the evening news that it was in the nineties in

New York. At Stan and Kitty's urging, she had invited Tom
Plummer to Maine. There was nothing he liked better than
poking his nose into a murder, and it looked as if a murder
was what they had. Since writing *Murder at the Morosco*,
he'd been making his living writing about real-life crime.
His latest book, about a family that had been terrorized by a
gang of thugs, had been another best seller and a critical success as well. It was about time that journalists started paying
attention to the victims of crime for a change, the reviewers
had said. She was glad the pendulum of public opinion was
finally swinging the other way. In many respects she was a
liberal, but when it came to crime she was a sobersided old
Yankee conservative. She'd always felt ill at ease among
people who excused antisocial behavior on the grounds of
environmental deprivation. How did they explain the fine
people who came from deprived backgrounds? To her mind,
it was a view that denied will, energy, and spirit.

She was looking forward to Tom's arrival. Since her
divorce, he had been meeting the one major need in her
life: compatible male companionship. If she wasn't cut out
for wifedom, she was at least entitled to a male companion.
In the European tradition, every elegant older woman had
her *cavaliere servente*, her gallant, and Tom was hers. It was
a symbiotic relationship: like shark and pilot fish, though
which was which she wasn't sure. As her companion, Tom
was exposed to the glamorous society that was hers as a
star. Being a star, her second husband used to say, was like
having a first-class ticket to life. Carrying the bag once in
a while (or was it the old bag, she thought wryly) was the
price Tom paid for going in style. For a couple of years
now it had been working out very well.

Friday was the day that Kitty and Fran usually went into
town to take care of their herb business. They had decided
to keep to their schedule, at Tracey's urging. "Carry on as
usual," he had said. Not only would it help take their minds
off the situation, it would also help quell gossip. The State
police had not officially acknowledged that they were con-

ducting a murder investigation, but their presence, under the direction of a handsome detective named Gaudette, couldn't help but set tongues wagging. Including Stan's. He couldn't understand why Kitty was choosing to associate with a suspected murderess. But Kitty was putting any suspicion of Fran completely out of her mind, for the moment at any rate. "Innocent until proven guilty," she told him.

Fran arrived mid-morning looking chipper—unsuitably so, thought Charlotte, in light of the fact that her uncle had probably just been murdered. But maybe that was her overactive imagination at work again.

Her green eyes shone behind the thick lenses of her glasses, and pink lipstick brightened her papery-white complexion.

Carrying a brown paper bag over to the long pine table, she carefully lifted out a large object wrapped in newspaper. "This is for you, Kit," she said as she unwrapped it. "A witch's wreath." She lifted out the wreath, which filled the kitchen with a spicy aroma.

"Oh, Fran, it's lovely," said Kitty, taking it from her. She gave her a peck on the cheek. "Thank you so much."

"It's made of mugwort, vervain, St. Johnswort, southernwood, elder, rue, willow, and valerian—the traditional herbs of the summer solstice," explained Fran. "I'm putting it in the catalogue. I think it will sell very well. People like to hang wreaths on their doors in summer too."

"That's a marvelous idea," gushed Kitty. She held the wreath out in front of her by its wire hanger. "Charlotte, isn't it just divine?" she said. "I'm going to hang it on the front door."

"Why is it called a witch's wreath?" asked Charlotte as she leaned over to smell the fragrance.

"The wreaths used to be singed in the Midsummer-Night bonfires and then hung on the door as a protection against lightning and the power of witches," she explained. "Witches are exorcised by fire: if you make a wreath of certain herbs and throw it in the fire, it will keep them away."

"Like the incense at the Midsummer-Night festival?" asked Charlotte.

"Exactly," replied Fran. "Oh, and look at this. This is the first of these I've made, but if it sells, we can make more for Halloween. A witch's broom. The handle is made of ash, which keeps the witch from getting her feet wet; and the sweeping part is made of birch, which holds the evil spirits." She held it up. "If you lay it across the threshold, it will prevent the witches from entering," she continued. "Of course, you can accomplish the same thing by hanging a dead black chicken from the doorjamb," she added cheerily, "but I think a wreath or a broom is so much nicer, don't you?"

Charlotte and Kitty readily agreed.

She briskly wrapped up the broom and returned it to the paper bag. "We've got to get going, Kit," she urged, heading toward the door. Turning to Charlotte, she said: "It was a pleasure seeing you again."

After gathering up her belongings, Kitty scurried out after her.

Charlotte sat for a moment after they had gone, looking out at the cove. She marveled at Fran's energy, and wondered briefly if there was an herb she prescribed for it. She decided she wouldn't want to take it even if there was. Outside, the gulls swarmed around the garbage cans. The gull, like man, had learned to adapt to its environment, she reflected as she watched a charred English muffin and a leftover chunk of lamb from their barbecue disappear into a down-turned beak. An eating machine with wings, it dined on everything from periwinkles to shish kebab with equal relish.

The phone rang as she was washing up the breakfast dishes. It was Tracey, with a report on the progress of the investigation. The results of the tests on the tea and the cookies had already come back. They were negative, meaning that the poison had probably been added to the teapot. The results on the tissue samples weren't in yet. He sounded harassed, and no wonder: taking statements from murder suspects was hardly his everyday fare. She had just finished reading the "Police Beat" column in the *Bridge Harbor Light*: sick moose on the beach, set of screwdrivers stolen, littering at the town pier, and a couple of driving-while-intoxicated arrests was about it—for last week. Next week's column would be a different story.

As she hung up the phone she decided to spend the rest of the morning following in Tracey's footsteps. He had urged her to talk with whomever she wanted, on his authority. She would start with the simplest task: Grace and Felix, the suspects with no apparent motives. But she suspected her task wouldn't be as simple as it seemed. For one thing, it bothered her that Grace had been so reluctant to call an ambulance. Perhaps she had wanted time for the poison to take effect. She even wondered if Grace had actually given Thornhill his nitroglycerin pill, as she had claimed. For another, there were the books. And no one knew more about books than Felix Mayer. She was anxious to hear what Tom had found out about him. She wondered if he'd really reported the book theft. If he *had* stolen the books, he could have feigned making the report, manufactured a phony provenance, and passed the books along to an innocent—or not so innocent—customer. If he was desperate for money, he might even have poisoned Thornhill. Hadn't Thornhill promised to let him handle the sale of his collection after his death? Maybe there was a reason why he had the reputation of being able to hear the death rattle before the doctor was called in. Collectors thrive among the dead—quote, unquote the great Felix Mayer.

After eating a light lunch by herself (Stan was playing golf), she headed up to Ledge House under a porcelain blue sky. It was a day to lighten even the heaviest of hearts, as if a benignant power were trying to make amends for what had gone before. Ten minutes later, she was ringing the bell at Ledge House. A witch's wreath was already hanging on the door. Good—if any dwelling needed protection from evil spirits, it was Ledge House. Grace answered the door and ushered her into a large, bright, old-fashioned kitchen, which looked much as it must have in the thirties. Taking a seat at an enamel-topped table, Charlotte explained that she was there at Chief Tracey's request, and asked Grace to review the statement she had given the police.

At the mention of Thornhill's name, Grace pulled out a handkerchief and dabbed at the swollen eyes under her rhinestone-studded glasses. Charlotte waited patiently. The smell of chocolate cake baking in the oven, the fern fronds bobbing in the open window, and the familiar theme music from *Guiding Light* reminded her of her childhood and of the afternoons she'd spent listening to the soap operas while she waited for her mother to get home from work.

Finally Grace lit a cigarette with shaking hands gnarled by arthritis and shiny-red from years of being immersed in hot water. "Honey, I can't tell you how heartbroken I am," she said, lifting the cigarette to a mouth outlined unevenly in red lipstick. "He was a fine, fine gentleman."

"I know," said Charlotte sympathetically. Grace had not looked away from the little television set on the table since Charlotte sat down. "I'd like you to tell me everything that happened on Tuesday afternoon," Charlotte prompted, "starting with when you began to fix the tea."

"I don't mind, honey," Grace answered, exhaling twin streams of cigarette smoke from her nostrils. "Anything to bring a villain to justice. Poor Frank—I mean Dr. Thornhill." She sighed, looked briefly at Charlotte, and returned her gaze to the television set.

"The tea?" said Charlotte.

"Oh, yes. I told that handsome State policeman, Detective Gaudette, all about it. I think he looks like a movie star, don't you?" Without waiting for a reply, she continued: "But land-a-goshen, what a mess they made with that fingerprint dust. It'll take me days to get it all cleaned up."

"I'm sure your work will have served a good purpose," Charlotte assured her. In fact, however, the fingerprinting had been no help at all, according to Tracey. What few good prints the police had found belonged to members of the household.

"We were talking about the tea," prompted Charlotte again.

"Oh, yes. I put the kettle on at about three thirty," Grace continued. "To have it ready at four. Frank—I mean Dr. Thornhill, God rest his soul—was very particular. He was every inch a gentleman, and we ladies know how a gentleman wants everything just so." She winked conspiratorially.

Charlotte smiled in acknowledgment. Poor Grace—a woman of fifty or more trying to be a Southern belle of eighteen. She couldn't understand this frantic effort to hold back the clock. The most horrible fate she could imagine would be to look the way that some stars did in their old age: lifted, powdered, and mascaraed into hideous caricatures of their former selves. She didn't mind getting old. True, she was a bit heavier than she used to be; true, she no longer wore the slinky sheaths she used to; true, the catty columnists sometimes referred to her "fading beauty" or called her an "aging goddess" as if she had betrayed her public by growing old. But as far as she was concerned, a lot of living had gone into the lines on her face, and she was proud of them.

She brought her attention back to Grace, who was still absorbed by the television. "What do you mean 'just so'?"

"I mean, he insisted on having his beer and sandwich on the dot of noon, and his tea—he called it his tisane—French, you know—on the dot of four. If I didn't have it ready . . . land-a-goshen, what a fuss he'd raise."

Then the fact that he took his tea at four was probably common knowledge, thought Charlotte, which meant that anyone could have recognized teatime as the perfect opportunity for a poisoning.

Grace glanced over at the counter, and then got up and fetched the tea tray. "Everything had to be in a certain place," she said, showing Charlotte the tray, which was all set up. "The teapot had to be here, the vase here, the sugar and milk pitcher here, the cookie plate here. I swear, he could drive a woman crazy sometimes. He was particular

about his cookies too," she continued as she returned the tray
to its place. "He always had two: coriander sugar cookies on
Mondays, Wednesdays, and Fridays and ginger biscuits on
Tuesdays, Thursdays, and Saturdays."

"It sounds as if he was a man of habit," said Charlotte
drily.

"Law, yes," she bubbled. "He was a gentleman, as I said.
With very particular habits, *refined* habits. He was also a
man of honor, the kind of man a lady of breeding could trust
with her reputation. He never would have taken advantage,
if you know what I mean. Not that I would have let him."
She raised her chin in an expression of virtuous hauteur.
"I'm not the type to let my emotions run away from me."

Her words had the fulsome ring of a script for *Search for
Tomorrow*, thought Charlotte. She also sounded a little like
Blanche DuBois.

"I worshiped the ground that man walked on," she continued in a maudlin tone, sniffling into a hankie. "He was
so like Mr. Harris—he passed away in 1962—so smart and
clever at explaining things. I was so lucky to have been
able to come to Ledge House. Before I came here I was
just at sixes and sevens all the time without a man to take
care of me. And now this. It's just too much." She leaned
forward to touch Charlotte's arm. "Honey, this conversation's mighty hard on me. Since Frank's death, I've just
gone to pieces. You wouldn't mind if I had just a wee tad
of bourbon to calm my nerves, would you? Mind you," she
added, rising from her seat, "I don't ordinarily touch spirits,
but my nerves are just worn to a frazzle."

"Please, go right ahead," said Charlotte, declining a drink
herself. She noticed that Grace's nose was rubricated with
the telltale broken blood vessels of the heavy drinker. Judging by the level of alcohol in the bottle of Old Grand-dad
she fetched from a bottom cupboard, it had been resorted to
on more than one occasion as a tonic for frazzled nerves.

Pouring herself a tumblerful, Grace quickly emptied more
than half of it in a series of demure sips. "Oh, yes," she
said, with a little shiver of pleasure. "Makes me feel like

a schoolgirl on a Saturday night." She giggled and looked around her as if the world had suddenly come into focus.

"What kind of tea did Dr. Thornhill drink?" asked Charlotte.

"He always had one of Fran's herb teas. He didn't believe in caffeine, you see. He said it poisoned the system." A shadow passed over her face at the mention of the word poison. She continued: "He had a different tea each day. Rose hip, peppermint, chamomile, lemon verbena. His favorite was lovage; it tastes kind of like celery."

Lovage was the herb that Kitty had mentioned in connection with the poisoning case in Belgium, the herb that monkshood had been mistaken for.

"Do you remember what kind of tea Dr. Thornhill had on Tuesday?"

"I can't recall the name," she said, reaching out a shaky hand to tap her cigarette ash in the ashtray, and missing. "It was a new one that Fran had just brought over that afternoon. I'd show you the package, but the police took it. She likes to test her new blends on the family. Come to think of it, I don't think she told me what was in it."

"Did you prepare it, or did Fran?"

"Usually, I do, but Fran did on Tuesday, because it was the new blend."

Why a new tea on that particular day? Charlotte wondered. And why had Fran prepared it? But if Fran was guilty, why call attention to herself by preparing the tea? She could have just let Grace do it as usual, and slipped the poison in later. Her attention drifted off to the subject of poison, while Grace's drifted off to the soap opera. Poisoning was reputedly a woman's crime, but she wondered if that was accurate. True, poisoning required cunning and subterfuge, the traditional weapons of the powerless. She was reminded of another case of monkshood poisoning that she had read about in one of Thornhill's books. It involved a group of wives in a Hungarian village whose husbands were called away to military service. When the husbands returned and started demanding their wives' submission, they began mysteriously dying off. More than sixty husbands were poisoned by their wives, one of the largest mass poisonings in history. Now *that* was a woman's crime. But even more important than cunning and subterfuge, she thought, would be the murderer's feeling that he or she could get away with it, the feeling of infallibility. And that feeling, she reflected, was distributed in equal measure in both sexes.

"Anyway, he didn't like it much," Grace continued. "He said it tasted kind of peppery. Do you think that was the poison in it?"

"Could be," replied Charlotte. She remembered that the alkaloid aconitine had been described as having a hot, sharp taste. "Mrs. Harris," she said. "Think carefully. Do you remember any time that afternoon during which someone could have added the poison to the teapot?"

"Lordy, yes," said Grace. She leaned back and crossed her arms. "I told that State policeman all about it. I was carrying the tea tray out to Frank when the doorbell rang. It was Wes Gilley delivering the lobsters I'd ordered for Frank's birthday party. I was going to serve lobster thermidor."

"What happened then?"

"Well, I set the tray on the sideboard in the parlor and answered the door. Wes didn't have change for a twenty. That's when I went upstairs to see if I could get change from you girls. I figure someone could have added the poison to the tea while it was sitting there on the sideboard."

The perfect opportunity, Charlotte thought. The poisoner must have concealed the poison on his or her person. But how? The crushed root, which is what she supposed he had used—it was the most poisonous part—would be moist and runny; it would require some sort of container.

"Did you see anyone in the parlor when you came down?"

"No, but that doesn't mean anything. The tea tray was just sitting there for a good five minutes. I remember worrying about its getting cold. Frank was a bit perturbed when I finally brought it. You see, it was past four by then. I know because *The Edge of Night* had already started."

"One last question, Mrs. Harris, if you don't mind."

"Of course not, honey," she said, patting Charlotte's arm affectionately. "Anything to bring a villain to justice."

"Did you know that Dr. Thornhill had plans to remarry?"

"Lord-a-mercy—that man," she said, shaking her head. "I knew there was talk of it, but I didn't believe it, not for one minute. You see," she said, leaning forward, "I knew Frank would never have *married* a woman like that. Just between you and me and the lamppost, she was nothing more than a common you-know-what. When she was up here over Memorial Day weekend, she didn't even go through the *pretense* of sleeping in her own bed." She leaned back with a self-satisfied air and poked a finger through her lacquered curls to scratch her scalp. "Oh, Frank would have remarried eventually," she continued. "Why, he was a real man, if you know what I mean. Goodness knows a man like that needs a woman in his life. But what Frank needed was a woman of culture and refinement"—she paused to pat the spot she had just scratched—"not a trashy gold digger like her." She nodded confidently. "He would have come to his senses eventually. Take it from me."

"I'm sure he would have," Charlotte agreed.

Grace leaned forward again, a fresh cigarette dangling from the fingers of her limp-wristed hand. "Of course," she said, her blue eyes glittering, "There's not much chance of that happening *now*, is there?" She smiled smugly and leaned back again, puffing on the cigarette she held between her twisted fingers.

Guiding Light had ended, and she switched the channel.

"*General Hospital*'s on now," she said.

"Thank you for your cooperation," said Charlotte, rising to leave.

"I'm happy to help. Anything to bring a villain to justice." She paused and then added, "You know, my Ellie Sue will be just thrilled to hear I met you. You wouldn't mind giving me your autograph for her, would you? She'd just love to have it. She has a little autograph collection."

"Not at all."

"Oh, wonderful. I have a picture of you right here," she said, reaching into her handbag and withdrawing a photo from an old magazine interview. "Just write 'To Ellie Sue: I'll always remember the good times I shared with my dear friend, your mother. Wishing you love and happiness, Charlotte Graham.' "

Charlotte wrote the message across the corner of the picture in her bold scrawl, adding another name to the ranks of her good friends across the world.

"Thank you," said Grace, retrieving the picture and putting it back in her handbag. "That's my baby," she said, pointing to the snapshot of a young mother with her two children that was taped to the refrigerator door.

"She's very pretty," said Charlotte politely.

"Oh, yes, she was homecoming queen at Georgia Teachers College. Her boys are Bobbie and Chuckie. I've got five grandchildren. My other daughter, Mary Ann, has three." She held up the locket that she wore around her neck, and showed Charlotte the picture of a baby. "This is the youngest, my little Betsy."

Charlotte admired the pictures of the grandchildren, and turned down Grace's offer to show her the other pictures of her grandchildren in her room. "I'm afraid I have to be going," she apologized. "Maybe some other time."

"I'm always here," she said, getting up to check the cake in the oven. "Always right here."

·9·

ON THE WAY back through the parlor, Charlotte stopped to study the layout. The room had access to the kitchen and the dining room on one side, the library on the other side, and the veranda at the rear. Then there was the front door and the twin staircases. Grace couldn't have picked a more vulnerable spot to leave the tea. That is, *if* the tea had been poisoned by someone else. The suspect with the least motive had turned out to have a strong motive after all. It was clear that Grace had had romantic designs on Thornhill, however delusional they might have been. And, like Fran, she knew a good deal about herbs. It might have been a case of, "If I can't have him, nobody else will."

As Charlotte was standing there John entered the front door. He was dressed in khaki shorts and a khaki drill shirt and was carrying a tripod in one hand. A 35mm camera hung from around his neck.

"You look as if you've been out in the African bush shooting pictures of wild game," she said with a smile.

"No, only out in the Gilley Island bush shooting pictures of wild waves crashing against the rocks."

"For Stan?"

He nodded.

"He showed me some of your photos. They're very good."

"Can I take that as an indication that you wouldn't be

averse to my photographing you?" he said, with a suave little smile.

Damn. She'd opened herself up to that one. "Okay," she said brusquely, "but let's do it right here, shall we?"

"Fine," he said. "It's nice light, soft. It will just take a minute. Why don't you sit there?" He pointed to one of the wicker chairs. "I'll get a close-up against the Chinese screen—a profile, maybe; it should be very nice, with your black jacket and your black hair."

"How's your work going?" she asked as he removed a roll of film from one of the film containers taped to his camera strap.

"Well, very well in fact," he said as he loaded the film. He paused. "I don't know if I should be confessing this to someone who's helping the police with their investigation, but Frank's death doesn't exactly hinder my career. He wasn't a great champion of my work, as you know." He smiled. "However, I'd appreciate it if you didn't come to the conclusion that because I stand to benefit from his death, I was the one who killed him."

"I'm finding out that there are a lot of people who stand to benefit from his death—you're not alone in that."

"Strangely enough, I miss him now that he's gone," he continued as he tried out different angles. "The man you love to hate, and all that."

It was odd how people missed their enemies, she thought as he snapped the shutter. The spouse who is hated is as deeply mourned as the spouse who is loved. Hate or love, the ties were equally strong.

"Now you can do something for me," said Charlotte, once he had finished.

"What's that?" he asked as he rewound the film.

"Repeat for me what you told the police about Tuesday afternoon."

"Sure. What do you want to know?"

"What you saw when you came downstairs."

"Nothing. I didn't even notice the tea on the sideboard. Chief Tracey asked me about that."

"Did you go out the front door?"

"Right out, and over to the gardener's cottage."

"And you didn't see anyone?"

"No one. Not even Wes Gilley, although his truck was parked out front. Chief Tracey kept asking me if I was sure I hadn't seen anyone at the front door. It was obvious that he thought I should have seen Gilley."

Then where was Wes? she wondered. He should have been at the front door, waiting for Grace to come back with his change.

"I'm afraid I'm not much help," he continued. "Would you like to join Daria and me for some tea? Hopefully, we'll live through it."

Charlotte smiled at the black humor; everyone had suddenly become very suspicious of their food and drink. She declined, and thanked him for his help. As he headed up the stairs to the bindery she reflected that there were only three possible reasons why John hadn't reported seeing Wes. One, Wes had left the door for some innocent reason; two, Wes had concealed himself to avoid being caught in the act; and three, John was lying. She suddenly realized how little she knew about him, and made a mental note to ask Tom to check him out.

She found Felix stretched out in a chaise on the veranda, with a book in one hand and a glass of Scotch in the other. He was fastidiously dressed as usual in a white suit, but he had made some concessions to the country in the form of large, dark sunglasses and a floppy white duck hat, the combination of which made him look like an Arab potentate traveling incognito. Settling herself on the chaise beside him, she asked what he was reading.

"*Moby Dick*," he replied as he lifted the book, a finger marking his place. "My favorite chapter—'The Whiteness of the Whale.' "

Surveying the white expanse of his stomach, Charlotte thought that reading about white whales must be right up his alley.

"For pleasure I read Melville, Dickens, and last but not

least, detective stories. The detective story has been called the ordinary recreation of noble minds. I am a great fan of the police procedural. With regard to our interest in police matters, we have something in common, *nicht wahr*, Miss Graham?"

"As a matter of fact, that's why I'm here."

"I thought as much. The case of the poisoned book collector. Very tragic—my oldest and dearest client. And I suppose you want to know my whereabouts at the time of the murder?"

Charlotte nodded. She knew full well he had been in the same place that he was now, but she wanted to see what his answer would be anyway.

"I was right here, reading *The Moonstone* by Wilkie Collins, one of the great classics of detection. A first edition, and quite valuable. The detective story has been overlooked as a collector's item, but it is finally gaining the recognition it has long deserved. Especially the early detective stories, which are becoming valuable indeed. Take the work of the father of the detective story, the great Edgar Allen Poe. Only a few copies are still extant of his *Murders in the Rue Morgue*, a little pamphlet printed in 1841. Very valuable. And then there's the *Beeton's Christmas Annual*. . . . "

"Can you tell me if you saw or heard anything unusual?" interrupted Charlotte, knowing that once he got started on collecting detective fiction she would have a hard time getting him back on the subject of Thornhill's murder.

Reaching into one of his many inside pockets, he withdrew a cigar. Charlotte observed that one of his pockets would be a good place to keep a container of poison at hand for dropping into a teapot.

"I'm sorry, no. I was immersed in my book." He paused, and lifted the cigar to his mouth to moisten it. "I must correct myself. I did hear what sounded like an altercation. Franklin and someone else, in the library. Followed by the sound of a door slamming."

"Did you hear what the quarrel was about?"

"It seems to me that I heard the other party say something

like, 'You'd better leave it to me, you understand?' Oh yes, and I heard the doorbell ring. I believe it was answered by Mrs. Harris."

The same words she had heard, she thought as she gazed out over the urns of geraniums to the lawn. She wondered whether Thornhill and Chuck had been arguing about the will. "Leave it to me," sounded as if Chuck was talking about the Ledge House property. But wouldn't he have said "Leave it to us," referring to him and Marion, if he was talking about the will? Thornhill had presumably left his house and grounds to his daughter, but until his will was retrieved from a Boston safe-deposit box they wouldn't know for sure. She wondered whether Thornhill would have left the property to Marion, knowing that Chuck would probably sell it to Chartwell. Perhaps he had threatened to include a clause prohibiting development. Or he might have threatened to leave the property to the public. In either case, Chuck would have the strongest motive. The use of poison to dispose of affluent relatives had a long history, and the property—valuable as it was—was only a fraction of the total estate.

"Does that help you, Miss Graham?" asked Felix, who had gone through the elaborate ceremony of lighting his cigar.

"Yes, thank you," she replied. "Mr. Mayer," she continued, turning to face him, "Have you any idea of the value of the Thornhill collection?"

"That depends on whether or not the incunabula are recovered," he said. "As we discussed the other day, the incunabula alone are worth in the neighborhood of four hundred thousand dollars."

"If the incunabula are recovered."

"The Thornhill collection contains about five thousand volumes, of which perhaps half can be considered rare. Such a collection, Miss Graham, is unique; it ranks among the finest botanical collections in the country. For that matter, the world. In today's market, such a collection would be worth, in my estimation, a minimum of four million dollars."

Charlotte was surprised.

"You see, Miss Graham," he went on, "when it comes to collecting books, the whole is worth far more than the sum of the parts."

"Have you any idea what will become of the collection now?"

"That remains to be seen, doesn't it? However, Franklin often told me that he would rather sell it than donate it to an institution, despite the persuasive arguments of our young scholar. You see, he was not a man of great wealth: the bulk of his estate was tied up in his books. To have bequeathed his collection to an institution would have been to deprive his heir—namely his daughter Marion—of her rightful inheritance."

"Then you think his will stipulated that the collection should be sold—probably through you—with the proceeds to go to Marion."

"That is what he led me to believe. You heard him say it yourself the other day. He always promised me that upon his death I would handle the sale of his collection. However, he always said I would be the first to go. It was a joke between us: who would outlive the other." He smiled, his hazel eyes twinkling. "I know what you're hinting at. It's true that I stand to make a substantial commission on the sale of his collection, the kind of commission that comes along once in a lifetime. But to kill an old and beloved friend for profit? Business is bad, yes"—he shook his head slowly—"but never that bad."

"Thank you for your help," said Charlotte, standing to leave. "I'm sorry I've had to disturb you with these questions."

"I understand. We are all suspects. But *you* must understand that a book dealer's good name is his stock in trade. The business of bookselling is a business that is rife with opportunities for the unscrupulous. The book dealer is constantly being faced with temptations: to accept a stolen book, to pay a gullible seller less than a book is worth, to purloin a valuable book from a collection he has been entrusted to appraise. The book dealer who yields to such temptations may make a profit in the short run, but he will not be in business very long. It is the book dealer who builds a reputation for honesty and fair play who survives and prospers." He took a deep, self-satisfied puff on his cigar. "It is exactly because my reputation is *sans peur et sans reproche* that I am considered one of the world's greatest book dealers."

Charlotte thanked him again and left. Like Grace, Felix had turned out to have a strong motive after all. He flaunted his good name like a badge of innocence, but she couldn't help thinking that reputation, as the bard had said, is "oft got without merit, and lost without deserving."

On her way back to the Saunders' house she stopped to rest in what had become one of her favorite spots: a bench under a big old oak tree overlooking the bar, which was now buried ten feet beneath a high tide. Out on the bay, the islands lay like lily pads on the calm silver surface of the sea. It was these islands that gave the Maine coast its character. In an era in which the sea had been an open highway, the islands had been its way stations. In the Saunders' living room was a nineteenth-century map of the area. The islands were heavily dotted with the little black squares that indicated residences, while the mainland had practically none. But today, many of the islands were ghostly relics of their former selves. All that remained of once-prosperous homesteads were filled-in wells, fields grown up to poplar and pine, and tiny family cemeteries like the one on the Gilley Road. She shivered as she rose to leave: the death of centuries seemed close at hand on this island of Gilleys past.

As she stood up her reverie was interrupted by a peal of girlish laughter accompanied by the blare of rock music. Two girls—one carrying a radio the size of a small suitcase—were skipping down the road from the direction of Ledge House. A few minutes later they had caught up with her. The younger girl, who looked about eleven, ran right up to her. Like the other girl, whom Charlotte recognized as Wes's daughter, she had the kind of careworn, old-young face that is often found among the children of the rural poor.

"Are you the movie star?" she asked. She was a scrawny little thing in dirty shorts, with a light brown ponytail.

"Shut up, Kim," said the older girl from behind. "Maybe the lady don't wanna be pestered by the likes of you."

"You don't mind, do you?" Kim said imploringly. She fingered the fine silk of Charlotte's jacket. "I like your outfit. Ain't it pretty, Tammy?"

The older girl, who looked about thirteen, had drawn alongside with the radio, which she carried in front of her like an armload of firewood. She had a pretty face and her father's far-off light blue eyes.

"What's your name?" asked Kim.

"Charlotte," she replied, with a smile. "And I bet you're Kim and Tammy. How do you like living on an island?"

"Ugh," replied Kim, with an expression of disgust. "We hate it, don't we, Tammy? There ain't nothin' to do." Her accent was almost as thick as her father's.

"Our friends are all in town," Tammy concurred.

Charlotte was reminded of a young couple from Brooklyn she had once met who had just returned from a honeymoon in Bridge Harbor. There was nothing to do, they complained. No discos, no boutiques, no beach (actually there was a beach, but not the kind they were talking about). Kim and Tammy clearly shared the young couple's feelings, magnified a thousand times by their isolation. They were trapped between the anachronistic world of their parents and the world they knew only from Kitty and Stan's television.

"We've got one friend out here," observed Kim. "Kevin. He gave Tammy that radio," she announced proudly. She clung to Charlotte's side. "Will you come visit?" she pleaded. "We ain't never had a movie star come visit."

Charlotte agreed, thinking it would be a good opportunity to ask their father some questions. They had reached the Saunders' house, and Charlotte stopped to open the gate in the white picket fence.

"Please promise you'll come," said Kim. She hung on the gate as Charlotte swung it shut. "Pretty please?"

"I promise," said Charlotte with a smile.

"There's someone here to see you, Charlotte," said Kitty as Charlotte entered the kitchen a minute later.

Tom Plummer was already comfortably settled in at the Saunders' kitchen table, beer can in hand and potato chips and dip within arm's reach. She greeted him and asked him about his trip—she hadn't expected him until later that evening—and then fetched herself a glass of lemonade.

Kitty had been filling him in on Thornhill, Tom said as Charlotte joined them. For years, the Saunders had lived in the same Boston suburb as the Thornhills, and their acquaintance had been one of the reasons the Saunders had retired to Bridge Harbor. In fact, they had bought their property from Thornhill.

"Excuse me," said Kitty, rising from the table. "I'm just going to see how Stan's doing in the studio. I haven't seen him all day. Besides, I imagine you two have plenty to talk about. Tom, we're delighted to have you here," she added. "Please let me know if there's anything you need."

"You've provided for me very well, thanks," replied Tom, raising his beer. "And thanks for the information. I wish I had such an informative source for all the stories I work on."

Kitty smiled, and, after fixing a tray with a glass of beer and a plate of potato chips, padded off to the studio.

"Okay, Plummer," said Charlotte, once Kitty was gone. "What have you got?"

He smiled mischievously, stroking his mustache with smug self-satisfaction. "Lots of *very* interesting stuff," he replied.

He was a stocky young man who looked as if he would be more at home coaching midget football than writing about crime. Boyishly handsome, he had an enthusiastic grin; a broad, open face; and a thick head of light brown hair that

was parted down the middle. He didn't fit the stereotype
of the new journalist: the brash, trendy young reporter on
the make, but it was precisely this open, innocent quality
that made him so good at what he did. He had the cheek
to talk his way into any milieu from board room to barrio,
and the persistence to hang in there asking questions that
nobody wanted to answer. But the naturally abrasive nature
of his profession was tempered by his warm personality.
People trusted him, and rightly so. He wasn't the type to
fawn all over his subjects one minute and stab them in the
back the next. Even the subjects of his unflattering portraits
respected him. They often told him that what he wrote was
true, much as they didn't like it.

"I know how you delight in keeping me on tenterhooks."

He rocked his chair back against the chair rail on the
wall, his beer can cradled in his hands. "First," he said,
"Mayer did report the books missing. But," he continued,
"your hunch about his finances was right on the mark."

Charlotte raised an eyebrow and took a drink of lemonade. She was thirsty after the walk from Ledge House. "Go
on."

"First, a little background. He's a third-generation book
dealer. His father and grandfather were book dealers in
Vienna. He emigrated just before the war and went into
business in New York. He's done very well for himself:
he's considered the top dealer in the country. A man of great
culture, shrewdness, and mystery. Apparently he's always
flying off on secret journeys to clinch million-dollar deals.
He's the book dealer who handles all the really big stuff,
especially manuscripts and early printed books. But . . .
he told you he sold the Gutenberg Bible for two point two
million?"

Charlotte nodded. "The price he paid for it, or so he
said."

"He lied. He sold it for two point one million. He lost a
hundred grand on that deal. He originally put it up for sale
for two point seven. Then he lowered the price to two point
five, and then to two point three. Finally he sold it at a loss

because he needed the cash to buy stock he could move."

"But a hundred thousand dollars isn't that much to lose these days; certainly not enough to risk going to jail for."

"That's just the beginning. He's been acting like a bettor who keeps raising the stakes in hopes of recouping his losses. The next loss was Audubon's *Birds of America*. He bought it for one point two million and sold it for fifty grand less. If he'd sold the plates individually, he could have made a pile, but dismembering a classic plate book for profit is one of the worst sins a self-respecting book dealer can commit."

"He was telling me how much he prides himself on his reputation."

"You bet." He continued: "He also took a beating on the Pratt Collection, a collection of nineteenth-century first editions. I could go on, but I won't bore you. In short, a string of bad guesses and misjudgments, none of them terribly serious in and of themselves, but together adding up to financial disaster. In a better economy he might have pulled out of it all right, but not in the middle of a recession."

"How did you find all this out?"

"I did a little checking around," Tom replied vaguely. "I found out some other interesting stuff too. He's a notoriously slow payer. He's also notorious for returning books to the auction house for trivial imperfections: if a book isn't *exactly* as it's described in the catalogue, he returns it. The auction house doesn't want to go through the hassle of putting it up for auction again, so they give it to him at a reduced price."

"Wait a minute, I thought that when you bought something at an auction, you paid for it then and there."

"You do, and I do, but people like Felix Mayer don't. The auction houses extend a line of credit to their best customers. It's an arrangement that works to their mutual benefit: the auction house can assure the owner of the merchandise that it will bring a decent price, and the favored dealer can afford to bid a bit more than his competitor because he has more time to scout around for a prospective buyer before he has to pay up."

"I see. And Felix hasn't been paying up?"

"Right. The book owners are clamoring for their money, and the favored dealer is behind on his payments. The auction houses are caught in the middle. They're willing to live with a certain amount of this, but when a dealer falls as far behind as Mayer has, they've no choice but to sue."

"Which they have?"

Tom nodded. "He's got five suits pending against him."

"Five! How much is he in the hole?"

"As nearly as I can tell, about four hundred grand."

"Exactly what the missing books are worth."

"Yup."

"What happens to him now?"

"Unless he comes up with the money, the court will order an auction of his stock. Book dealers tend to be cash poor: most of their cash is invested in books. But Felix is even more so than usual. He hasn't a dime, but his stock is worth a fortune. From what people tell me, he buys expensive books even when he doesn't have a customer in mind for them. He likes to have them on hand just in case someone wants them. It's a form of status, I guess."

So, Charlotte reflected, Felix had been something of a liar when he told her he was immune to the drive to possess that is the demon of bibliomaniacs. When it came to acquiring stock for his business, he was as much of a bibliomaniac as his customers.

"The point to keep in mind is that there's more at stake than just the survival of his business," Tom went on. "His family honor is also on the line. The business was founded in the mid-nineteenth century. His grandfather was probably selling books to Freud. Can you imagine the ignominy of being the guy who runs the family business into the ground after three generations?"

"But if he did take the books, how would he dispose of them? Foist them off on an unsuspecting customer?"

"I doubt it. The risk would be too great. But the underground markets are there, if you know where to look. Some collectors are so hungry for books that they don't ask any questions. South America. Behind the Iron Curtain. Look at the famous paintings that are stolen from museums. They surface mysteriously years later. Nobody's able to account for what's happened to them."

"Funny how that figure of four hundred thousand keeps turning up," Charlotte said. "I was just up at Ledge House talking with him. He admits that Thornhill promised to let him handle the sale of his collection after his death. He estimated that the collection is worth four million. At ten percent, that's four hundred thousand dollars."

She remembered Felix asking Fran at the Midsummer Night scrying session whether the consignment he was anticipating would come through, earning him a big commission. Fran had told him that it would.

Tom rocked his chair back against the chair rail again and drained his beer can. "What you're saying is that A: he pinched the books to pay off his debts, or B: he knocked off Thornhill so he could make the commission."

"Or C: both of the above," said Charlotte. She paced around the kitchen, a cigarette in hand.

"What do you mean both?" asked Tom.

"I mean that maybe there's a connection between A and B. Let's just suppose for the moment that Felix took the books. Maybe Thornhill discovered that he took the books and confronted him with the theft. Which would also explain why Thornhill didn't report that the books were missing."

"Very good, Graham," said Tom, picking up the thread of her thought. "Thornhill threatens to turn him in, and Felix kills him, figuring he'll save his own skin and make the commission in the bargain."

"He could sell the stolen books on the underground market and collect the commission on the rest. Or, if he didn't want to run the risk of selling the stolen books, he could just report that they'd been recovered . . ."

"And collect the commission on the whole works," Tom

interjected. "A few holes, but a workable hypothesis none-theless."

"*Non fingo hypotheses*," she replied, grinning.

One of Tom's maddening habits was quoting proverbs in Latin. It was the only use he could find for his classics degree from a fancy institution of higher learning, other than translating the inscriptions on the pediments of museums and banks. She took great pleasure in tossing them back at him every once in a while.

"Newton," he said. " 'I do not form hypotheses.' " He smiled sheepishly. "*Touché*, Graham."

·10·

THE MEMORIAL SERVICE early that evening was a brief, low-key affair, attended only by close friends and relatives, but it offered some new insight into the personalities of the players in the drama of Thornhill's death. Marion attended with Chuck, but that was the extent of her dealings with him. When she was put in the position of having to speak directly to him at the gathering at Ledge House afterwards, she had done so with contempt. Clearly the source of their estrangement ran deeper than the stress of recent events. Fran maintained her herb-lady role even in the ritual of death, passing out sprigs of rosemary, the herb of remembrance, to the mourners. Charlotte was surprised to find her chatting at the gathering after the service with Thornhill's fiancée. Apparently Fran didn't find her nearly so unpleasant now that the threat of her marriage to Thornhill had passed. Although Charlotte, who also talked a bit with her, thought her references to her other (still living) wealthy suitors displayed an astonishing lack of taste and sensitivity in a putatively bereaved fiancée. When it came to scheming gold diggers, the vamps were no match for ladylike suburban widows with ailing bank accounts.

The next morning found Charlotte in the Ledge House library once again, this time with Tom. They had volunteered to help Daria assemble the documents needed to put together descriptions of the missing books. Daria had been called back to New York on business for a couple of days, so she was just getting around to the task to which Felix had assigned her of sorting through Thornhill's papers. She had found a willing assistant in Tom, who had lost no time in acquainting himself with the only single (young) woman on the island. One thing was reasonably certain, Charlotte reflected as she turned to the stack of papers that Tom and Daria had set on the table in front of her: the murder was probably related to the missing books. She reminded herself to keep that thought at the forefront of her mind. The links between the murder and the vandalism, the poison-pen letters—even the death of Jesse (from where she was sitting, she could see the hole where Jesse's body had been dug up)—were still all suppositional. As for the motives of the suspects—greed, envy, passion (if that's what you'd call Grace's banal sentiments)—they really didn't amount to much. Once you started digging into the affairs of a murder victim, you were apt to unearth all sorts of motives. But the books were different: Thornhill is taken ill, and the books turn up missing. Charlotte's New England horse sense told her the connection was too obvious to ignore.

After a half hour of sorting, she had distilled half a dozen documents relating to the missing books from a stack of academic papers with deadly titles like "*Solanum Tuberosum* [The Potato] and Its Use for Food" by J. Franklin Thornhill. Taking a break, she leaned back to watch Daria and Tom, who were emptying the last of the filing cabinets. She would wager that Tom would give John a run for his money. The signs were all there, she observed as Daria carried a stack of papers over to the table with her long, leggy stride: he, an appraising look; she, a self-conscious relaxation of the step, an inviting sway of the hips, a coquettish tilt of the head. The almost imperceptible signals that the male and female of the species are programmed to follow through to their immemorial end. She remembered Fran's prophecy that love was in the air, and smiled to herself. Of Daria's two suitors, Fran had said, she should choose the stocky one with the brown hair. "He's your lucky guy," she had said.

"Well, I guess that's it," said Daria, laying the last stack of papers on the table and taking a seat opposite Charlotte.

Pulling up an overstuffed club chair, Tom lit a cigarette

and tossed the match into an ashtray with the panache of a professional basketball player. He carried a lively spirit of youthful camaraderie around with him that infused his surroundings with the atmosphere of a big city newsroom.

"What I can't figure out is this": said Daria, "if the books were missing two weeks ago when I first noticed they weren't in the vault, then Dr. Thornhill must have known they weren't there. And if he knew they were weren't there, why didn't he report that the books had been stolen?"

"We wondered about that too," replied Charlotte. "The only explanation we've been able to come up with is that he knew, or suspected, who the thief was, and wanted to confront him himself. He might even have threatened to turn the thief in, which would have provided a motive for the murder."

Daria nodded. "Do you have any idea who might have stolen the books?" she asked. Then she added: "I guess Chuck is the obvious suspect."

"Why Chuck?"

"Because of the argument."

A possibility, thought Charlotte. Chuck's words, "You'd better leave it to me, you understand?" could have referred to his theft of the books. He could have been warning Thornhill of the consequences if Thornhill turned him in. He could even have been offering to return the books, or repay the debt.

"But why would Chuck steal the books?" Charlotte asked. "He doesn't appear to need the money; he has a successful insurance business."

"That doesn't mean anything," said Tom. "He could be up to his eyeballs in debt, just like our friend the book dealer."

"I see one problem with the Chuck theory," said Daria. "The poisoning would have required premeditation, and Chuck quarreled with Dr. Thornhill just before the poison was put in his tea.",

"Maybe Chuck hoped to convince Thornhill not to turn him in, but took along the poison just in case he wasn't

successful," said Tom. "Then, when Thornhill made it clear
he wasn't going to let him get away with it, Chuck decided
to use it. The tea just happened to be sitting there."

"Kind of far-fetched, isn't it?" said Charlotte.

"Non est fumus absque igne," he said with a devilish grin.

Charlotte rolled her eyes in mock exasperation. "What he
means is," she said, translating for Daria, "where there's
smoke, there's fire."

"Thanks," said Daria, flashing Tom a smile.

"Then there's always the chance the books were taken
on the night everyone was at the hospital," Charlotte continued, standing up to divide the rest of the papers among
them. "In which case, there are two explanations. The first
is that Thornhill was murdered by mistake."

"What do you mean?" asked Daria.

"The symptoms of monkshood poisoning mimic those of
heart disease. The thief might have intended to induce a
phony heart attack with the aim of getting everyone out of
the house, not knowing that the difference between a dose
that produces the heart attack symptoms and a lethal dose
is very small."

"What's the second?" asked Tom, shaking his head skeptically.

"The second is that someone took advantage of the fact
that Fran and Grace and Daria were all at the hospital to
steal the books from the vault. John and Felix were both
here, and anyone else could have walked in; the door wasn't
locked. The 'casual thief,' Felix called him."

"In which case, the book theft has nothing to do with the
murder," said Tom. "Speaking of book theft, what exactly
are we supposed to be looking for?" he asked, gesturing at
the stack of papers in front of him.

"Anything to do with the missing books," said Daria.
"Descriptions, inventories, catalogues, bills of sale, notes.
Here's a list of the titles," she added, sliding a sheet of
paper across the table.

Silence fell as they turned to the tedious task of sorting
through the rest of the papers. Charlotte's newest pile con-

sisted mostly of old auction house catalogues. They had
been annotated in Thornhill's tiny, square handwriting with
the amount of the high bid and the name of the high bidder. Several contained listings for other copies of the missing books. She set these to one side. They would provide
some guidelines on the values of the missing books. She
was down to the middle of the pile when she came across
a manila envelope containing a sheaf of notes written in a
tall, slanting hand. The first page was headed "Der Gart der
Gesundheit," and gave a detailed description of that book,
along with comments on its historical importance. The other
pages were each headed with the names of other books,
including the four other titles on the missing list. Why were
the notes written in a different handwriting? she wondered.
Her question was answered by the next document in the
stack: a bill of sale for the books MacMillan had sold to
Thornhill. It was written on MacMillan's letterhead, and
signed by MacMillan in the same tall, slanting handwriting.
Then it dawned on her: the notes were the notes for the
catalogue that MacMillan had been working on at the time
of his death, the notes that Felix had referred to when he'd
talked of the irony of MacMillan's having begun work on a
catalogue in the weeks prior to the diagnosis of his illness.
But why would MacMillan's notes be among Thornhill's
papers?

She was about to dismiss the question from her mind—
MacMillan had probably just handed the notes over with the
books—when something puzzling caught her eye. The notes
were dated December, 1959, which wasn't a surprise—
Felix had said that MacMillan died on Christmas Eve—
but the bill of sale was dated June, 1959. If MacMillan had
sold the books to Thornhill in June, why had he included
them in the notes he was making for a catalogue six months
later? Slowly, bits and pieces of conversation from the
herb luncheon began to bubble up to the surface of her
consciousness: how MacMillan had outwitted Thornhill at
auction to purchase *Der Gart*, how Thornhill had vowed to
never let a book he wanted slip through his fingers again.

And from the conversation the next day with Daria: how
the botanical society had asked Thornhill, as the board
member most knowledgeable about botanical collecting,
to oversee the transfer of the MacMillan collection to their
library. Suddenly she realized that the bits and pieces all fit
together: Thornhill had stolen the books from the MacMillan
estate!

The conversation from the luncheon came back to her
now in more detail: Thornhill saying how MacMillan had
decided to sell his prizes to his rival because he would
appreciate them, and how the dying man had entrusted
them to him with the words, "Take care of them, Frank.
They are my children." The words had struck her as phony
at the time, but she had written their phoniness off to imagi-
native storytelling. She imagined Thornhill going through
shelf upon shelf of MacMillan's books, and then coming
upon *Der Gart*: the book he had wanted above all others.
She pictured him lovingly picking it up, and then hastily
putting it down as his conscience flirted with temptation.
"Who would know if I took it?" *No one.* "What if someone
found out?" *I could say that he sold it to me.* "How would I
prove it?" *I could forge a bill of sale on his stationery.* Then,
upping the ante: "If I'm going to take *Der Gart*, why not
take the others too?" And finally, making the grand ration-
alization: "The botanical society will never be able to appreciate these books the way I do."

She doubted he had felt remorse. He had probably thought
Der Gart was his due because he'd been tricked out of it by
an obscure auction-house rule. He had also probably thought
he was doing society a service by rescuing the books from
the unworthy patrons of the botanical society's library. She
remembered what Felix had said about Thornhill possessing
all the attributes of the winning player in the collecting
game. He might have listed deceit and arrogance along with
skill, patience, and boldness. But she did suspect that deep
down inside Thornhill had been afraid: afraid that he would
be found out, afraid that he might slip out of the groove
again. In retrospect, his life of scholarly rectitude and self-

less public service seemed to have been erected as a bulwark against the sinful strain in his honorable Puritan heritage, and the achievements recorded in his obituary—Chairman of the Board of Trustees of the New York Botanical Society, past President of the Society of Economic Botany, founder of the J. Franklin Thornhill Plant Science Center, author of dozens of highly respected books and articles—stockpiled like weapons against the possibility that he might one day be exposed for the thief he was.

Realizing that she was still holding the papers, she looked down again at the signature on the bill of sale. The line was not firm and bold as it was on MacMillan's notes, but wavering, as if it had been traced. The risk had really been very slight: it was, after all, not a string of bad checks he had forged, but one signature on a quasi-legal document. The chances were that it would pass all but the closest scrutiny. For further protection, he must have simply taken the catalogue notes, knowing that it would be incriminating to leave them among MacMillan's effects. He should have destroyed them, but he probably couldn't bring himself to throw them away: they contained valuable information about the books that were now in his possession. Maybe he had even planned to issue a private catalogue of his own someday, using MacMillan's notes as a foundation. She wondered if he'd taken the catalogue manuscript as well. Felix had said that the completed manuscript was about to go to the printer's at the time of MacMillan's death. If it could be found, it would be further proof that Thornhill had taken the books. She riffled through the rest of the stack of papers in front of her, but it wasn't there.

Was the fact that Thornhill stole the books related to his murder? she wondered. As Daria and Tom sifted through the other papers she slipped the notes and the bill of sale into her bag. She wanted to talk to Tracey before revealing to Daria that her former employer was a book thief.

"I've got an inventory here that was taken last year," said Daria. "Does anyone else have anything?"

"I've got some old auction house catalogues with listings of other copies of the missing books," said Charlotte, passing them across the table.

"Actually," said Daria, leafing through the catalogues, "between what we've got here and the card catalogue, we probably have enough."

"How about you, Tom?" asked Charlotte, hoping he might have turned up the catalogue manuscript. "Find anything?"

"*Nada*," said Tom, tossing the rest of his stack of papers on the reject pile at the center of the table. "Is that it? I'm ready for some lunch."

"I guess so," said Daria.

She escorted Charlotte and Tom to the door, where they ran into John, who was entering. He was carrying a wicker picnic hamper. It was obvious that he and Daria were about to go off on a picnic.

"John, I'd like you to meet Tom Plummer. Tom is Charlotte's friend. He's helping her out on the case," said Daria. "Tom, this is John Lewis, Dr. Thornhill's scholar-in-residence."

"Nice to meet you," said Tom politely, removing his hand from its resting place at the small of Daria's back and extending it to John.

Charlotte noticed John's gaze follow Tom's hand. They exchanged pleasantries, but their mutual distrust was obvious.

"See you tonight," said Tom to Daria as they left.

Stan and Kitty had invited Daria for a barbecue. Kitty was playing matchmaker. Not that she needed to—the forces of nature were already at work.

Charlotte and Tom were about to sit down to lunch when Tom was summoned to the telephone by Stan. He returned to the table a few minutes later.

"That was my book contact in New York," he said. "He called to tell me something he'd forgotten to mention the other day."

"Well?" said Charlotte as she bit into a tuna fish sandwich.

"Good stuff. The scuttlebutt in the book world is that Thornhill didn't buy those books from MacMillan—he stole them from the MacMillan estate. MacMillan was putting together a private catalogue at the time of his death that included the books he'd supposedly sold to Thornhill months before. I haven't the faintest idea where we would get our hands on it, but if we could . . . And get this. Guess who his source was."

"Who?" asked Charlotte.

"Felix Mayer."

"Felix!" exclaimed Charlotte, her hand pausing midway between plate and mouth, "Now that *is* interesting."

Of course! Felix had known all about it. She remembered the feeling she'd had at the herb luncheon, that Felix was goading Thornhill: the description of Thornhill as a collector of "uncommon daring," the anecdote about the Spanish monk who had murdered for a book, the odd observation that Thornhill's collection as it stood today surpassed MacMillan's as it stood at the time of his death. Even the conversation in the library about the missing books was mined with references to the theft: Felix's observation that the most difficult thief to catch is the thief who steals out of the drive to possess because he thinks he has a right to a book, and how such a thief usually keeps the books in a place under his direct control—"such as a vault." And in his conversation about the importance of a book dealer's good name, he had talked about the many temptations facing the book dealer, among them the temptation to purloin a valuable book from a collection he had been entrusted to appraise. Why had he kept on dropping these references after Thornhill was dead? Charlotte wondered. Had he wanted to tip them off that Thornhill stole the books, or was he simply so accustomed to needling Thornhill that he did it almost without thinking?

"What about the rest? Not easy to impress, are you?"

Tom complained. Getting up, he fetched another beer and then sat down again at the table.

"That's because I'm one step ahead of you." Charlotte smiled, and reached into her handbag for the catalogue notes. "Here," she said, handing the papers to him.

He started leafing through them.

"They're papers I pinched from Thornhill's library this morning," she explained, putting on her glasses. "I came across them in the middle of a pile of auction house catalogues that were annotated with Thornhill's notes. I noticed that the handwriting on these was different from Thornhill's."

"MacMillan's?"

Charlotte nodded.

"Then, these are the notes for the catalogue?"

"Yes. Felix had mentioned that MacMillan was working on a catalogue at the time of his death. Otherwise, I never would have guessed what they were. Now," she said, retrieving the other piece of paper from her purse, "this is the bill of sale for the books, signed by MacMillan. Compare the dates."

He examined the papers. "The catalogue notes are dated December, and the bill of sale is dated June." He looked at the papers again. "I get it. Thornhill steals the books from the estate, forges a phony bill of sale, and backdates it to six months prior to MacMillan's death."

"Exactly. The question is whether this is just an interesting fact about the honorable professor or whether it's related to the murder. I have a sneaking suspicion it's the latter."

"Now we know why Thornhill didn't report the theft," said Tom. "The chances of his being caught were too great. Some savvy book dealer might have decided to do a little research on the history of the ownership of the books, and Thornhill would have been in big trouble."

"I've got an idea," said Charlotte.

"I'm listening."

"The person who knew that Thornhill stole the books—namely our friend Felix—would have the perfect opportunity of stealing them himself. The risk would have been minimal: he could have stolen them knowing that the chances of Thornhill's reporting the theft were almost nonexistent."

"Very good, Graham, but you forgot one thing. Why was Thornhill murdered?"

"I haven't figured that out yet," she said with a smile.

They sat in silence, finishing their lunch. Charlotte faced the cove, where she could see Wes making his way from one to another of the red-, white-, and black-striped buoys that marked the spots where his baited traps rested on the ocean floor. The round of Gilley Cove was his last; it was an announcement to his wife that he would soon be home for dinner. He tended his traps with the dexterity that comes from years of experience: gaffing the warp, winching the trap over the side, checking the contents. The keepers—the lobsters that measured over a certain length—were tossed into a barrel in the cockpit, and the undersized lobsters were tossed back over the side. The trap was then rebaited and lowered back overboard.

The lobster trap was a clever contraption. Tracey had explained to her how it worked, on their walk up to Ledge House. Lured by the smell of decomposing fish, the lobster entered the first compartment, the kitchen, through a funnel-shaped net, or "eye," that prevented it from backing out. In its confusion, it crawled through another eye into the second compartment, the fatal bedroom. There, it crawled aimlessly, unable to find the narrow end of the eye, which was located well above the floor.

Just so, she thought, had Thornhill been lured by the bait of his tea ritual. The question was, who had baited the trap?

The silence in the kitchen was interrupted by the sound of a knock on the door. It was Tracey—on foot, since the tide was up.

Since the discovery that Thornhill had been poisoned, Tracey had had his hands full. Charlotte hadn't seen him since Thursday afternoon, when the police had taken her statement, but she'd talked with him on the phone several times, including the evening before when she'd called to tell him what Tom had discovered about Felix. He had been impressed by Tom's legwork, and delighted he would be meeting the author of *Murder at the Morosco*.

Now she and Tom filled him in on what they had since discovered, namely that Thornhill had taken the books over twenty years ago and that Felix, for one, knew about it. She made sure that Kitty and Stan were out of earshot. Much as she loved her, she knew Kitty had a tendency to talk. And for the time being she thought they should keep this newfound fact about Thornhill under their hats, just in case it turned out to have something to do with the murder. Tracey wasn't especially shocked that a respectable citizen had turned out to be a thief. Charlotte supposed he was accustomed to seeing the underside of people's public personas. Also, he was too tired to be shocked by much. The sparkle was gone from his eyes, and the skin beneath them hung in grayish-violet folds. He'd been assigned all the routine work: checking the names on hotel registers, parking tickets, and credit card receipts against criminal records; checking out the boats that had been in the vicinity. All to no avail. For the moment, he'd given up on the murder and was pursuing the book theft instead. He'd been calling rare book dealers on the off chance that the books had been sold to a dealer who wasn't aware that they had been stolen. At least he could make the calls from home, enabling him to spend some time with his wife and two boys, who hadn't seen much of him of late.

However, he said, the sparkle coming back into his eyes, one avenue of exploration had bore fruit—the background checks of the suspects. Two of the people in the house on the day Thornhill had been poisoned had criminal records. One was John, who had a record of several arrests in connection with left-wing political demonstrations.

Charlotte wasn't surprised, but arrests for civil disobedience hardly indicated a propensity for murder. "Who's the other?" she asked.

"Now," he said, with a little smile. "The other's much

more interesting—an assault and battery case. The person in question served some time; appears to be quite a dangerous customer, though you'd never suspect it."

"Who is it?"

"Well, it's someone we excluded from the original list of suspects, which shows how misleading appearances can be," Tracey continued, with a little smirk. "The incident in question happened quite some time ago, but . . . "

"He's talking about you, Charlotte," interrupted Tom, with a smile.

"Oh," said Charlotte, with a grin. "You found out about that?"

Tracey nodded. "I'll tell you," he said, "if I were a gentleman of the press, I'd have second thoughts about associating with Miss Graham."

"Well, I can't fault you for being thorough." Charlotte now looked back on the incident with amusement, although she hadn't found it funny at the time. In frustration at his constant harassment, she had once decked an obnoxious paparazzo. He had filed charges against her and she'd filed countercharges. They had both won: she'd been ordered to spend twenty-four hours in jail, to the delight of the tabloids, and he'd been ordered to stay away from her. In her opinion, a day in jail had been a small price to pay to get rid of the pest.

"What other skeletons did you unearth?" she asked coyly.

"That's it. Apparently you've led a pretty blameless life."

"Thanks," she said. "Are you here solely for the purpose of confronting me with my past misdeeds, or is there something else?"

"A little of both," he said. "In the latter category, I came to report that the lab tests are back. The poison that killed Dr. Thornhill was monkshood, or rather, aconitine, the poisonous alkaloid in monkshood, just as we suspected. It was aconitine that killed Jesse too."

"Have you found out anything about the will yet?" asked Tom.

"Ayuh. The bulk of the estate, including the house and grounds, was left to Marion. Fran Thornhill received a substantial cash settlement, and there were small bequests to Grace Harris and to Maurice, the handyman."

"What about the books?" asked Charlotte.

"The entire collection was bequeathed to the New York Botanical Society, along with money for cataloguing, shelving, repair, and other expenses incurred as a result of the acquisition."

"So much for Felix's commission," said Tom.

"Yes," said Charlotte. *And so much for the Ledge House property*, she thought. Without the money from the sale of the collection, Marion would be forced to sell the property in order to pay inheritance taxes. She wondered why Thornhill had changed his mind about selling the collection. Maybe he'd had a belated crisis of conscience. It was odd how he'd called in Daria to spruce up the collection, as if he'd had a premonition of his death.

"Ironical, isn't it?" said Tom. "If the stolen books are recovered, they'll come to rest in the very place they were been destined for over twenty years ago. Like overdue books returned to the library on one of those no penalty days for delinquent borrowers."

· I I ·

THE AIR WAS balmy as Charlotte, Tom, and Daria crossed
the channel in the Ledge House runabout after dinner. They
were on their way to the public hearing on the tax abatement
proposal. Charlotte wanted to see how deeply community
feeling ran on the issue, and Tom and Daria were along for
the ride. It was an intoxicating evening, the kind of summer
evening that is as rare in Maine as a thaw in January. The
setting sun suffused the sky with a glow of shrimp pink, and
the windowpanes of the houses of Bridge Harbor glinted like
topazes in their setting of dusky purple hills. Even the gulls
had ceased their restless circling and crying; they floated
quietly, several hundred black silhouettes bobbing on a sea
of molten silver.

For Tom and Daria, too, the evening was special. The
romance that Kitty had plotted had taken off like one of
the Roman candles that was being launched from the town
pier. Tom sat at the wheel, his hair blowing in the wind.
Now and then he would take his eye off the water to glance
at Daria, who smiled like a schoolgirl who's been handed a
valentine. The romance made Charlotte feel old and cynical.
In the evening quiet the young couple seemed to sparkle and
sizzle like one of the Roman candles. But she knew that the
fireworks never soared as high as you expected them to, and
that the sizzle eventually sputtered out. And then, black-
ness. For years she had sought the flame, and for years she
had been consumed by it. Until now. She had finally learned
to live in the darkness, to take comfort from its shroud of
security. She was a lonely old lady, or rather an old lady

alone, since she had grown to treasure her solitude.

The town pier was now in sight. Cutting back on the throttle, Tom steered the boat into the dock. After disembarking, they walked up a ramp to the pier, which was at the foot of Main Street. The town was done up festively for the upcoming Fourth: the Stars and Stripes hung from porch columns; miniature flags were planted in flower boxes; and red, white, and blue bunting draped the storefronts. The street was crowded with strollers, mostly vacationers staying in the town's hotels and guest houses or camping in the nearby State park. They browsed in gift shops, watched the fishermen unload the day's catch, or dined on boiled lobster at the rustic lobster pounds lining the waterfront. From a pub that was the hangout of the young and the young-at-heart came the muted strains of a Dixieland melody. The only note of incongruity in this atmosphere of relaxed gaiety was struck by the brisk strides and sober expressions of the townspeople who were heading up the hill to the Town Hall, with a very unvacation-like seriousness of purpose.

As Charlotte entered the meeting hall with Tom and Daria the room grew hushed as the townspeople craned their necks to get a glimpse of their famous visitor. Most of them knew who Charlotte was, the *Bridge Harbor Light* having run a notice of her arrival in the "Social News and Notes" column. The few who didn't turned to their neighbors to find out, for it was obvious that she was *someone*: in her rakish fedora and elegantly tailored suit, she stood out like a diamond in a tray of paste. Somewhere else, her appearance might have set off a stampede of autograph hunters, but the townspeople of Bridge Harbor were held back by their New England restraint. She was approached by only two fans, a little blue-haired old lady who remembered Charlotte's first movie, and a punk rocker with hair combed into stiff, shiny spikes. Much to her amusement, she had recently become a cult figure among the rock set, as a result of the fact that the fashions she had helped to popularize—the man-tailored shirts and broad-shouldered jackets of the forties—were again in vogue. Signing her autograph in a large, bold scrawl, she chatted graciously with the old lady and the punker. Unlike today's stars, she came from a tradition in which scorning one's fans was not acceptable behavior. She was a relic of the old Hollywood studio system in which a star was a queen and her fans her royal subjects. The lack of privacy that was the complaint of today's stars was no more an issue for her than it would be for the Queen of England. She had been raised to think of herself as a public figure, to always be gracious, glamorous, and in command—even if she was just running out to the supermarket. She had succeeded in that system because its standards were also her own. She felt an obligation to her fans, that she owed them an image— even now. If they wanted to see Charlotte Graham, the star, they would see a star, not a slob in a T-shirt and dungarees. To her, being a star was a business first and a privilege second. Her fans were her bread and butter. They had paid their money's worth, and they deserved to get it.

After signing the autographs, she looked around the hall. The house was full: the extra folding chairs that had been set up at the rear were occupied, and the late-comers were still streaming in. Among them were Stan and Kitty, looking glaringly suburban among the workshirts and fishing boots of the locals. Just behind the Saunders came Fran, whose outfit provoked some curious stares. She was wearing a green skullcap and an ankle-length green robe; around her neck hung a jeweled talisman in the shape of a pentagram, the symbol of the witch. Chuck was present, but not Marion. The turnout was evidence of how seriously the townspeople took their civic responsibilities, a phenomenon that was generally attributed to their form of local government, the New England town meeting. One of the country's last vestiges of true democracy, the town meeting was truly government of the people, by the people, and for the people. The dealings with a big corporation such as Chartwell might have necessitated the formality of a public hearing, complete with microphone, reporters, and court stenographer, but the tax abatement proposal would still stand or fall on the vote of the citizens themselves.

The concept of the town meeting had a certain romance—it was in just such meetings that the foundations of the Constitution had been laid—but Charlotte knew from her years in Connecticut that it was often less romantic in fact than in theory. The drawback of democracy in its purest form was that it was often cumbersome and inefficient, to say nothing of downright uncivilized: fists had been raised on more than one occasion over a proposal as seemingly benign as the restriction of dumping hours. One thing was certain, Charlotte thought as she settled in: a town meeting was rarely boring.

The meeting was called to order with a bang of the gavel by the First Selectman, a middle-aged man who looked uncomfortable in his coat and tie. After reading the proposed ordinance, he invited the audience to state their views at a microphone in the center aisle. The first person to come forward, a lawyer for the Chartwell Corporation, read a long, dull statement describing the benefits the project would bring. He was followed by a pleasant-looking man who identified himself as the proprietor of the local drugstore and president of the Citizens for the Chartwell Corporation.

"Fellow townspeople," he said, taking the microphone, "I think most of you know me. I've lived in this town my whole life. Now, there's nobody who's more reluctant to speak ill of our town than me. But I think we've been fooling ourselves long enough. I'm standing up here this evening because I don't want to see our community die. And it *is* dying, whether we want to face it or not. In the last five years, the cannery's closed and the boatyard's closed, and now the shoe factory's laying people off. Even the tourist trade isn't what it used to be. How much longer are we going to sit around before we do something about it? The Chartwell Corporation is offering us a chance for a prosperous future, and I think we should grab hold of it, if not for ourselves, then for our children. I, for one, don't want to see my boy have to go out of state to find a job, and I think the same goes for the rest of you."

The speech met with enthusiastic applause. "Thank you," said the speaker. After nodding to the First Selectman, he returned to his seat.

The reference to native sons being forced to leave the state to find work could be depended upon to touch a responsive chord in Maine, whose young people were often forced to seek better lives elsewhere. The next two speakers touched on the same theme: one was a high-school teacher who viewed the jobs the development would create for teenagers as a panacea for a host of social problems, and the other was an unemployed shoe factory worker who spoke of his reluctance to uproot his family to find work elsewhere.

The first person to speak against the proposal was the president of the Coalition to Save Gilley Island, a tanned, athletic-looking young woman who gave her occupation as student and her address as the Shore Road. Charlotte recognized the address as the stretch of shoreline known as Millionaires Row. She read from 3 by 5 cards in a crisp, businesslike tone:

"Six thousand years ago the Red Paint People canoed down our rivers to spend their summers on our beautiful coast, to feast on its plentiful harvest, to delight in its natural beauty. They were the first of the summer visitors who have sought out our coast over the centuries for respite from the tension and routine of their everyday lives. Until recently, our coast has been bountiful with its resources, but now those resources are threatening to give out under the sheer weight of demand: the peace and beauty that we cherish is being eroded by those who would seek its refuge. Our coast is at a crossroads, and how we vote on this issue will be one factor in deciding our future. Will we sacrifice our spiritual sanctuary for material gain? or will we preserve it for the generations to come? I say we have a sacred trust to preserve it for our children and our children's children, as an unspoiled reminder of the fragile beauty of nature. If our coast continues to serve as a lifeboat for the hordes seeking salvation and peace, the lifeboat will sink. And with it will disappear the very qualities that we, as its caretakers, most cherish."

The speech was applauded, but not as heavily as those of the previous speakers—the CCC forces were obviously in the majority.

The young woman's speech was appealing in its idealism, but there was a mendacious tone to it that Charlotte didn't like. The Coalition to Save Gilley Island reminded her of the residents of a tract development who oppose construction of an identical development next door, under the sanctimonious guise of protecting the environment. Or, to use the speaker's own analogy, lifeboat passengers who would keep other shipwrecked passengers from climbing aboard, to protect their own comfort and safety. The other aspect of the argument that bothered her was its anti-progress bias. She didn't think Maine's future lay with unimpeded development, but neither did she think it lay with subsistence farming and arts and crafts, particularly when it was one of the less prosperous states in the Union.

Once the hubbub caused by the young woman's speech had died down, the next speaker, Chuck Donahue, made his way to the microphone. He stalked up the aisle with his head down like a bull on the attack.

"Charles Donahue, Gilley Island, insurance broker," he said, identifying himself to the stenographer. "First," he said, taking the microphone, "I'd like to know what right the previous speaker has to preserve Gilley Island for her children, her children's children, or for anyone else. In case you weren't aware of it, young lady," he said sarcastically, "Gilley Island is private property, just as your property is private property. You have no more right to preserve it than I have to camp in your backyard. The only people who have a *right* to preserve it are myself, Mr. Gilley"—he nodded at Wes—"and the other owners of property on Gilley Island."

"Way to go, Chuckie baby," hooted Wes. He was standing up like a bettor cheering on his horse at the track.

Bang bang went the gavel. "Please sit down, Mr. Gilley," said the First Selectman. "Mr. Donahue has the floor."

Wes complied, casting a mocking smile at the young woman.

"Second," continued Chuck, "I'd like to point out to the young lady and to the other members of the Coalition to Save Gilley Island that the Chartwell Corporation is not planning to build a factory." He paused. "Or an oil refinery." He paused again. "Or a nuclear power plant." His voice had risen with each statement. "What they are planning to do is invest seventy-eight million dollars in what will be the finest resort on the coast of New England. I doubt very much that they'd be willing to invest that kind of money in the destruction of the environment. The Chartwell Corporation is just as interested—probably even more interested—in preserving the natural beauty of our coast as the Coalition to Save Gilley Island."

Turning his broad back on the microphone, he stalked back to his seat amid a thunder of applause.

Next came Wes Gilley, who rolled up the aisle yawing like a lobster boat in a heavy sea. He was dressed as usual in a navy watch cap and a faded red sweat shirt, his white belly hanging over his belt like rising dough over the lip of a bowl. As he passed, Charlotte could smell his odor: a not unpleasant mixture of beer, brine, and freshly cut wood. At the front, he gripped the microphone with one hand and hitched up his pants with the other. Then he stood silently for a minute, balancing himself with the aid of the microphone stand.

"Name, address, and occupation, Wes," prompted the First Selectman.

"John Wesley Gilley the third, Gilley Road, Gilley Island," he replied in a nasal growl. "Lobsterman. The way I figure it is this: there was this person who was ballin' up the works. You know who that was." He pointed at the First Selectman. Then he pointed at his chest. "*I* know who that was. So we don't have to go namin' names. Excuse me, Chuck," he said with a nod to Thornhill's son-in-law, "but that's the truth of it. Now, due to certain circumstances, the person we're talkin' about is out of the picture. So what's the problem? Let's get on with it."

It wasn't a very coherent speech, but Wes wasn't exactly in a condition for clear thinking.

He turned to walk back to his seat and then changed his mind. "Forgot something," he mumbled, taking the microphone again.

Tracey stood at the side of the hall. Charlotte noticed his expression change from relieved as Wes terminated his speech, to worried as he resumed it. She suspected he'd had to throw Wes out of more than one public meeting.

"I'd like to tell Miss Richbitch that she don't have no more right to preserve Gilley Island than I have to *piss* in her backyard," he said. He looked around him with a proud grin, swaying from side to side.

Bang bang went the gavel. "You're way out of order, Wes," said the First Selectman.

"Don't I know it," he replied, still grinning. "If I was in order, I'd have a hell of a time holdin' this much beer."

The audience chuckled.

"That's enough, Wes," said the First Selectman. "Now sit down and shut up."

Wes smiled broadly, hitched up his pants, and staggered back to his seat with a distinct cant to leeward.

The testimony continued for another hour, but it was tame by comparison with that of Chuck and Wes. Most of the speakers touted the development's benefits. But there were a few who spoke against it, including a high-school history teacher who called it welfare for the rich, and an Audubon Club spokesman who claimed, in a variation of the payroll or pickerel theme, that it posed a threat to the island's bird life. Charlotte was glad she had come. The people whose temperatures ran the hottest on the issue were clearly Chuck and Wes. If any of the island's recent events could be linked to the development controversy, it would most likely be through either of them.

The next day, a Monday, dawned cool and crisp and electric, the kind of summer day that presages fall. After a late breakfast Charlotte and Tom set out to visit Wes. To reach his front door they had to make their way across a yard littered with broken lobster traps, rusting fifty-gallon oil drums, old tires, castoff auto parts, even a broken toilet. The door, which was posted with an orange BEWARE OF THE DOG sign, was answered by a slovenly but cheerful-looking woman, whose thin, light brown hair was pulled tightly away from her face in a ponytail. She had the prematurely old appearance of women who have given birth too young and too many times.

"Hello," said Charlotte, "My name is Charlotte Graham and this is Tom Plummer. We'd like to have a word with your husband, if he's not busy."

"The girls told me you might be comin' over," she said in a thick accent. She turned toward the interior of the house. "Tammy, Kim," she shouted.

The younger girl appeared in the doorway behind her mother, carrying a little boy who was chewing on a crayon. In his other hand, he was holding a drawing that had been scribbled in red crayon on a brown paper bag.

"Yippee, you came," Kim said, seeing Charlotte. Handing her brother over to her mother, she threw her arms around Charlotte's waist and clung to her side. "I didn't think you would. Honest, I didn't."

"Kim Gilley, show your fetchin' up," scolded her mother.

From inside came the yipping of a small dog. Tammy appeared at the door, carrying the huge radio in one hand and cradling a Chihuahua, which must have been the ferocious dog to which the sign referred, under her other arm.

"You girls take the lady and gentleman out to your father," ordered their mother.

They found Wes sitting on a bench at the rear of a ramshackle bait shed, painting lobster buoys in stripes of red, white, and black. The already-painted buoys lay spread out around him, drying in the sun.

"Papa, look who's here," said Kim excitedly, running ahead. "It's Charlotte, the movie star I was tellin' you about. And this is her friend, Tom." She turned to face him. "Right?" she said, with a disarming smile.

"Right," said Tom, charmed.

Wes continued painting. Charlotte noticed that the hand that gripped the paintbrush was scarred and calloused from the burn of the pot warps.

Collecting a group of the lobster traps, Kim arranged them in a semicircle around her father, as if she were arranging a tea party for her dolls. After showing Charlotte and Tom to their seats, she took one of her own, while her sister sat down on the bench next to her father.

Wes looked up. "Get," he said to the girls.

He was met with a chorus of whines. "We was the ones that asked Charlotte," protested Kim. "She come to see us, too."

"Don't make no damn's odds who asked her," he replied. "Now, go sandpaper the anchor," he bellowed, raising his paintbrush threateningly and baring his teeth in an expression of mock ferocity.

The girls retreated reluctantly to a grassy plot at the foot of the wharf to watch the proceedings from a permissible distance, sitting like the patrons of a movie theatre on a castoff automobile seat.

After settling in on his makeshift seat, Tom inquired about the lobster catch. If he thought he was going to get a short reply, he was wrong. When it came to the state of the lobster industry, the taciturn toiler of the sea was apt to become as loquacious as a New York cabbie. No matter how good or bad the market, the lobsterman could be depended upon to find something to complain about, the perennial favorites being the size of the catch, the price of bait, and their exploitation by out-of-state interests. Like the farmer, the lobsterman wore his poverty like a badge of honor. Hearing Wes refer to his traps as "poverty boxes," Charlotte was reminded of Tom's story about Diogenes the Cynic, the Greek philosopher who, upon seeing the nobles of Athens in their finery, snorted, "Affectation," and, upon seeing the poor in their rags a few minutes later, snorted,

"More affectation." She suspected Wes's littered yard was as much an affectation as Chuck's expensive automobile.

Taking advantage of a pause in the conversation, Charlotte asked Wes what he thought of the meeting.

"All right," he said tersely.

She waited.

He looked up at her and smiled broadly. "I guess I really gave that rich bitch a rakin' over." Chortling to himself, he reached down to dip his brush into a can of paint.

"I assume that the person you referred to in your speech, the person who was balling up the works, was Frank Thornhill," she continued. "You didn't like him much, did you?"

He stopped painting and looked out over the water with the far-off look in his pale blue eyes that came from a lifetime of gazing out to sea. "Can't say that I did," he replied, leaning over the edge of the wharf to spit a brown stream of tobacco juice into the water.

"Why's that?"

He nodded in the direction of the Gilley Road. "See them cement pillars over yonder? He put 'em up. To mark the boundary."

Charlotte turned to look at the cement pillars that flanked the road midway between the Saunders and Gilley properties. They were about six feet high and shaped like the Washington Monument. On the walk over she and Tom had wondered who had put them there and why.

"The island was settled by my great-great-great-grandfather. He had two sons, and he divided the land between 'em. The line was sighted through a knothole in an apple tree. The tree is long gone, but the Gilleys have always held that the line followed that stone fence over yonder."

Charlotte and Tom turned to look at the stone fence, which intersected the road about fifty yards from the monuments in the direction of the Saunders' place.

"I owned all the land to this side of the fence—or thought I did—and the old man owned all the land to the other side. He bought the Ledge House property and the Saunders property from my cousin; it was all one piece back then. Anyways, I was out cuttin' cordwood one day," he continued, nodding toward the pillars, "and who comes drivin' up but Howard Tracey. He serves me a summons—for cuttin' wood on the old man's land."

"The land you thought belonged to you," said Tom.

"Damn straight I thought it was my land. Still do. Well," he went on, "the old man gets himself some big Herb of a lawyer, and we go to court about it. He dredges up some old maps to prove that the tree was fifty yards this side of the fence, though how anyone could know where that tree was beats me. I lose. Fifteen acres, including the most beautiful little stand of white pine you ever seen—it's as quiet as a church in there." He turned around to look at the pillars. "Some day I'm goin' to get me some dynamite and blow 'em all to hell. I shoulda done it before the old geezer croaked."

Charlotte wondered if the pillars would have been next on the list of vandalized property. "Do you have any idea who might have killed him?"

"It weren't me, if that's what you're thinkin'. What's it to you, anyways?" he said, turning suspicious. "Why're you snoopin' around?"

"Chief Tracey asked us to help him out with the investigation," said Charlotte, "You're under no obligation to talk with us if you don't want to."

"I already talked to Howard and to that royal boy."

"Royal boy" was Maine parlance for a State policeman, Kitty had said. The State police wore hats modeled on those of the Royal Canadian Mounted Police. "I know," said Charlotte. "But I'd appreciate it if you could go over it again for Mr. Plummer and me."

"Well," he said. "I guess if Howard says it's all right, it's all right. It coulda been anybody. The old bastard weren't very popular around here."

"Why was that?"

"Oh, he was the hoity-toity type. He insisted that everybody call him doctor, like he was a medical man or something."

"Mr. Gilley, did you see anyone other than Mrs. Harris at Ledge House while you were waiting at the door?"

"Only that fat joker, the book dealer. He was out back on the veranda. He was settin' on a lounge chair just outside them French doors."

"Were you waiting at the door the entire time that Mrs. Harris was upstairs getting your change?"

"No. I went out to look at my truck. Thought she might be leakin' oil—my oil pressure was low."

"How long were you gone?"

"Only a couple of minutes."

If Wes was telling the truth, it would explain why John hadn't seen him when he came out of the house, she thought. "Did you see anyone else?"

"Ayuh. I seen Chuckie comin' out of the library. He'd been arguin' with the old man. Goin' at it tooth and nail by the sounds of it. Then, two, maybe three minutes later I seen that guy Lewis comin' through the parlor."

"Through the parlor. You mean from the back of the house?"

"Ayuh."

"Where were you when you saw Chuck and Lewis?"

"Kneeling down behind my truck."

"From that position, you were able to see into the house? To see Chuck coming out of the library, and John coming through the parlor?"

"Ayuh."

Looking into his far-off blue eyes, Charlotte knew distant, dusky parlors would present no challenge to his eyesight. "Do you know what Chuck and Thornhill were arguing about?"

"Nope. But I can guess."

"The development?"

"Ayuh," he replied, spitting another stream of tobacco juice over the side. "Chuckie wanted the old man to sell out to Chartwell. The people from Chartwell say they won't go ahead with the development without the old man's land. They say it wouldn't be worth their while."

"But that's old news," said Charlotte. "They've been arguing about that for a long time. There must have been something else."

"There was," said Wes, massaging the wad of tobacco under his lip with his tongue, like a cow chewing its cud.

"Well?"

"I suppose it don't matter none if I tell you," he said with a shrug. "Bound to come out eventually, anyways." He paused. "Chuckie was pissed about the will. The old man said he'd rather leave his property to the State park than leave it to Marion and see it turned into a resort development."

Then the words, "You'd better leave it to me, you understand?" *had* referred to the will, thought Charlotte. "But Thornhill didn't change his will—the house and grounds were left to Marion," she said.

"He didn't have no chance, did he?"

·12·

AFTER LUNCH, CHARLOTTE and Tom headed out toward
the Donahue cottage. Once past the wooded Ledge House
property, the rutted track of Broadway opened onto bar-
ren headlands whose bold, bare granite cliffs rose steeply
from the waters of the bay. From this site more than from
any other, one had a sense of the island's vulnerability to
the elements. The sea breeze carried the chill of icebergs
and arctic wastes, and the waves crashed against the stony
flanks of the rocks with a fury that sent plumes of salt spray
skyward. On the bay, the pale gray mass of a fog bank
hovered threateningly over the outer islands, waiting for a
northeasterly wind to push it inland. The minute world of
pure perfection had been besmirched, and the island itself
now seemed in some way menacing. Even the sky and air,
which had once seemed to expand in widening circles of
time and space, now carried a stony, heavy malevolence.

Charlotte's thoughts were interrupted by a shout from
Tom, who had wandered over to the cliff's edge. "Seals,"
he said, pointing to the water below, where three shiny
black heads bobbed in the heavy swells.

They appeared to be playing a game of hide-and-seek in
the waters of a channel created by a fissure in the granite
bluffs. Their white-whiskered faces with their glistening,
puppylike eyes disappeared underwater, only to pop up minutes later in another spot. On a rocky ledge at water level,
the porcine form of a large seal—the mother, perhaps—
kept a lazy watch, until, alarmed at their presence, she awk-
wardly wriggled her ungainly torso into the water, where

she was transformed into a creature of grace and agility. On the rocks on the opposite side of the channel, a group of large, long-necked cormorants stood with their wings outstretched. Popular wisdom had it that the hapless water bird would sink unless it dried out its wings, for its dense feathers lacked the protective oils to keep them from becoming waterlogged.

The scene was primeval in its beauty: just so must the Red Paint People have found the coast on their summer visits thousands of years ago. What would happen to the seals if the condos were built? Charlotte wondered. Would they stay to entertain the occupants with their play, or would they flee to the peace and quiet of a more remote island? She thought of the great auk—the giant, flightless, gooselike creature that had once been the most powerful water bird in North America. Hunted at first for its eggs, then for its flesh, and finally for its feathers, which were used for comforters and pillows, it was driven to take refuge on ever more remote islands. Finally it made its last stand on a remote island off the coast of Newfoundland before succumbing to extinction early in the nineteenth century.

As they resumed walking their conversation turned back to the murder. It had been almost a week since Thornhill was poisoned, but they had no leads. All they had was a plethora of suspects, each with reason to want Thornhill dead, and each with means and opportunity. But if Charlotte and Tom were frustrated at their lack of progress, Tracey was even more so. His many hours of tedious labor hadn't yielded a single clue.

They had just rounded a bend in the road when Daria and John came into view at the cliff's edge. After scrambling up the scree, they ascended the last few feet to the top. John was carrying a picnic basket, and Daria her sketch pad. Spotting Charlotte and Tom, they waited for them at the roadside.

Daria was certainly taking care to portion out her company evenly, Charlotte thought. She had picnicked yesterday afternoon with John, dined last night with Tom at the

Saunders, and was now out with John again. She supposed it would be Tom's turn again tonight. At least Tom got the evening hours.

Charlotte and Tom caught up with them a few minutes later. Daria explained that John had been taking photographs of waves for Stan and she had been sketching waves—her homework for Stan's class.

"John's just been telling me about the wildflowers of New England," she continued. "He says that every species we can see from here has a significant medical or nutritional use. I'm testing his knowledge," she added with a dazzling smile. "He's going to tell me of what use these wildflowers are." She held out the bouquet she had gathered from the roadside.

"Well?" said Charlotte, smiling at John and raising her signature eyebrow.

"Anyone have hemorrhoids?" asked John with his lop-sided smile. "An ointment made from fresh buttercup leaves is very effective." He studied the bouquet. "How about bloating? Yarrow tea is a strong diuretic. Nervous? Try valerian, the nineteenth-century answer to Valium."

"And the lupine?" asked Charlotte, gazing across the road at the field blanketed with the tall white, pink, and lavender spikes of one of New England's most beloved wildflowers.

"Aha! It used to be grown in Europe for fodder, but isn't much anymore. Too many accidents. The mature seed of certain species is poisonous. A lot of common flowers are poisonous, but I don't want to get into that for fear of incriminating myself. Speaking of which, how's the investigation going?"

They chatted for a moment more and then separated: Daria and John were headed back to Ledge House.

"Stalking the healthful herb, or maybe the not-so-healthful herb," said Tom as they resumed their walk. "So . . . what do you think of our plant hunter?"

"A wonderful photographer," replied Charlotte. That morning, John had dropped off the photos that he had shot in the parlor at Ledge House. The close-ups of her face against the background of the elegant Chinese screen were among the best that had been taken of her in recent years.

"I'm surprised you let him take them," replied Tom. "Didn't you tell him that it might be hazardous to his health?"

Charlotte smiled. "Why are you asking about him?" she teased. "Jealous?"

"Maybe."

"An ideologue, but with a certain amount of charm," she replied. "He didn't like Thornhill, which he freely admits. But I don't think that's motive enough for murder, if that's what you're getting at."

"Not even if you view it psychoanalytically? Thornhill could represent the father—you know: authority, power, privilege. By killing Thornhill he could be setting the world aright, patricide as a political act."

"Plummer, the wild man," she said. In Mack Sennett days every Keystone Kops story conference had had its wild man, whose function it was to toss out outrageous ideas. The idea was to get the juices of creativity flowing. Tom's being her wild man was their private joke. But maybe John could have killed Thornhill out of some twisted desire to get even with the system. "Why is it that I have this funny feeling you've been out turning over rocks again?" she asked. "What have you found out this time?"

"Nothing terribly revealing," Tom replied. "He has an up-and-coming reputation. He won the Asa Gray award when he was in graduate school—it's a prestigious award for the best doctoral dissertation in botany—and he's been awarded a couple of grants to study the herbals in European libraries. But things haven't been going too well for him lately. A couple of research grant applications were recently turned down, and his latest book was just turned down by the outfit that published his earlier books. I guess times are tough in the ivory tower."

Charlotte remembered Thornhill's allusion at the herb

luncheon to the difficulty John was having in getting his work published.

"Apparently there's even some question whether he'll be granted tenure," Tom continued. "In some universities these days being granted tenure is the equivalent of being awarded the Nobel Prize, and Lewis's politics aren't the sort to earn him points with his older colleagues."

The Donahue house was now in sight, a shingled cottage with a glass-enclosed porch of the type found at seaside resorts up and down the East Coast. It perched forlornly on a grassy shelf near the end of a jagged, rocky point that sloped steeply down to the shoreline.

"Here we are," she said.

A few minutes later they had come to the opening in the cedar hedge that set off the house's apron of lawn from its rocky surroundings.

The door was answered by a bewildered Marion, who seemed unaccustomed to having guests. She ushered them through the hallway into a living room that had the musty odor of vacation homes that are closed up for much of the year. Charlotte sat on a couch opposite her, while Tom sat at a desk on the other side of the room where he could unobtrusively take notes.

Charlotte noticed that Marion's face was deeply etched with lines; worry and suffering had left their mark. She also seemed strangely impassive. Charlotte wondered if she was on tranquilizers. They were chatting about the fog when they heard the sound of a trail bike in the driveway.

"My son Kevin," explained Marion.

In a minute Kevin entered the hallway. He was dressed in the same outfit he'd worn the other day: a studded leather jacket and a knapsack emblazoned with the name of a rock group. He carried his motorcycle helmet under one arm. He had his mother's fair skin, and thick dark hair, which reached to his shoulders.

"Kevin," said Marion, "we have some guests. Would you like to meet them?"

Tossing his helmet and knapsack onto a chair, he glanced curiously into the living room, and then walked defiantly up the stairs. If Charlotte had been the mother of such an ill-mannered child, she would have knocked some sense into him, but Marion seemed inured to his insolence.

"Is Kevin your only child?" Charlotte asked. She immediately regretted her words, remembering something Tracey had said about another son.

"Yes," she replied. "I had another son, Patrick. But he was killed in an accident last year. He was on his bicycle. A hit-and-run driver."

"I'm sorry," replied Charlotte, genuinely. She glanced around the room, waiting for the awkward moment to pass.

The room was tastefully decorated with an eclectic mix of country and modern furniture. Although it was designed for beauty and comfort, its air of neglect made it seem dreary. The surfaces of the furniture were coated with a fine layer of dust, and the carpet was littered with the dried-up leaves of dead plants. The draperies were drawn over all but one window, obscuring what must have been a magnificent ocean view. Like its occupant, the room seemed sapped of its vitality. The exception was the baby grand piano that stood in a position of prominence at one end of the room. Charlotte remembered the piano lessons—what a comedown for someone who'd once aspired to be a concert pianist. The sun that streamed in through the one unshielded window warmed the piano's walnut surface to a honey glow, and a crystal vase of fresh flowers graced it like the flowers on an altar.

"Do you play?" asked Charlotte, nodding at the piano.

"Not so much anymore. I used to perform professionally, but I haven't in years." She lowered her head, touching her hand to her brow.

"Chief Tracey has asked us to . . . "

"Yes," she replied simply.

"Do you have any idea who might have wanted to kill your father?"

"No," she said, hesitatingly. And then more firmly: "No, I don't."

"You're aware that one of the suspects is your husband."
She nodded.

"Did you know that he quarreled with your father just before your father drank the poisoned tea?" asked Charlotte softly.

She looked up, her eyes welling with tears. Returning her hand to her brow, she cast down her gaze. "No, I didn't," she said quietly, pulling out a tissue to wipe the tears that were slipping down her cheeks.

She gave the impression of being overwhelmed—by her father's death, but also by lost opportunity and dashed dreams. Her sadness bespoke a career that had been sacrificed to marriage and children. And now the marriage had gone sour, and one child was dead and the other was out of control, leaving her nothing to fall back on in her grief. How difficult it was for women to find the middle ground that most men took for granted, Charlotte thought. The popular view was that times had changed, but Charlotte suspected there was still a heavy price to pay for trying to have it all. For Charlotte, it had been the other way around: the marriage and children had been sacrificed to her career. She had survived and prospered, but Marion reminded her of the long-necked cormorants who didn't have enough oil in their plumage to keep them from sinking. For Charlotte, the antidote to the disappointments in her personal life had always been her work, and she suspected, seeing the piano graced with its vase of flowers, that the same might be true for Marion. Like the cormorant, all she needed was some time and sunshine to dry out her wings.

"Do you think it was about the property?" she asked gently.

"Probably," Marion said with a sigh. "They didn't see eye to eye." She paused, and then continued: "Chuck says that the pressures for development are such that the island will be developed eventually anyway. He thinks it's better for us to be involved ourselves, so we can retain some control."

"It must not have been easy, being caught in the middle."

"No, it wasn't," she murmured, casting Charlotte a rueful smile.

"I don't understand one thing. Why was it so important to your husband to develop the property now? Your father wasn't young, and he wasn't healthy. If your husband had waited until your father's death, he would have had the land to do with as he pleased, without your father's opposition."

Marion shrugged. Her hands fingered the tissue in her lap, quietly tearing it to shreds. She sighed, and then reached for a pack of cigarettes. "I think he may have needed the money," she said finally. "I'm not privy to his financial affairs, so I can't say for certain."

Charlotte wondered why Marion was confiding in her, and decided that it was because she suspected her husband. By unburdening herself, she was putting the responsibility for determining his guilt in someone else's hands. No wonder she was a mess—the strain of the suspicion must have been unbearable.

"What makes you think that?" she asked.

"In recent years, he's become involved in horse racing," Marion said, adding, "I don't know why I'm telling you this."

"Because you need to confide in someone," said Charlotte. "His financial situation probably has nothing to do with what's happened. But the thought that it might is a terrible thing to have to keep to oneself."

"Yes," said Marion, wiping her eyes. "That's it—exactly." She sat for a moment, struggling to regain her composure. She lit a cigarette, and then continued: "He started going to the track years ago with his colleagues, on Wednesday afternoons, the way doctors play golf. Then he started buying shares in racing syndicates. Small shares at first, but in the last few years, he's been investing heavily. He says it's a tax shelter."

"Is he losing money?" asked Charlotte, mentally congratulating herself on pegging him as a racetrack type.

"I don't know. It's true that the cost of keeping these horses is enormous, but I don't think it's that as much as

his lifestyle. He's trying to keep up with people who are
way out of our league. These are the kind of people who buy
and sell million-dollar horses the way most people buy and
sell . . . I don't know, stocks and bonds or something." She
spoke more animatedly now, carried along by the momen-
tum of getting her story off her chest.

"For instance?"

"For instance, he flies all over the country to watch his
horses race. Last year, he bought a share in a stallion syn-
dicate in Ireland, so now he's flying over there all the time.
I don't know—the fancy hotels, the entertaining—I don't
think we have that kind of money."

"Is that how he met the Chartwell people?" asked Charlotte. The family that controlled the Chartwell Corporation
was known for its horse breeding.

"Yes," she said. "Meanwhile, he's been neglecting the
business. He hardly spends any time at the office anymore."

From outside came the sound of a car pulling into the
driveway.

Marion looked up in alarm. "He would kill me if he knew
I was telling you this," she said earnestly. "You won't tell
him, will you?"

"No. Don't worry."

In a moment, Chuck entered. Seeing them, he paused in
the doorway, his hands in his pockets and his burly frame
propped up against the doorjamb. He bared his teeth in
a smile, the cold blue-gray eyes behind his wire-rimmed
glasses squinting in contempt. "My, my! What do we have
here? An inquisition?"

He may have been hobnobbing with millionaires, but he
still had the smell of Southie about him, Charlotte thought.
The streetwise hustler with a deal always in the works and
big dreams of striking it rich on the next horse, or the next
picture. In Hollywood, they were a dime a dozen.

Marion nervously introduced Charlotte and Tom, and
explained that they were helping the police with the investigation into her father's death.

"And what have you been telling them, Marion dear?

About how well your beloved hubby got along with dear
old dad?"

Marion sat frozen to her seat.

"She's been telling us about her whereabouts on the afternoon of the murder," lied Charlotte. "We'd like to ask you
the same question."

"Oh, you would, would you? Well, I'd like to ask you
a question or two myself," he said belligerently. "Starting
with what the hell gives you license to go poking your nose
into other people's business?" He pointed at the door. "Get
out of my house," he bellowed. "Now."

"Why don't you call the police?" Charlotte suggested.
"I'm sure Chief Tracey would be interested to hear how
you refused to answer questions about your quarrel with
your father-in-law." She added: "In case it's escaped your
attention, that quarrel makes you a prime suspect in his
murder."

He leaned back against the doorjamb in a relaxed pose,
but his fists were clenched inside his pockets. "Who says I
quarreled with him?"

"I do. I heard you. And so did Daria Henderson, John
Lewis, Felix Mayer, Grace Harris, and Wes Gilley, to name
just a few."

"Then you must know what the argument was about."

"No, we don't. But we've been told you might have been
arguing over your father-in-law's will. Our source told us
that your father-in-law wanted to change his will, leaving
the Ledge House property to the State instead of to Marion.
To prevent your selling it to Chartwell against his wishes."

Chuck's ordinarily florid complexion turned lobster-red.
"Who told you that? That sot Gilley?"

Charlotte nodded. She wondered how accurate it was.
Why would Chuck have told Wes about the will? Then
again, why not? They were old buddies and unofficial
partners in the Chartwell venture.

"Did that lying son of a bitch also tell you that he was
the one who let the air out of the jeep's tires, that he was
the one who shot out the library window, that he was the

one who sent the poison-pen letters? Put that in your pipe and smoke it, Miss Hollywood Sleuth."

Their eagerness to implicate one another reminded her of the bandits in the Westerns who give the game away the minute the heat's applied. "So I can assume that you did quarrel with your father-in-law over the will."

"You can't assume a goddam thing," shouted Chuck. "As a matter of fact, we quarreled about something else."

"What was that?"

"None of your goddam business. Now," he said, "get out before I have to throw you out. I'd do it, too."

"Gladly," she said, rising from her seat. She headed toward the door, followed by Tom. "Thank you for your cooperation," she said icily. She marched out with all the dignity of a dethroned monarch.

Between Wes and Marion, a lot of questions about Chuck's motives had been answered, she thought as they headed down the walk. He needed the money, he needed it immediately, and there was a good chance that Thornhill was about to cut him, or rather, his wife, out of his will.

"I've been thrown out of better places than that," said Tom jauntily as they left. Once they were beyond the hedge surrounding the house, he took a piece of paper out of his pocket. "Look at this," he said, handing it to her.

It was a piece of stationery bearing the letterhead of Carolyn Freeman, bookbinder. The text, headed "Der Gart der Gesundheit, Peter Schoeffer, Mainz, 1485," contained detailed descriptions under various headings, including "Condition when received," "Work done," and "Binding materials used." The text ended with the sentence: "This job was completed in my studio on December 16, 1959." Underneath was the signature of Carolyn Freeman.

"Where did you get this?"

"From Chuckie baby's desk," replied Tom. "It was in with a bunch of other papers, telephone bills and that sort of thing. If you spend enough time sitting at desks waiting for politicos to get off the phone you can learn all sorts of important skills. I can also read letters upside down. . . . "

"Plummer, shut up for a minute," said Charlotte, who was studying the piece of paper intently. "Do you know what this means?"

"I think it means Chuckie baby took the books," said Tom smugly.

Charlotte smiled. "My, aren't you proud of yourself."

"They're called binder's reports," he continued, leaning over her shoulder. "Daria puts them in the books she works on. I figure this one either fell out of *Der Gart* by accident or was removed deliberately by the thief—namely our friend Chuckie baby—before he sold it."

"And you think Chuckie baby stole the books to keep up his fancy lifestyle, figuring that, if he was caught, Thornhill would be reluctant to press charges against his own son-in-law. Right?"

"Right."

"Well, there's something else about his little piece of paper I'll bet you haven't figured out," she teased, waving it in front of his nose.

"What?" he asked, annoyed that he'd missed something.

"Daria told me that her mentor, Carolyn Freeman, had worked on *Der Gart* when it was still part of the MacMillan collection. But this report is dated December, *after* the books were supposedly sold to Thornhill."

"Another piece of evidence incriminating Thornhill as a book thief?"

"Exactly."

They walked side by side in the dusty wheel tracks, which were separated by a swath of green dappled with hawkweed and buttercups. (What a shame—she would never be able to look at buttercups again without thinking of hemorrhoids.) Overhead, the air was filled with the strident screeching of the gulls, intermingled with the soft mewing of the terns. Their wheeling silhouettes were black specks against the meek, feeble sun, which seemed to be fading in submission to the mass of gray fog that stood poised offshore.

"Tom," said Charlotte after a minute. "Remember the

other day when we found out that Felix knew Thornhill had stolen the books?"

Tom nodded. He was walking with his hands in his pockets, deep in thought.

"We figured that the person who knew Thornhill had stolen the books—we were thinking in terms of Felix then—could have stolen the books himself, counting on the likelihood that Thornhill wouldn't report the theft for fear of being exposed as a book thief himself."

"Do you think Chuckie baby knew that Thornhill stole the books?"

"I don't know. But let's forget the books are missing for a minute. Let's say that someone knew that Thornhill had stolen them. Now, let's say that that person wanted something important from Thornhill, like, for instance, his cooperation in a scheme to develop Gilley Island."

"Blackmail. Very good. Chuckie baby says to Thornhill: 'Either you sell out to Chartwell, or I'll let everyone know that you're a book thief.' The binder's report is his proof that Thornhill stole the books."

Charlotte nodded. For that matter, she thought, the blackmailer could also have been Felix. He could easily have applied a little gentlemanly pressure to ensure that Thornhill followed through on his promise to let him handle the sale of the collection after his death.

She said as much to Tom.

"Or the blackmailer could have been any of the people at the Ledges on the day of the poisoning," replied Tom. "Wes, out of the same motive as Chuck; John, to advance his career; Grace, to promote her love life . . . "

"Even Daria, I suppose," interjected Charlotte with a mischievous smile. "She could have used her knowledge of the theft to encourage Thornhill to direct his bookbinding business her way."

"*Not* a likely scenario, Graham," said Tom, lifting an eyebrow in an imitation of Charlotte's famous expression. "I'll give you the blackmail theory. But the problem with it is that blackmail victims are more likely to kill their blackmailers than the other way around."

"This is true."

The wind blew at their backs, as if it were pushing them along. It was a steady, nervous wind, the kind that makes people pick quarrels with their best friends. Out on the bay, the fog crept slowly inward, swallowing the outer islands in its path, and reaching ghostly tentacles toward shore.

Suddenly they heard a sharp crack. For a moment, Charlotte's heart leapt into her throat: the image swept through her mind of Chuck shooting his wife in his anger over her betrayal. But it was only Kevin setting off cherry bombs in the yard. She and Tom exchanged relieved glances.

"I'm as nervous as a cat," he said.

"Me too."

·13·

ON THE WAY back from the east end they stopped at Ledge House to talk with Fran. She was the only suspect with whom Charlotte hadn't yet spoken. They looked for her in the herb garden, but she wasn't there. Passing through the witches' garden, Charlotte pointed out the monkshood bed to Tom.

"Does it have a fragrance?" he asked, leaning over to smell. Suddenly he pulled back and started sneezing, the tears streaming from his eyes.

"I'd be careful," said a voice from behind. "Even the pollen can make the eyes swell when the plant's in full bloom."

They turned to find Fran approaching from the direction of the barn. She was again dressed entirely in green, except for white tennis shoes.

"Hello," she said to Tom as she joined them in the witches' garden. She extended her hand and gave him a wide smile, "I'm Frances Thornhill."

"Glad to meet you," he replied, introducing himself. He wiped the tears from his eyes. "Pretty powerful stuff."

"Yes," she said. She bent over to rub a delicate, chrysanthemum-like leaf between her thumb and forefinger. "Try touching it."

Charlotte and Tom followed her example. Charlotte felt the same numbness that she had felt after touching the leaf at the Midsummer Night festival. "It's numbing, like the feeling in your gums when you've had Novocaine," she said.

"Exactly," said Fran. "In fact, monkshood is still used

in some places for dental surgery. Here, try rubbing some on your gums."

"No thank you," said Charlotte, "I'll take your word for it."

"The numbing effect is what makes it so effective in the treatment of rheumatism," Fran continued. "The danger is in getting the dose too strong."

"What do you mean?" asked Tom, who was rubbing a small piece of leaf on his upper gum. "The poison might be absorbed through the skin?"

"Yes. Witches used to rub their skin with an ointment made from monkshood and other plant poisons. They called it flying ointment because it caused the sensation of rising and falling—a hallucination, really."

The same sensation her uncle had had on his deathbed, but Fran didn't mention that. She spoke even more rapidly than usual. Charlotte wondered if she was nervous. In addition to rounding out the list, they had another reason for wanting to talk to her: Tracey had told them that the handyman, Maurice DesIsles (he pronounced the name *Dezizzle*, with the Yankee talent for making a hash of French names), had reported seeing Fran digging in the monkshood patch a couple of weeks before the murder. Initially he had refrained from saying anything out of loyalty to Fran, but had finally decided to come forward. The fact could mean nothing— Fran would naturally spend time working in her garden— but it could also mean that she had dug up the roots with the intent of poisoning her uncle. She had motive—no groom, no wedding. It was true that she would lose the herb garden either way, but with Thornhill dead she would at least have a stake to get started somewhere else. But despite her motives, she didn't strike Charlotte as a murderer. It seemed a fair enough assumption that the person who took out her anger against herself, which was what the herb garden was, would be unlikely to take it out against someone else.

They were still standing in front of the monkshood bed, which Maurice had replanted. Looking at the flower, Charlotte thought how menacing it looked now that she knew that it carried the deadly alkaloid in its delicate veins. Even the color seemed sinister: the luminous dark blue of nightmares, and death.

"Is this the black witches' garden, then?" asked Tom.

"Yes," replied Fran. "The poisons and drugs •that do harm. The cauldron is to suggest the witches' brews," she said. "I've given Maurice instructions to tear out the whole bed, though. I—" She shook her head. "I don't want to be reminded." She looked disgusted with herself, as if her uncle's death was her fault. Which, in a sense, it might have been.

"I know monkshood is often grown in herb gardens," said Charlotte. "But I'm surprised. Why do people grow a plant that's so poisonous?"

"Because the flower's so beautiful. On account of beauty, we're willing to overlook a lot of dangers, are we not?" she said. "However," she added, "there are precautions that should be taken. For instance, monkshood should never be grown by people who have young children."

"What about people who have pets?" asked Charlotte, thinking of Jesse.

"Pets aren't a problem. Animals know instinctively when a plant is poisonous. Cows will graze all around monkshood, but they won't eat it. The same goes for field mice, who will eat just about anything. It's only man who's deceived." She blinked, as if startled by her words.

"As you probably know," said Charlotte, coming to the point, "Chief Tracey has asked us to look into your uncle's death."

"Yes. I've already spoken with the police, but I expect you'd like to ask me some more questions."

Charlotte nodded.

Explaining that she was in the middle of drying some herbs, Fran invited them to talk with her in the barn. This was herb-gathering season, she said, the busiest time of her year. Following her through wide doors flanked by barrel planters overflowing with herbs and flowers, they entered the barn, whose dim interior was redolent with the scent of drying herbs. Charlotte still thought of Fran's herb business as something of a glorified hobby, but this was clearly not so. Herbs were everywhere—in baskets, tubs, and boxes. They hung from the rafters in bunches, creating a sweet-scented canopy in shades of green and brown. The room was set up like a store: one wall was lined with shelves displaying herb products—potpourris, herbal teas, herbal vinegars, herbal moth preventatives; another wall was lined with shelves of gift items—herbal wreaths, witches' brooms, dried herb arrangements, herbal sachets in calico bags. In a corner, a rack displayed pamphlets with titles such as *Halloween at Ledge House*, *The Witches' Handbook*, and *Favorite Ledge House Recipes* (this was co-authored by Grace). At the back stood a wood cookstove, above which were suspended several tiers of wooden screens on which herbs were spread out to dry.

It was here that Fran took her place. She was stirring the herbs vigorously with a wooden spoon. "Most herbs dry perfectly well by themselves," she said. "But a few—like chervil, dill, and fennel—have to be helped along."

Charlotte took a seat on a ladder chair next to the stove, while Tom leaned up against a counter displaying packets of herb seeds. The heat of the stove felt good. The weather had turned damp and chilly.

"Have you found out anything?" asked Fran as she stirred. "I was curious about . . . about how the investigation is going."

"Nothing significant," replied Charlotte vaguely. "One question we have," she continued, "is whether you remember discussing monkshood with anyone."

"I talk about its being used by witches in my lectures. And of course, I talk about the plants in the witches' garden being poisons and drugs, but I don't say anything about monkshood specifically. Unless someone asks, but I don't remember anyone asking recently."

"About the monkshood . . . I noticed when I was here for the Midsummer Night festival that someone had dug up the bed."

"Yes," she said. "I don't know who. I checked with Maurice to see if he had any idea, but he didn't."

"That's funny," said Charlotte. "He told the police that he saw you digging in the monkshood bed a couple of weeks before the murder."

Two bright pink spots appeared in the center of Fran's papery-white cheeks. "Oh—oh," she stammered. "I forgot. I guess I was. I was . . . " She paused. "That's right. I guess I was dividing the roots. The plants don't flower properly if you don't divide the roots now and then."

"I see," said Charlotte.

So she had lied. But that didn't necessarily mean she was guilty. It might only mean that she felt guilty, and guilt was a feeling that, like good luck and good health, often seemed to be meted out in inverse proportion to the degree in which it was deserved. The mere fact of being under suspicion was enough to induce guilt in sensitive people, and if Fran had dug up the monkshood bed, she had reason to feel guilty. Surely she must have wished her uncle's death, if only subconsciously. How must she have felt, then, when her wish was fulfilled, and with an herb husbanded by her own hand?

"I understand you were in the kitchen on the afternoon your uncle was poisoned," said Charlotte.

"Yes, I brought Grace a new blend of tea that I wanted Frank to try: liberty tea, made of tansy and some other herbs. The colonials used it instead of China tea, which was banned from many households. The colonials considered China tea unpatriotic, because of the tax."

"Was the liberty tea very bitter?" asked Charlotte. "What I mean is, could it have camouflaged the taste of monkshood?"

"Oh, yes, I never thought of that," she answered. "Very hot and peppery. Though the colonials used to enjoy it tremendously. I've often thought its lapse in popularity said something about how accustomed our tastes have become to sweets. Would you like to try some?"

"No thank you," said Charlotte, who considered herself

a trusting soul, but not trusting enough to try some tea offered by the person who had prepared the fatal tisane for Thornhill.

"Is there anything else?" prompted Fran.

"No, I guess that's all," replied Charlotte, rising from her seat. "Thank you very much."

Fran showed them to the barn door, where she stood waving goodbye with the wooden spoon that she still held in one hand.

"Bubble, bubble toil and trouble," said Tom as they closed the garden gate behind them. "You half expect her to start casting spells."

"It's 'double, double toil and trouble,' " corrected Charlotte, who hated to see the bard mangled. And then: "Yes, she is a bit much, isn't she."

As they headed down the road Daria emerged from the gardener's cottage. She was carrying a thick book under one arm. At the sight of her, Tom looked disheartened, as if he thought he was losing out in his bid for her affections. He wasn't one to give up easily, however. After excusing himself, he crossed the road to talk with her, leaving Charlotte to continue on. He caught up with her a few minutes later wearing an expression of smug success.

"Good news on the love life front?" asked Charlotte.

"On that front and on the book thief front," replied Tom. "At least I think it's good news. Daria says she meant to tell us about it when she saw us out on the East End. She says we should call Tracey right away."

As they entered the Saunders' kitchen a short while later they were surprised to find Tracey sitting at the table, "mugging up"—Maine parlance for a coffee break—with Kitty. They were discussing the Gilley Island Fourth of July clambake, an annual event that was being hosted for the third consecutive year by the Saunders. Kitty reported that Tracey would be coming but that he wouldn't be able to stay because he was needed in town. The Bridge Harbor fireworks, he explained, attracted viewers from all around.

And with so many people, some were bound to "get notional," as he put it.

Charlotte and Tom joined them at the long pine table. "What brings you over here?" asked Charlotte, curious about the news.

"I guess you could say that we've solved the case of the missing books," he replied. "Though its not going to help us a whit with the murder."

"Really!" exclaimed Charlotte. "Who took them? Donahue?"

"A Donahue," replied Tracey, "but not the one you're thinking of."

"What do you mean?" she asked, baffled.

"Kevin Donahue."

"The son!"

"Ayuh. Last night while I was at the hearing the partner of one of the rare-book dealers I had talked with called. When I called back, he said that a kid had been in with an old herbal. He described the kid as looking like a juvenile delinquent, and right away I thought of Kevin."

"Did the dealer buy the book?" asked Tom.

"No. The kid said his grandfather had given it to him as a junior high-school graduation present. The dealer thought the book might have been stolen, and asked him to leave it, using the excuse that he would have to consult with his partner. But the kid got suspicious and left."

"And here we thought it was Chuck," said Charlotte, shaking her head. She was pleased, though, that Tracey's diligence had paid off, even if it hadn't brought them any closer to the solution of the murder.

"It turns out that he has a juvenile record as long as your arm," continued Tracey. "Petty vandalism, possession of marijuana, breaking and entering. Just goes to show that you should always be thorough. I checked the criminal records of everyone on the dad-blamed island but him."

"Yes, I'm well aware of that," said Charlotte drily.

Tracey smiled at her, his blue eyes twinkling.

"Did Thornhill know he'd taken the books?"

"Ayuh. And so did his parents."

No wonder Thornhill hadn't reported the theft. He would have been accusing his grandson of a crime of which he was also guilty. There was something Gothic about it: the sins of the fathers being visited on the sons.

"I went out to Donahues' as soon as I got off the phone," Tracey continued. "The minute I asked to see Kevin, I knew I had the right person. Chuck owned up to the theft right away. Evidently he'd found the books in the boy's room. He'd discussed the matter with Dr. Thornhill. In fact, that's what they were arguing about on the day of the murder. Chuck had promised Dr. Thornhill that Kevin would return the books himself, but the kid was stalling, and apparently Dr. Thornhill was tired of waiting."

Then, the words "Leave it to me, you understand?" had referred to Chuck's efforts to discipline his son, rather than to the will, Charlotte thought. "Why didn't Chuck and Marion say anything after Dr. Thornhill died? They knew we were looking for the book thief."

"I asked the same question. I was some put out, let me tell you. After all that work. They'd planned to make Kevin return the books to his grandfather himself, but after the old man died, they didn't know what to do, so they didn't do anything. I think they were happy to turn them over to me, which is probably what they would have ended up doing anyways."

"So he just lifted the books from the vault when he was visiting his grandfather, on impulse?" said Tom.

"Ayuh. Just stuck them in that knapsack he was always carrying around. The amazing thing is that he actually sold a couple. Not the herbals, but some of the less valuable ones. A dealer gave him a hundred and fifty dollars for them. He used the money to buy a radio for one of the Gilley girls. He's a generous kid, anyways, even if he is a peck of trouble."

Charlotte remembered Kim telling her that Kevin had given Tammy the radio. She should have wondered where he got the money. She felt totally confused: for nearly a week, she'd been operating under the assumption that the book theft was related to the murder. But she also had the feeling that if she tugged on the right string, the complex knot that was Thornhill's murder would start to unravel. The news about Kevin simplified the matter enormously. In fact, it was a philosophical maxim of some kind that the simpler an idea is, the closer it is to the truth. It was called Occam's razor—Tom was always quoting it. For instance, they could throw out the theory that Felix or Chuck had stolen the books to pay off their debts, as well as the theory that Thornhill had been murdered by a book thief who had been caught in the act. They could also throw out the farfetched theory that Thornhill had been accidentally poisoned by someone who had really wanted to induce a heart attack with the aim of getting everyone out of the house. Which didn't leave them with much.

"Is the botanical society going to press charges?" asked Tom.

"No," replied Tracey. "I don't think they could. The books were stolen from Dr. Thornhill, not from them. All they're interested in anyways is getting the books back in good shape. They suggested that Daria examine them to make sure none of the plates had been cut out or anything. Which she did."

"And they're okay?" asked Charlotte.

"Ayuh. I took them over to her last night after I left Donahues'. She's locked them up in the vault until someone from the botanical society can pick them up, except for the one that John has been working on."

"You can tell her to lock this up with them," said Charlotte, removing the binder's report from her purse.

"What's this?" asked Tracey.

"A binder's report," said Charlotte. "It's further proof that Dr. Thornhill stole the books." She explained about the dates. "We were out at Donahues' earlier this afternoon. Tom found it on Chuck's desk. He thought Chuck might be using it to blackmail Thornhill into selling out to Chartwell."

Tracey looked up at Tom. "You took it from his desk?" Tom nodded.

Tracey's mild blue eyes turned cold with disapproval. "I don't approve."

"Kevin took it, didn't he?" said Tom. Then he shrugged. "I'm sorry. I guess we should have notified you."

"I guess you should have," said Tracey.

"This changes the whole picture, doesn't it?" said Tom, artfully changing the subject. "The fact that it was Kevin who stole the books, I mean."

"Yes, but maybe it will simplify matters," said Charlotte. "We've gotten rid of one messy complication."

"*Entia non multiplicanda praeter necessitatem*," he said. "Occam's razor: all unnecessary facts in the argument being analyzed should be eliminated."

Charlotte smiled with the triumph of a trainer who has successfully put a performing seal through a difficult trick.

"What's going to happen to Kevin now?" asked Kitty, who had returned to the table. She had been making arrangements for the clambake.

"Nothing," said Tracey. "But I don't think he'll cause any more trouble. He's had the living daylights scared out of him."

"How's that?" asked Tom.

"The State police really put him through the wringer this morning. They thought he might know something about the murder."

"I feel sorry for him," said Kitty. "He must be a confused boy."

"I can't say that I disagree with you there, Mrs. Saunders," Tracey concurred. "The problem is that he hasn't got anything to occupy his time. His father doesn't pay any attention to him, and his mother's still so torn up over the other boy's death that she isn't able to."

"Maybe he should get a summer job," said Kitty, who could always be depended on to look for the bright solution.

"As a matter of fact, I've been looking into that," said

Tracey. "I've asked a friend of mine who does some lobster-
ing to take him on as bait boy. I'd ask Wes Gilley, but
he's already got his girls helping him out. Some honest work
won't do Kevin any harm, and it might just do him a lot of
good."

As Charlotte was getting ready for bed she stood looking
out at the cove. A full moon hung above the black tips of
the spruces on Sheep Island, bathing the room in its soft
light. She felt as if she could walk out to the island on the
flickering silver path of its reflection. She loved the cozy
room, with its lovely view, its antique furnishings, and its
wide plank floors; it was gracious and unassuming, like the
people of Maine. Tracey, for instance. How many police
chiefs would have taken a juvenile delinquent under their
wing? The people of Maine were often like that, noble and
generous. She thought of them as natural aristocrats. They
had little, but they were rich in spirit—the legacy, it was
said, of the days of the great sailing ships. The sailors of that
era had visited hundreds of ports in a lifetime, and knew that
the world was bigger than their own little towns. Their wide
horizons lived on in their descendants. Of course Maine, like
anywhere else, had its share of bigots and backbiters, but
it was nevertheless remarkably free of the narrow-minded
prejudice typical of other rural populations.

Still another appeal of Maine, she thought as she snuggled
under the antique quilt, was its belief in the old-fashioned
values, values like pride in workmanship, self-reliance, and
perseverance. Looking up at the rafters, she could see the
marks left by the adze that the barn builder had used to
hew a square beam from a round log. He had been just a
simple craftsman putting up a functional building. But he
had created a structure with such dignity of form and purity
of line that it was as beautiful a hundred and fifty years later
as on the day it was built. She was not a believer in genius.
Like Edison, she believed that genius was ten percent
inspiration and ninety percent perspiration. She had been
taught from her youth to do her job well and to do it with

humility; it was a lesson that had brought her tremendous success. With the years, she had come to see that it was the same in any profession. The greats were great because they were always the first on the job in the morning. Like the barn builder, they were dedicated craftsmen whose creations withstood the test of time. Things were different today: nobody wanted to pay their dues. The bright young stars expected to start at the top and often did, but what they failed to recognize was that their so-called genius would wither away unless it was nourished by skill, effort, and diligence.

Thornhill had paid lip service to the Yankee values, she reflected, her thoughts shifting back to the murder. He had professed to be a man of plain living and high thinking, of pure ideals and earnest effort, in the best New England tradition. But he had betrayed those values: he had wanted the books, and he had wanted them now. He hadn't been willing to wait to acquire them honestly. She remembered Felix's taunting words at the herb luncheon: "It is not the yielding to temptation that oppresses me, but oh the remorse for the times I yielded not." Perhaps the betrayal had cost Thornhill his life.

Soft, fitful puffs of fog blew in through the screen, dampening her pillow. The fog bank that had hovered offshore all day was creeping toward land. Before long, the moon would be swallowed up. In the distance, she could hear a foghorn; its hoarse, haunting call sounding base to the clanking rhythm of a bell buoy, like a tin can being kicked along an empty street.

She had just drifted off to sleep when she was suddenly awakened by heavy pounding on her door. "What is it?" she called, her heart beating wildly.

"It's Tom," answered an urgent voice.

She sat up in bed, alarmed. Her clock dial read eleven thirty.

Tom opened the door, and stood silhouetted in the light from the stairwell, one hand on the doorknob and the other on the doorjamb. "It's Daria," he said. He was out of breath.

"She's missing. She went out in the runabout to paint the island by moonlight. She was supposed to meet me in the parlor at Ledge House at ten, but she hasn't come back."

For one drowsy minute, Charlotte wondered why Tom was meeting Daria at ten o'clock, but then she remembered that he had spoken with her that afternoon. They had probably made a date then. The rest took a little longer. The channel! The current was most treacherous in the hour before low tide. She made a quick mental calculation. The tide had been out just before ten, when they had set off for Wes's. Which would mean that the current would have been at its strongest around nine, just as Daria was about to come in. And the moon was full. Ordinarily the tidefall was twelve feet, but with a full moon it would be a couple of feet more, making the tidal current all the more swift.

She threw aside her covers and sat up, groping for the pair of trousers that was draped over the back of a chair. The room was dark—the light of the moon had been extinguished by the advancing fog. She glanced out the window—a wall of white. How would they ever find her? "Damn. Did you call Tracey?"

"Yeah," he replied briskly. "He's going out in the police launch, and he's calling the Coast Guard. I already stopped by the gardener's cottage. Lewis is going out in Donahues' boat, and I thought I'd go out with Wes. I'm headed over there now. Can you and the Saunders search in their boat?"

Charlotte nodded.

"Thanks," he said as he turned to leave.

"Did you search for her on the Ledges? Maybe she fell down and hurt herself on the path or something."

"Yeah. All the way down to the landing. She wasn't there."

·14·

THE FOG SMOTHERED the island in a shroud of white. It was an unearthly world—cold, wet, and strangely dark. A world of no bearings and no dimensions. A world of ships crashing on hidden ledges. A world without comfort or safety, in which the senses were heightened to danger, the eye more keen, the ear more sharp. Even the sea birds spinning out of the mist seemed like sinister emissaries from the underworld.

Charlotte rubbed her hands together. Her skin was cold and clammy. She had been out all night in the Saunders' boat, searching for Daria. At daybreak, Stan and Kitty had dropped her off to search the shoreline, on the chance that Daria had managed to swim ashore. She couldn't see anything: the fog obscured everything outside of fifty yards. "So thick you could stick your knife in it to mark the passage back," Tracey had said. She had circled the island once and was now on her second circuit, just past Ledge House where the road opened up onto the headlands that marched out to the point at Donahues'. She had never realized that the sea had so many voices: the deep, angry roar of the breakers as they crashed upon the rocks; the rumbling of the rounded rocks on the shingle beaches as they were sucked back into the sea; the undertone of hoarse gasping. Occasionally, there was a sound like a pistol shot as a big wave slapped against a granite bluff, sending a plume of foam skyward. From the edge of the cliff came the slow, steady hiss of the wind that carried the fog toward land. What was it she was listening for? she wondered. A cry, a moan, the thud of an oar? The sound of an empty boat splintering against the rocks?

At the side of the road ahead emerged the silver, skeletal shapes of a forest of dead trees; it was the *dri-ki*, the word the Indians used for the trees that die when a beaver dam raises the level of water in a pond. They stood like an army of ghosts, their bones clothed in a miasma of fog, their feet rotting in the dark, fetid water. She was reminded of a legend Kitty had told her about the seamen who'd lost their lives in shipwrecks on the ledges surrounding the island: their ghosts were said to haunt the island when the fog was thick. "Cobweb-shaped creatures," Kitty had called them. She imagined she could hear them moaning, but it was only another of the sea's many voices. She hastened her step; the place made her uneasy. In a minute, she had left the *dri-ki* behind in the fog. She walked in a trance, her thoughts dwelling vaguely on the death that was omnipresent in the wind, the fog, the sharp rocks; the death that demanded the sacrifice of the youngest, the most fair. By turns, she fought off the succession of feelings—outrage, impotence, poignant sadness—that are left to the living when youth and beauty are taken before their time. Thornhill, yes, he had lived his life, but not Daria.

She had been missing now for nearly twelve hours. The only explanation for her disappearance was that the boat's outboard motor had failed. The boat was equipped with oars, but the consensus was that her chance of overcoming the treacherous tidal current was slim; strong men had lost their lives in its grip. "As swift as a mill race," Tracey had called it. She thought of another local legend related by Kitty, the legend of a schoolteacher who'd been engulfed by a wave while she was reading on the rocks. Her body had washed up on shore a week later, looking as neat as if it had been laid out in a funeral parlor, her bonnet still tied under her chin, her shawl still neatly pinned across her breast. She shuddered, and pulled up the collar of her jacket against the damp. Looking out over the cliff's edge, all she could see was waves crashing on the rocks, and an angry swirl of white foam that reminded her of one of Stan's paintings: the elemental battle between land and sea. But the sky was brightening: the sun had tentatively begun to shine through the gauze-like fog, tingeing it with a pearly luminescence. She could hear the invisible gulls greeting the morning with their raucous cries . . . and another sound. She cocked an ear: could it be a groan?

It seemed to come from the channel where she and Tom had watched the seals at play. She walked over to the edge, half believing that her ears were deceiving her, that it was the sound of the sea, the clamoring of the voices in the waves. But it was not: there, on a rock, was Daria, her slim body thrown up on shore like a piece of flotsam. She lay face-down on the slab of granite where the mother seal had sunned herself, the cheerful red of her sweater strangely incongruous in the grim, gray scene. One leg was skewed at an awkward angle, like a rag doll's, and the rising tide was lapping at her feet.

Slipping and sliding on the seaweed and algae, Charlotte clambered down the cliff. "Please let her be alive," she prayed. Her hands and shins scraped against the sharp shells of the mussels and barnacles that clung to the rocks, but she barely noticed. Reaching Daria, she gently pulled her dank, fishy-smelling hair away from her face. "It's Charlotte," she said. "Everything's going to be okay." Daria opened her eyes and nodded weakly in response. Beneath her tan, her face was drained of color, and her lips were an alarming shade of gray.

Removing her jacket, Charlotte draped it over Daria's slender shoulders.

Once Charlotte had called the police from the Donahues' house, Daria's rescue was quick work. A rescue squad plucked her off the rock within half an hour, and she was now resting in the hospital with Tom at her side. Fran's prognostications had been accurate in one respect:

Tom was Daria's lucky guy. If he hadn't been there to notice that she hadn't come back, she would probably be dead. Instead she had a broken leg—a simple fracture—a couple of cracked ribs, and contusions and abrasions, which meant that she had taken a beating on the rocks. But she would be all right. The breeze that had driven the fog inland had been her salvation. Once the tidal currents had eased, the breeze had blown her back toward land. She had been guided by the lights at Donahues'. Thank God Marion was an insomniac. But she hadn't made it all the way. The boat had been grounded on a ledge exposed by the tide—one of the ledges on which so many ships had met their doom. She had been forced to swim to shore. It was only through the grace of God that she'd ended up in the channel, where she was protected from the waves. Charlotte had found her just in the nick of time. Another hour and she would have been drowned by the rising tide.

Charlotte was now sitting in Tracey's office, waiting for him to finish a phone conversation about a stolen piece of lumber.

Hanging up the phone, Tracey asked how Daria was doing.

"Fine," said Charlotte. "The doctors say she'll probably be able to go home tomorrow or the next day."

"Good. I can talk with her then. I was supposed to go over the report on the book theft with her this morning, just to check some facts."

"Have you recovered the boat?" asked Charlotte.

"Ayuh. Stove all to hell—the prop's sheared off, the lower housing's knocked out. Drove on a ledge just east of that little channel. She's a lucky girl," he continued. "I thought we'd seen the end of her, sure as shooting. It would have been the end of her, too, if it hadn't been for that breeze."

"I wonder if she's as lucky as you say," said Charlotte.

"What're you driving at?" he asked, curious.

"Do you know anything about engines?"

"Depends."

"She said that the engine ran fine on the way out, but

that she couldn't get it started again when she was ready to come in."

"Do you think someone might have tampered with it?"

"Maybe."

"There's only one way to find out," said Tracey, standing up and reaching for his windbreaker. "She's down to the town pier."

The sun was shining brightly through the fog as Charlotte and Tracey walked down the steep slope to the town pier.

"Looks like it's going to scale off," said Tracey, squinting in the glare. "Good weather for the fireworks tomorrow."

The pier was aswarm with volunteers helping the crew from the fireworks company set up for the Fourth. Metal stands in the form of a waterfall, a pinwheel, and the American flag had been erected for the set displays, and sand-filled oil drums and steel cylinders were being set into place for the launching of the rockets. The fireworks were expected to draw a crowd of four thousand or more, at least half of which would be tourists. The fireworks could always be depended upon to create a controversy, Tracey complained. Every year, someone raised the issue of whether the tourists ought to be allowed to view the fireworks at the expense of local taxpayers, and every year the Chamber of Commerce defused the controversy by raising the money for the fireworks fund, on the theory that fireworks were good for business.

It was going to be a busy day: the schedule of festivities included a lobster feed put on by the Rotarians; a parade with prizes awarded by the Chamber of Commerce for the best float; and a field day at the ballpark. The annual lobster-boat race would be held in the afternoon. Two dozen lobster boats would be challenging the defending champion, Wes Gilley. The fireworks would be preceded by a band concert and a reading of the Declaration of Independence by the local Catholic priest, whose recitation could always be depended on to bring a collective lump to the throat of his audience. Following the fireworks, there would be a square dance on the town pier, with a demonstration by the Bells and Buoys Square Dance Club. All of which meant extra work for the police, Tracey complained.

At the end of the pier they headed down a ramp to the docks where the boats were moored. They found the Ledge House runabout in a slip near the end of the dock, her bow splintered where she had hit the ledge. Maybe she was being paranoid, Charlotte thought, as she watched Tracey check the fuel line and then unscrew the gas cap. Who would want to kill Daria? Her paintbrushes were still scattered on the floor of the boat. Picking up one of the longer ones, Tracey stuck it handle first into the gas tank. Could someone have added something to the gas? she wondered. Sugar, or water? As she watched him rub the liquid on the paintbrush handle between his fingers, she knew from the frown that crossed his genial face that her hunch had been right.

He stepped back onto the dock a few minutes later carrying a spark plug in one hand, which he held out to show her. "Somebody put chain saw bar oil in the spare tank," he said. "See how the plug's all gummed up? The main tank's okay: she had enough gas to get out there, but once she switched tanks, she was in trouble." He wrapped the plug in a handkerchief, and put it in his pocket.

They turned to walk back up the ramp.

"Hard to fathom why anyone would want to kill her."

"I've been thinking about that. The only reason I can think of is that she knew something incriminating about the killer."

Tracey looked at her with a quizzical expression.

"There are a couple of other explanations. One is that this is more of the same mischief, that there was no intention of harming anyone."

"I'll buy that. What's the other?"

"That Daria wasn't the intended victim. The innocent bystander theory."

"But if she *was* the intended victim, because, as you say, she knows something, wouldn't she have told us?" asked Tracey.

"Maybe she doesn't know that she knows."

"You mean that she said something or did something that made the murderer think she knew he had poisoned Dr. Thornhill."

"Exactly."

It was strange how both she and Tom had the feeling that the murderer wasn't finished. But maybe it wasn't so strange: he was being hunted, and the natural response of the prey is to defend itself. If the murderer *had* tried to kill Daria, maybe he was beginning to panic. Thornhill's murder had been an act of cunning; the risk of detection had been very small. But tampering with the boat's gasoline tank had the smell of recklessness about it. On the other hand, the killer's boldness might also be a manifestation of the sense of infallibility that comes of having committed a serious crime and gotten away with it. In either case, his chances of making a misstep were increasing.

Tracey and Charlotte parted company at the foot of the pier. He was headed back to the station to report their latest findings to Detective Gaudette, and she was headed up to the hospital to see if she could find out what had prompted the attempt on Daria's life.

Charlotte sat in a chair at Daria's bedside, watching a nurse arrange the flowers that had been presented by her well-wishers; she had already received visits from John, Felix, and the Saunders. As she waited for the nurse to finish she found herself hungrily eyeing the remains of Daria's lunch, and remembered that she hadn't eaten since the night before. Putting the thought of food out of her mind, she turned her thoughts back to Daria. She and Tom had been asking Daria about her activities over the last two days. The only facts to come to light that might be connected to the attempt on her life—if that's what it was— were one, that she had spent Sunday afternoon wandering the island with John and yesterday lunch picnicking on the rocks with him; two, that she had told several people that she planned to paint the island last night by moonlight; and three, that she had spent yesterday getting the herbals ready for presentation to the botanical society.

The first didn't tell them much—she couldn't remember seeing anything unusual. The second told them only that anyone who wanted to kill her would probably have known she was going out alone in the boat. But the third just might be a clue: the nagging thought still lingered in Charlotte's mind that the murder was somehow connected to the books.

Daria cupped her hands around a cup of tea and shivered. "I just can't seem to get warm," she said, reaching out to pull up the blanket.

"No wonder," said Tom, who was sitting on the edge of her bed. "Taking a moonlit dip in fifty-degree water. What do you think this is, Miami Beach?"

She smiled at him. The brown eyes that had seemed so dull and lifeless on the rocks had regained their golden sparkle.

"Daria," said Charlotte, after the nurse had gone, "I'd like to go over exactly what you did yesterday, step by step."

"Okay," she replied. "I was getting some documents together. The chairman of the board of the botanical society had called to say that someone would be flying up from New York this afternoon to pick up some of the books."

"Which books?"

"The incunabula. The rest of the collection won't be shipped until they have their shelving ready, but they wanted to take possession of the incunabula immediately. They're a bit nervous, on account of the theft."

"So you were assembling documents relating to the incunabula?"

Daria nodded.

"What documents?"

"The bill of sale, the notes for some sort of a catalogue—they looked like they might have been written by MacMillan . . ."

Charlotte nodded. They were the papers she had returned to Daria, the papers that had tipped her off that Thornhill

had stolen the books. She was surprised Daria hadn't noticed
the discrepancy in dates, but she probably hadn't looked at
them that closely.

" . . . binder's reports, auction catalogues, cards from
the card catalogue, that sort of thing," continued Daria.

"Where were you doing this?"

"In the library. The documents were spread out on the
library table, and the books too."

"Did anyone see you?"

"Yes," she said, thinking. "Grace came in twice: once
with a phone message from Chief Tracey, and once to ask
if I wanted some tea. Actually, three times: she also brought
me the tea. I guess she can't get out of the habit. And Fran—
she came in to consult a book about herbs. And John, and
Felix."

"Did you tell anyone what you were doing?"

"No. No one asked. They're used to seeing me working
in there."

"Did you leave the room at all?"

"I had lunch with John out on the East End—where I
saw you. I was gone for maybe an hour and a half. Later
on, I went over to pick up *Der Gart* from the gardener's
cottage—John had been working on it. He was out taking
pictures somewhere. That's when I saw you again; it was
just about four. Just before tea. I drank my tea out on the
terrace. I also read a bit. I was gone for about forty-five
minutes, I'd say. Maybe a little more."

Someone might have seen the documents spread out on
the table and put two and two together, just as Charlotte
had. Especially if, like Felix, they already suspected that
Thornhill had stolen the books. But that still didn't explain
the attempt on Daria's life.

"What then?" asked Charlotte.

"Then I got the books together and put them in the vault."

"What about the documents?"

"I put them in the vault too, with the books. And then
I locked it. I'm not taking any chances when it comes to
these books."

Charlotte sensed that the solution to the riddle was to be found in the library, if it was to be found at all. It was like playing the role of a famous person: you could read all the biographies in the world, but until you walked the ground they had walked on, sat in the rooms they had lived in, and read the books they had read, you really couldn't get a sense of who they were.

"Daria, I'd like to look at the books," she said. "Do you think you could give me the combination? I won't tell a soul."

Daria wrote the number on a slip of paper and handed it to Charlotte, who promised to destroy it the minute she was finished.

An hour later, she was back at the library. As she turned the dial on the combination lock, she felt a little as if she was plundering an Egyptian tomb. This was Thornhill's *sanctum sanctorum*, its contents the treasures for which he had risked his reputation, maybe even his life. They were the earliest examples of a technology that had revolutionized learning, making knowledge accessible for the first time to the common man.

At the click of the final tumbler, she opened the door. The books were stacked in a pile, each in its linen-covered box. They ranged in size from the Gerard, which was as thick and weighty as an old family Bible, to the *Herbarius Latinus*, which was the size of a large paperback. The documents were lying on top of the books in a manila folder. She looked inside. They were all there, just as Daria had said—the bill of sale, the catalogue notes, the binder's reports, and so on. She carefully removed the books and carried them over to the table, where she took a seat in one of the baroque armchairs. She decided to look at *Der Gart* first. Gently, she slipped it out of its box. It was good-sized, measuring about 8 by 11 inches, but surprisingly light. The wooden boards, or covers, were covered with calfskin stamped in a flower pattern and riddled with the tracks of nearly five centuries' worth of bookworms. They were held together by leather straps affixed to a clasp of tooled brass. Unlatching the clasp, she opened the cover. Between the cover and the flyleaf was a sheet of paper giving a description of the book and a translation of the dedication on the first page:

"Now fare forth into all lands, thou noble and beautiful Garden, thou delight of the healthy, thou comfort and life of the sick. There is no man living who can fully declare thy use and thy fruit. I thank thee, O Creator of heaven and earth, Who hast given power to the plants and other created things contained in this book, that Thou hast granted me the grace to reveal this treasure, which until now has lain buried and hid from the sight of common men. To Thee be glory and honor. Now and forever. Amen."

She reread the words, " . . . this treasure, which until now has lain buried and hid from the sight of common men." Even after five centuries, they made her shiver. Turning the page, she drew a sharp breath: she could see why Thornhill had been willing to steal for this book. It bore no more resemblance to a modern book than a magnificent hand-worked tapestry does to a cheap synthetic fabric. The thick rag paper was stiff and creamy. Except for a few water stains, it might almost have been new. Against it, the ornate Gothic lettering was black and shiny. The headings and capitals were hand-lettered in red ink, the delicate curlicue embellishments showing care and love and even a sense of whimsy. But the most remarkable part of the book wasn't the hand-lettering but the woodcuts, which depicted plants and flowers simply outlined in heavy black, like the pictures in a child's coloring book. They were colored in by hand with painstaking delicacy and accuracy. To some, they might have seemed crude, but to her, they had a delightful innocence and charm. They were the first printed illustrations to be drawn directly from nature, John had said, forming the basis for all subsequent botanical illustration. There were woodcuts of parsley, onion, dandelion, violet, chive, scallion, grape, daffodil, squash, hop, rose, lily of the valley, and strawberry. There were even animals: real animals—the rabbit, the stag, and the wolf—and imaginary animals—a horselike creature with horns and tusks, a dragon with webbed feet and breath of fire, and a strange elephantlike creature with a long nose.

The index at the back (even the earliest printers had seen the value of an index, she noticed) was the most time-worn part of the book. The pages were well-thumbed, and the margins were annotated in a minute Gothic script that resembled that of the text. She could make out the words *melancholie*, *complexion*, and *für das Herz*. Also something about Tegernsee, a Bavarian lake-town known for its ancient Benedictine monastery, which she had once visited. She remembered its flower-bedecked houses and the white sails dotting the lake. The notations had probably been made by a monk whom the peasants had sought out for treatment of their ailments—their depression, their acne, their heart problems. The book even seemed to have an ecclesiastical smell, she thought, an observation that she wrote off to her imagination before identifying it as a smell from her youth: the musty odor of the hymnals and prayer books that she used to help carry up from the church basement for the extra worshipers who always showed up on Christmas and Easter.

Midway through the index, the pages opened up on a manila envelope that had been inserted into the book. Opening it, she found a slim manuscript with the title: *The Charles W. MacMillan Collection of Rare Botanical Books—A Short Title Catalogue*. The neatly typed text duplicated the handwritten notes she had found among Thornhill's papers. It was the typed manuscript of Mac-Millan's private catalogue, the manuscript that she had presumed to exist but had been unable to find. Not only did it include the books that MacMillan had supposedly sold to Thornhill, it even included a reproduction of the iris woodcut from *Der Gart*, along with a disquisition on the influence of *Der Gart* on botanical illustration. And it was dated December, 1959, proof positive that Thornhill had stolen the books from the MacMillan estate.

But what was it doing stuck in *Der Gart* like a bookmark? It couldn't have been there when Kevin stole it: Tracey had said that Daria examined the books afterwards. She would have found it and put it with the other documents. Then she realized that "like a bookmark" was exactly it: someone had absentmindedly used the envelope as a bookmark, like the reader of a library book might use Aunt Ethel's postcard from Myrtle Beach. She was returning the manuscript to its envelope when a loose page slipped into her lap. As she picked it up she realized that it wasn't part of the manuscript, but a sheet of letterhead stationery on which was typed a list of seven names. Next to each name was a "yes" or a "no." In some places, the "no" had been crossed out and a "yes" substituted in its place, for a total of five "yeses" and two "noes." The names meant nothing to her, but the letterhead did. "That's it," she said to the stone-faced portrait of John Gerard. The pieces fit together as neatly as the mortised rafters on the roof of the Saunders' barn. She now knew who had murdered Thornhill, and why. All it would take to confirm her theory was a phone call or two.

But, she thought as she sat down at the secretary to make the call, her theory didn't explain who had tried to kill Daria. And then she discovered the answer to that question as well. On the secretary was a "While You Were Out" message pad with a message for Daria from Chief Tracey, dated yesterday. The message, which had been taken by Grace, said: "Chief Tracey wants to change meeting time. Will meet you tomorrow at ten."

·15·

As CHARLOTTE SAT on a driftwood log, watching Stan prepare the lobster bake, her thoughts turned to the Red Paint People, who had held their clambakes on these shores when lobsters were still so plentiful they could be picked up by the dozens off the rocks. Named for the red ochre with which they painted the bodies of their dead, they had disappeared mysteriously around 4000 B.C., replaced by the ancestors of the modern day Penobscot and Passamaquoddy tribes. Each spring, after planting their crops of corn and squash and beans, they had paddled down river in their birch bark canoes to camp on the coast and feast on the plentiful seafood. The grassy slope that led down to the bar at the foot of Broadway had once been one of their campsites. For many years a shell heap had marked the spot, but it had long since disappeared, the crushed shells hauled away to surface local roads. In the old days, Stan had said, one could still see the stone circles that had surrounded their campfires.

The preparations for the clambake had been going on all day. The Saunders were going the traditional route. Not for Stan the fifty-gallon oil drum, the aluminum trash can, or the sealed barbecue grill. This would be an authentic bake, right down to the stones used for cracking open the lobster claws. The time-honored method had begun with the gathering of round stones worn as smooth as softballs by the waves. Next came the driftwood fire, which had been built on a bed of round stones on the rocky shore at the foot of the Ledges. Once the fire had burned down, it had been covered with damp rockweed. Then had come the food: first the clams and lobsters, which provided moisture for the steam, then the hard-boiled eggs, the foil-wrapped vegetables, and the corn on the cob. Wes and Virgie had donated the clams and lobsters, carrying bushel after bushel over from Wes's lobster boat, the *Virgie G.*, which was docked at the Ledge House landing. The bake would now be covered by another layer of rockweed, sealed with an old sailcloth, and allowed to steam.

Charlotte surveyed the scene. The cast was nearly complete. Wes and Virgie were supervising Kevin and the Gilley girls, who were collecting more rockweed from the shore. Felix had just appeared at the foot of the Ledges. He looked like a Disney elephant-ballerina as he tiptoed across the rocks in fear of scuffing his shoes. Grace was right behind him, Felix appearing to have taken the place in her fantasies that had been previously occupied by Thornhill. Chuck and Marion were still descending the Ledges, Chuck carrying a large cooler. Behind them came Fran and John, who were loaded down with other supplies destined for the tables on the landing.

The only members of the cast who were still missing were Tom and Tracey, but they were both in sight. Tom was approaching in the Saunders' runabout with Daria, who sat in the stern with her leg outstretched. Her cast made it impossible for her to negotiate the Ledges, so Tom had driven her over in the boat. Tracey was approaching in the police launch with Detective Gaudette and another police officer. All three would be armed. She hadn't been an actress all these years without developing some talent for staging a performance. And she wanted Tracey and his colleagues waiting in the wings for the final scene. There was even music: the sound of the community band tuning up drifted clearly across the channel on the light offshore breeze.

"Looks like the weather's going to hold," said Stan to no one in particular as he pitched another forkful of rockweed onto the bake.

Rain had threatened all day, but it had held off, the threat of cancellation only adding to the anticipation.

"We've got the best seats in the house," Stan continued, nodding at the crowd of early birds who had already set up their folding chairs and blankets in the park overlooking the town pier.

Charlotte smiled wanly. They had good seats for the show all right, but it wasn't the one they were expecting. The show they were about to get was apt to be a lot more explosive than the fireworks.

The new arrivals headed directly for the drink table, which, with Kitty as barmaid, was doing a brisk business. Chuck was reminiscing with Kitty about past clambakes, their conversation punctuated by his braying laughter. Grace, already in her cups, was making sheep's eyes at Felix, who looked as if he couldn't decide whether to be annoyed or flattered. And Wes, who had given up supervising the kids, was lovingly tending the spigot of the keg of beer that he had tapped for the occasion. For that matter, thought Charlotte, she could use a little snort herself. She got up to fetch herself a drink.

An hour and a half later, the bake was nearly gone. Stuffed with seafood, the group sat on logs around the fire that Stan had rekindled. Here and there, the last stubborn morsels of lobster flesh were being sucked out of a leg or picked out of a claw. To one side was a shell heap that, if it failed to rival the Red Paint People's, was nonetheless a respectable accumulation for one evening's feasting. Tracey and the two other policemen had put away their fair share. Their presence had aroused no suspicion: it was assumed they would be leaving shortly to deal with the fireworks crowds. In addition to Gaudette, looking resplendent in his State police uniform, Tracey was accompanied by one of his own men, a dim-witted young man named Rodgers, with glasses that kept slipping down his nose and a severe overbite that gave him a rodentlike appearance. No wonder Tracey had been so eager for Charlotte's assistance.

"Can I get you a drink?" asked Tom, who had risen to replenish his glass.

"Thank you," she answered. "Gin and tonic, with lots of ice."

Sweet Tom, she thought. He knew what she was going through. It was called stage fright, that paralyzing fear of failure that turns the legs to Jell-O and makes the voice a feeble croak. Ever since she'd first set foot on the boards, at the tender age of eight, she'd struggled to conquer her fear. Her case was a mild one: she'd never been completely paralyzed like some—some of the best. Oddly enough, it was the better actors who were the most susceptible to stage fright, because it was they who were the most likely to open up every nerve to the demands of the part. Nor was a good performance necessarily a cure. On the contrary, it sometimes made it worse. It was one of the mysteries of the stage that only rarely was a performance infused with the kind of electrifying power that turned it into an experience that audiences would talk about for years to come. But such a performance was a gift from God: if you strove for it, it eluded you. Like water in the Zen proverb, the harder you tried to grasp it, the more quickly it flowed through your fingers.

Tom brought her her drink, and she took a long swallow. He'd been coached to be her prompter, but it turned out to be Stan who delivered her cue. After whistling to get everyone's attention, he stood up to address the group: "One week ago today," he said, "we were shocked to learn that our good friend Frank Thornhill died as a result of poisoning. We are all aware that the police, with the assistance of our guest, Charlotte Graham," he said, nodding at Charlotte, "have been conducting an investigation into the murder. But few, if any, of us have been informed as to the progress of their findings. I wonder if we could take advantage of your presence here, Chief, by asking you to fill us in on what's happening. I think you can understand that this matter has been a source of great anxiety to us all."

Charlotte recognized the speech as a mild reproof. The

Saunders were put out at her failure to confide in them.
She hadn't done so partly because she didn't feel right
about revealing the details of a police investigation, but also
because she hadn't had much to tell them—until now.

Stan's speech cast a pall over the gathering, reminding
them of events they had been trying to put out of their
minds.

By arrangement, Tracey, who had been sucking on a lobster leg, deferred the question to her. "I'd rather leave the
explaining up to Miss Graham—she's the one who figured
it all out," he said.

Rubbing her moist palms against her thighs, Charlotte
put down her drink and stood up, whereupon her audience
stopped eating and rearranged their positions, as if settling
in after the rise of the curtain.

"Let me start by saying that we know the identity of Dr.
Thornhill's killer," she said bluntly.

It was a startling opening line. The audience stared,
dumbstruck.

"From the beginning," she continued, turning to slowly
pace the long, flat slab of granite at one side of the fire,
like a professor delivering a lecture, "we thought that the
death of Dr. Thornhill was related to the theft of the books.
But we were wrong, as you know."

The eyes of the audience turned to Kevin, who was playing with the Gilley girls some distance away.

It was better that the kids wouldn't be around for what was
coming up, thought Charlotte. "But we weren't as wrong as
we thought," she said, stopping to look out at the group.
"The murder of Dr. Thornhill *was* related to a book theft,
a book theft that took place in a mansion in Worcester,
Massachusetts, more than twenty years ago. And the thief
was Dr. Thornhill himself."

"Frank?" said Fran, bewildered.

"You mean that Frank *stole* some of the books in his
collection?" asked Stan incredulously.

"Yes. Dr. Thornhill was the rival of another botanical
book collector named Charles W. MacMillan. MacMillan

was the owner of a rare German herbal called *Der Gart*, which Dr. Thornhill wanted for his collection. In fact, it had once been the subject of an auction room battle between the two of them. *Der Gart* and four other early herbals were the prizes of MacMillan's collection; today, they are the prizes of Dr. Thornhill's collection."

"How did Frank get them?" asked Stan.

"In December, 1959, MacMillan died after a long illness. Having no heirs, he bequeathed his collection to the New York Botanical Society, of which he was a trustee. The Board of Trustees of the society, not being familiar with the contents of the collection, asked one of their members— a well-known collector of botanical books—to inventory the collection and oversee its transfer to the society's library."

"Frank Thornhill," said Stan.

Charlotte nodded. Her audience was spellbound, but some looked faintly puzzled, as if they were wondering what all this had to do with the murder. Comfortable now in her role, she picked up the pace.

"Dr. Thornhill probably didn't have theft in mind when he came across *Der Gart* in MacMillan's library," she continued. "But once the thought had occurred to him, there was no putting it out of his mind. If he stole the book, who would know? And if someone did find out the book was missing, who would dare accuse him, an eminent botanist and a trustee of the society? Once he had decided to steal *Der Gart*, it was only a small step to stealing the others."

From across the channel came the rousing notes of "Yankee Doodle Dandy." The band concert was in full swing.

"Charlotte dear, I should think someone would have found out. Wouldn't MacMillan have kept some sort of record showing that he owned the books?" asked Kitty, who was standing behind Stan, her hands on his shoulders.

"Yes, he did. But Dr. Thornhill covered himself by drawing up a false bill of sale on MacMillan's stationery and forging MacMillan's signature to it. Then he took all evidence of MacMillan's ownership, including the handwritten notes for a private catalogue of his collection that MacMillan had been about to publish at the time of his death, and the typed manuscript of the catalogue."

"May I ask how you arrived at this conclusion?" asked Felix, who was puffing on a postprandial cigar, Grace at his side.

"We have you to thank for the first clue, Mr. Mayer— your account of the rivalry between Dr. Thornhill and MacMillan. Later I came upon the phony bill of sale among Dr. Thornhill's papers. It would never have aroused my suspicion, however, had I not also come across the notes for MacMillan's catalogue. The notes, you see, contained references to *Der Gart* and the other books that MacMillan had supposedly sold to Dr. Thornhill six months before."

"Let me see if I've got this straight," said Stan. "What you mean is that the books were still a part of the MacMillan collection at the time of MacMillan's death, that he had never sold them to Frank."

"Exactly," responded Charlotte.

"Thornhill backdated the phony bill of sale to six months prior to MacMillan's death," explained Tom, who was sitting with his arm around Daria. "We don't know why he didn't destroy the notes. He probably didn't anticipate that anyone would ever be looking through his papers."

"But Charlotte dear, how does all this relate to the murder of poor Frank?" asked Kitty.

"I'm getting to that." She stopped pacing, and resumed her seat.

The sky overhead had cleared, but the light of the sun, which was setting behind the low-lying clouds, had turned it a sickly shade of yellow. The little group was cast into shadow by the hillside.

"We discovered that Dr. Thornhill had stolen the books quite by accident," Charlotte continued. "What if someone else had made the same discovery? The person who knew that Dr. Thornhill had stolen the books would hold his reputation in the palm of his—or her—hand."

"Blackmail," said Stan, one step ahead of the narrative.

"Exactly," she said. "What would drive someone to blackmail Dr. Thornhill? To our surprise, we discovered that practically everyone at Ledge House on the afternoon of the murder wanted something from Dr. Thornhill, something that he might be forced to yield in exchange for keeping his secret."

Charlotte gazed out at her audience. She could feel their nervous anticipation, a mixture of curiosity, fear, and suspense.

"We'll start with Fran," said Charlotte, turning to Thornhill's niece, who was sitting to Charlotte's left.

Fran looked up, startled. She had been fiddling with the delicate skeleton of a sea urchin that she had picked up off the rocks. It cracked under the sudden pressure of her fingers, and she dropped it to the ground.

"Fran's motive was jealousy. Dr. Thornhill had announced his plans to remarry. Fran thought his new wife would make her life so unpleasant that she would be forced to leave. The knowledge that her uncle had stolen the books could have come in very handy in persuading him to change his mind."

Fran made no comment.

The band concert had ended with "It's a Grand Old Flag." It was followed by the priest's declamation of the Declaration of Independence. The words floated across the channel in the still evening air: "We hold these truths to be self-evident, that all men are created equal, that they are endowed by their Creator with certain inalienable Rights . . ."

Next Charlotte turned to Wes and Chuck, who sat next to Fran, large cups of beer in their hands.

"Wes and Chuck were the most obvious suspects," she continued. "Their motive was monetary gain, and they both needed the money, badly. With Wes, it was a chronic condition, but with Chuck, it was something new: he needed the money to keep up with the horse-racing crowd he'd become involved with."

Chuck shot Marion, who was sitting on the other side

of the fire, a dirty look, but she didn't notice. She stared blankly at Charlotte, as if girding herself for a shock.

"Since Marion was the heir to Dr. Thornhill's property, they stood to benefit not only from blackmailing Dr. Thornhill but also from his death. Adding to their motive was the fact that Dr. Thornhill had recently threatened to change his will, leaving his property to the State instead of to Marion."

"I didn't do nothin'. It was Chuck who was goin' to inherit the property, not me," Wes said angrily, pointing at the ground for emphasis.

"Oh yes, you did do something," replied Charlotte. "For years you've harbored a grudge against Dr. Thornhill. He cheated you out of some land, or so you thought. Now he was thwarting your get-rich-quick scheme. The development controversy provided the perfect opportunity for you to take your revenge. It was you who let the air out of the jeep's tires, who put a bullet through the library window, who wrote the poison-pen letters."

"Now you wait just a jeezly friggin' minute," Wes said threateningly, jumping up. "You can't prove I done them things."

"Yes I can. Stan saw you at the Ledge House barn the night the air was let out of the jeep's tires."

Wes looked over at Stan, who nodded. Then, sitting back down on his log, he took a long, insolent swig from his cup of beer.

"I also saw your son holding a drawing in red crayon on a brown paper bag," she continued. "The same red crayon and brown paper bag that were used for the poison-pen letters. I think you're subject to arrest on charges of vandalism at the very least. What do you think, Chief?"

"I'd say so," Tracey concurred.

Wes drained his cup, and crumpled it. Giving his wife a sheepish smile, he said: "I mighta done somethin' like that when I was a little oiled up, but I ain't never killed nobody."

Charlotte turned next to John, who was sitting by himself some distance away on a log near the landing. He was looking stylishly casual in white duck pants and a navy boatneck sweater.

"John's motive was also gain," she continued. "He was uncertain about being granted tenure at his university. But with one of the world's most prominent economic botanists on his side, his future would be assured."

John looked up skeptically. He had been tracing figure eights on the ground with a piece of driftwood.

"Even Daria had something to gain from Dr. Thornhill," Charlotte went on, continuing around the circle. "With a little pressure, Thornhill might have been induced to give her all his bookbinding business, to say nothing of that of his book-collecting cronies."

As Charlotte spoke Tom gave Daria a reassuring hug.

She turned next to Grace. "For Grace, as for Fran, the motive was jealousy. She didn't want to see Dr. Thornhill get married either. She had the illusion—I think we may safely call it that—that he was in love with her, and that he would some day marry her."

The audience looked over at Grace—some, like Stan, with amused smiles—but Grace was too busy flirting with Felix to notice.

"Finally," Charlotte continued, "there was Felix, who had known for years that Dr. Thornhill had stolen the books."

Felix looked up in alarm; it was the first time Charlotte had seen him lose his composure.

"What could he do with such knowledge? Well, first he could use it for his private amusement: needling Dr. Thornhill with references to the stolen books was one of his favorite pastimes. But no matter how pointed his barbs, they failed to draw blood. Because Dr. Thornhill had long ago convinced himself he was the legitimate owner of the books. He was a perfect example of the book thief Felix described, the book thief who believes he has a *right* to a stolen book." She paused. "But there was also another way Felix could put this knowledge to use. Dr. Thornhill had promised Felix that he would be the one to handle the sale of his collection after his death—if he died first, that is. What better way of guaranteeing Thornhill's promise than by threatening to expose him? For a man who scours the obituary columns of two continents for sources of consignment material, this was merely shrewd business practice."

The last light of day was withdrawing over the hills of Bridge Harbor, turning them a dusky purple. On Main Street, the storefront lights had been turned on, backlighting the audience that had assembled in the park. In the harbor, the boats were turning on their green and red running lights.

Charlotte rested a long leg on a rock. "Seven people. All present at the time of the murder. All with a motive for blackmail. The next question was, why would a blackmailer kill Dr. Thornhill? The answer was obvious, in retrospect. Not only did the blackmail scheme fail, it backfired."

From across the channel came the whoosh of a rocket being launched, followed by the staccato boom-boom-boom of a triple bomb that left spots dancing in front of their eyes. The explosions punctuated Charlotte's speech as neatly as if they had been written into the script.

Charlotte looked over at Tracey and his two assistants. They were on the alert; the final act was coming.

"What do you mean, backfired?" asked Stan.

Charlotte continued, pacing back and forth: "The blackmailer had threatened Dr. Thornhill with ruin, but what he hadn't foreseen was that Dr. Thornhill could ruin him."

"Thornhill refused to be blackmailed," explained Tom. "He thought his reputation was unimpeachable. But he wasn't taking any chances."

Charlotte suddenly spun around. "No books published, no grant money, no tenure. Isn't that true, John? Once Dr. Thornhill was finished with you, your career would be over."

The group stared at John. He sat quietly with his head down, scratching a rock with his stick.

"You thought you had Dr. Thornhill over a barrel: he sees to it that you're granted tenure in exchange for your keeping his little secret. But what you didn't count on was the bill of sale. It was forged, yes, but who would take your word against the word of one of the most distinguished men in his field? Dr. Thornhill wasn't about to take any chances, however. He set out to discredit you, to ensure that no one would ever pay attention to your story. It wasn't easy: you were capable, respected. He had to exert the full force of his professional reputation. He sat on the editorial boards of the academic journals, he sat on the grant review committees, he sat on the tenure review committees. He had enormous power, and he was determined to use it. At first, you didn't think he would carry through," she continued, as she resumed pacing. In that, he had miscalculated badly, she thought, remembering Felix's account of how Thornhill had outbid MacMillan for the nurseryman's catalogue. She continued: "But then you started getting indications that he was in earnest. A book that had been accepted for publication was inexplicably rejected; a grant application that you fully expected to be accepted was suddenly turned down; and your tenure appointment, which had been in question before, was now definitely out. Tom, you see, did a little research on your career."

John gave Tom a seething look.

"You began to realize that it was just a matter of time before your career was in ruins. Once you had slipped, there was no place for you to go but down; too many others were coming along to take your place. Instead of a faculty appointment at a prestigious university, you would have nothing to look forward to but an adjunct professorship at a community college, *if* you were lucky."

In the end, she thought, he had turned out to be a petty little villain, like the villains he so admired in the movies. He had killed simply to keep his job: she might almost have thought more of him had he killed out of some twisted political idealism. She turned to pace in the other direction. Night had fallen, and the faces of the audience shined in the light of the fire.

"The idea of using monkshood came from Dr. Thornhill's

book, which must have appealed to your sense of irony. It was the ideal means: not only was the risk of detection small, it was even more so in Dr. Thornhill's case because the symptoms would be mistaken for heart disease. Fran made it easy for you by digging up the roots; it was just a matter of picking them up off the ground."

"I was going to divide the roots so the plants would flower better," Fran explained defensively.

"Yes, but you knew you'd been irresponsible in leaving the poisonous roots exposed. Which led to your second mistake—withholding information from the authorities. Fortunately we didn't come to any false conclusions."

Charlotte turned back to John. "The problem was that the books were vague about dosages. How much crushed root would be required to kill an adult man within a short period of time? Being a scientist, you decided to conduct a little experiment—your subject was Jesse."

The audience stared at him, open-mouthed, except for Wes, who jumped up and looked for a minute as if he might take a swing at him.

"The experiment was a success. You forced Jesse to ingest the poison, probably with a syringe, and Jesse died shortly afterward." She continued: "To find the right dose for Dr. Thornhill, you simply extrapolated according to body weight. From that point on, it was just a matter of waiting for the right moment. Knowing that Dr. Thornhill was in the habit of taking his tea at four, you made a practice of hanging around Ledge House at that time. The right moment was provided by Grace. When you heard her coming upstairs after the doorbell rang, you figured that she might have left the tea steeping." She remembered how he'd glanced at his watch. "The front door presented a bit of a problem: you weren't sure if anyone was waiting there or not, but if someone had been there, you would simply have tried again another time. Another possible glitch arose when Chuck came bursting out of the library, but he was already out the front door when you reached the landing. By the time you reached the foot of the stairs, you knew your moment had arrived. The tea was sitting on the sideboard, steeping. No one was around. The poisoning itself took only a second—pop off the cap of the 35mm film container in which you kept the crushed root at the ready, and empty it into the teapot."

John had stopped playing with the stick and was sitting motionless, his head hanging. Throughout Charlotte's narrative, his eyes had shifted from side to side like those of an outnumbered fighter who's sizing up his adversaries. At one point, he had looked up at the Ledges, as if planning an escape route.

"No one around, that is, except Wes," she continued. "He didn't see you adding the poison to the teapot, but he did see you coming *through* the parlor. Why would you have been in the parlor at all if you had gone directly down the stairs and out the front door as you claimed, unless it was to poison the tea?"

She paused to stare at John, but he didn't look up.

"That was it, you thought. The teapot would be washed up, and the evidence along with it. How fitting that the deed had been carried out on Dr. Thornhill's sixtieth birthday, the same day the ancient Greeks administered a poisoned cup to those who had outlived their usefulness. The notion fit in nicely with your ideological convictions: not only was Dr. Thornhill a social burden, a parasite on the energy and creativity of the young, a dinosaur who had quit writing, quit thinking, quit innovating—to use your own words— he was also, in your opinion, a wealthy political conservative whose collecting had deprived the academic world of valuable works on early botany."

"He thought he was doing the world a favor," said Tom.

"Exactly. But, John, you must have had a harder time justifying the next murder attempt," she continued. "The attempt to kill Daria. When you thought Daria had found you out, you went after her too. By tampering with the boat engine."

The audience's attention shifted to Daria, who looked very shocked, and in the glow of the firelight, very beautiful.

And then it happened.

In an instant, John was gone. Taking advantage of the lapse in their attention, he had bolted for the landing. Before anyone realized what was happening, he had jumped into the Saunders' runabout, started the engine, and taken off. Avoiding the boats that had gathered in the harbor to view the fireworks, he headed straight down the channel toward the open bay.

The curtain had dropped much sooner than they expected.

·16·

THEY SAT FOR a second in stunned silence. Then, as a green rocket exploded, Tracey, Gaudette, and Rodgers sprinted toward the police launch. Tracey was the first to reach it. He jumped in and turned the key, but the engine wouldn't kick over. As the little group listened to the futile grinding, John raced toward the darkness of the open bay. On the fourth try, the engine finally started, and they were off under a blaze of rockets.

As the police launch took off Wes raced to the *Virgie G.*, gesturing for Charlotte and Tom to follow. He was probably trying to redeem himself in the eyes of the law, Charlotte thought. The boat must not have been as ramshackle as it looked, for it had won the lobster-boat race again that afternoon. Though slow in getting underway—they had to turn around first—they quickly closed the gap. The old boat shuddered with the effort of its speed.

"Don't worry. We'll catch up," Wes said reassuringly, leaning over to spit a stream of tobacco juice over the side. "This baby's fast." The engine, he explained proudly, had been custom-built from an old Oldsmobile engine.

The light of a bright rocket revealed that the police launch was closing in on John. "Looks as if Tracey will catch up with him all right," said Tom, leaning to the side to look out over the prow.

"He don't stand a chance," replied Wes, who stood at the helm with his teeth bared in a gleeful smile. "With that little thirty-five horsepower engine? Howard'll catch up to him in nothin' flat."

MURDER AT TEATIME

  209

Tom sat back down next to Charlotte, atop the wash rail that did double duty as a worktable for lobster pots. "There's still something I don't understand," he said, raising his voice above the noise of the engine.

"What?" asked Charlotte. She pulled up the collar of her jacket against the rush of the cold night air.

"Why did John want to kill Daria?"

"It had to do with the manuscript for the private catalogue of the MacMillan collection. Felix had said that MacMillan was about to send the manuscript to the printer's when he died. But when we looked through Thornhill's papers, we found the notes, but no manuscript."

"I remember."

"Well, I more or less forgot about the manuscript, but it turned out that it did exist and that John had it all along."

"He used it to blackmail Thornhill?"

"Yes. I don't know how John found out Thornhill had stolen the books. Maybe he heard the gossip, or maybe he noticed the discrepancy in dates, just as we did. In any case, once he started poking around among the papers in Thornhill's library, he found the manuscript."

Tom nodded.

"He realized he could use it to force Thornhill to pull strings on his behalf," she continued, "and he confronted him with it. He also presented Thornhill with a list of the names of the seven people on his tenure review committee, three of whom were subject to his influence."

The sky erupted into a giant pink chrysanthemum that seconds later spawned a bouquet of little chrysanthemums. The display prompted a chorus of *oohs* and *aahs* from the spectators lining the waterfront. By its bright light, they could see that the police launch was still gaining on John.

"The attempt failed, and John returned to his room with the manuscript and the list of names, which he stuck in an envelope. The envelope must have sat there for weeks, until he absent-mindedly picked it up while he was working on *Der Gart* Monday morning and stuck it between the pages as a bookmark."

Tom nodded. "I do that sort of thing all the time—use an old bill or a letter to mark my place."

"That's where I found it. I must have still been thinking along the lines of blackmail, because when I came across the list of names on university stationery, I was reminded that John, too, wanted something from Thornhill. Then it was just a matter of calling to confirm that the names were those of the tenure review committee members. The rest fell into place: it became obvious that the blackmail attempt had backfired, and that the reason John's career had taken a nose dive was that Thornhill was out to ruin him."

"But what about the attempt to kill Daria?"

"Okay. That sequence of events began when the botanical society called to tell Daria that they'd be sending someone up on Tuesday to pick up the books. Daria goes to John's room to fetch *Der Gart* in order to have it ready. Tracey told us that he was using it for his work, remember?"

Tom nodded.

"It was *Der Gart* she was carrying when you spoke with her Monday afternoon. She probably meant to tell John she'd taken it, but forgot."

"I think I'm beginning to see."

"John comes into the library while Daria's drinking her tea out on the veranda. He sees the book and wonders why she's taken it, not knowing that she's getting the books ready for the botanical society. Then he notices the envelope containing the manuscript and the list of names stuck in the book, forgetting that he was the one who put it there."

"He thinks she's assembling a case against him?"

"Yes. He wonders why she's taken this stuff from his room. And then he sees the other papers—the catalogue notes, the bill of sale, the binder's report—a whole sheaf of papers that, when examined closely, prove incontrovertibly that Thornhill stole the books."

"He must have freaked out. He thought he was the only one who knew Thornhill stole the books."

Charlotte nodded. "To him, it looked as if Daria had

figured the whole thing out: how Thornhill had stolen the books, how he had tried to blackmail Thornhill, and how, when that failed, he had murdered him. And to top it off, he thought she was about to go to the police."

"Why'd he think that?"

"One of those odd coincidences. Daria was due to go over the official report on the book theft on Tuesday with Tracey. He just wanted to make sure all the details were accurate. He called to change the time of their appointment, while she was out at lunch with John, and Grace took the message."

"And John sees the message: 'Chief Tracey called and wants to change meeting time.' "

"You've got it."

"So he figures he'll kill her before she has a chance to air her suspicions—or the suspicions he thought she had—to Tracey."

"Yes. He knew she was planning to go out on the water to sketch that night. He also knew that the tidal current was treacherous, and that it would be at its most treacherous at about the time she was ready to head in. It was a risk, but he thought he had to act quickly."

"Whew," said Tom. "What a creep."

"One other thing."

"What's that?"

"Revenge. He was in love with Daria, and he thought she was in love with him. Until she met up with you, that is."

Their conversation was interrupted by a shout from Wes. Suddenly they realized that the boom of the rocket explosions was interspersed with a lighter, pinging sound—the sound of gunfire. Moving up beside Wes, they looked out over the prow. By the light of a large orange rocket, they could see Gaudette crouched in the bow of the police launch with his revolver drawn. The launch was closing in on John, who was steering the boat in a zigzag path to avoid Gaudette's fire. But when the rocket faded out, so did their ability to see. For a moment, they raced toward their quarry in darkness and in silence.

Charlotte thought of the crowd waiting in silence for the thrill of the next rocket when a much more exciting display was transpiring in the darkness right in front of them.

Suddenly Wes let out a whoop. "They've got him," he said.

Charlotte marveled at the acuity of Wes's vision, the product of years of peering into the pre-dawn darkness. Then a pinwheel display burst into a hot, white light that revealed Tracey struggling with John on the deck of the Saunders' boat. Gaudette was covering Tracey from the police launch, which had pulled up alongside with Rodgers at the wheel. On the pier, a fountain display erupted into flame, raining colored fire. At the same time, they heard the boom-swish, boom-swish of rockets being launched one after another for the grand finale. Then the sky burst into a blaze of color.

"He's got him," said Wes, easing up on the throttle.

The noise of the finale was deafening, like the explosion of mortar fire. The explosions left spots dancing before their eyes and the acrid smell of gunpowder in their nostrils.

Tracey was holding John by the elbow—his hands were secured behind his back by handcuffs. He pushed him into the police launch toward Gaudette, who sat him down in the stern with a gun pointing at his chest. Then Rodgers moved over to the Saunders' boat to drive it back.

"I guess the show is over," said Charlotte as a red, white, and blue portrait of Uncle Sam transformed itself into an American flag and then burned itself out, casting the water into darkness.

Wes turned the boat around and headed back to the Ledge House landing.

"*Acta est fabula*," said Tom with a grin.

"He confessed everything," said Tracey as he sat at the Saunders' kitchen table two days later. "I guess he figured his career was over no matter what."

So much for Fran's prognostication that his tenure would come through, thought Charlotte.

"He says he wants to continue his research in jail. That's where he is now—he was released yesterday from the hospital."

"Was he badly injured?" asked Kitty.

"Nope. Gaudette just winged him. Enough to make sure he couldn't fight back when I boarded the boat. Didn't stop him though—he managed to whale into me nonetheless—sent me tail over bandbox. If he hadn't lost his balance, I would have been in a heck of a pickle."

Tracey had come to fetch Charlotte. The tide was up, and he had promised to take her across the channel in the police launch. But he was being kind enough to do it her way. She wanted to leave the island the same way she had arrived: via the Ledges. Stan had loaded her bag into the police launch at the Saunders' wharf nearly an hour ago. Then Tracey had driven around to the Ledge House landing, climbed the Ledges, and met her at the Saunders'. They would go back down the Ledges together.

Charlotte excused herself to answer the telephone. She was expecting a call from her agent. A few minutes later, she hung up the phone and entered the kitchen. She pulled a handkerchief out of her pocket, and waved it at the group sitting at the table. "My wish came true."

Tracey looked baffled.

"Fran Thornhill gave us handkerchiefs on Midsummer Night with a drop of sap from a dogwood tree on them," explained Kitty. "She said that if you carried the handkerchief around with you, your wish would come true."

"What was your wish?" asked Tracey.

"A wonderful script," said Charlotte. "A movie—one I've been wanting to do for a long time. That was my agent telling me I had the part."

Kitty and Tracey congratulated her.

Fitzgerald had been wrong when he said American careers have no second acts, she thought. Her career had had a second act, and a third . . . Probably she would go on until she dropped.

She would be flying back to New York with Felix, whom

she would be meeting later at the airport. He had left earlier in the day to see a client about handling the sale of his collection—maybe a big commission would be coming his way after all. He hadn't seemed terribly worried about his financial predicament. "God watches over the bibliophile," he had said. Tom would be staying on with Daria until she was finished with the transfer of the Thornhill collection to the botanical society. He was busy collecting material for a new book, on the Thornhill murder. She doubted anything would come of their relationship: they were both too independent to settle down. But it was bound to be a pleasant affair. Maybe that's the way she should have done it, she thought. But she doubted the studio would have approved. Better to keep on getting married than to have—God forbid—a scandal. The studio encouraged romances between the stars—it made for sizzle in the love scenes and simoleons at the box office—but it wanted the romances kept legal.

"Ready?" asked Tracey, interrupting her thoughts.

"Chief Tracey was just telling me about the chase," said Kitty. She turned to him. "I bet you'll go down in Bridge Harbor history for that."

Tracey looked down at the floor, embarrassed. In fact, however handsome Detective Gaudette might have looked in his State police uniform, it was Tracey, in his Red Sox baseball cap and navy blue windbreaker, who was the hero of the hour. His capture of the fugitive murderer was the talk of the town.

"I'll tell you, I was some anxious when that engine wouldn't start. It always gets notional when you need it the most."

He rose to leave. They said goodbye to the Saunders, who insisted that Charlotte come back soon. Tracey too invited her back, and she reciprocated by inviting him to the Big Apple. He was grateful, he said, but he'd only been outside of Maine twice, and had regretted it both times.

"I'll look out for your old movies on television, or maybe I'll see you in the movie theatre in this big new role," he said.

As they walked down the Gilley Road their conversation turned back to the case. "Did you know the town voted last night on the tax abatement proposal for the Chartwell Corporation?" he asked.

She'd forgotten. "How did it turn out?"

"They turned it down. But the Board of Selectmen is asking Chartwell to submit a new plan for a scaled-down development."

"But didn't the Chartwell people say they wouldn't go for a smaller development—that it was all or nothing?"

"That's what they said. But the selectmen did some checking around. They think Chartwell's bluffing, and they probably are."

"Will the town approve a scaled-down development?"

"I think there's a pretty good chance of it."

So, she mused, the big corporation thought that they could put one over on the country hayseeds, but the hayseeds had seen through their scheme. The wisdom of the people had triumphed: they would be voting to preserve the past, but they would be voting for the future too.

"I expect Marion will go along with it, despite her father," Tracey continued. "She's left Chuck, you know."

Charlotte looked at him in surprise.

"Ayuh. She went down to Boston right after the Fourth. The wife and I have volunteered to take care of the boy for the rest of the summer while she gets settled in an apartment. We're glad to have him. He's not such a bad sort."

"I suppose it's for the best."

"She's never been very happy with Chuck."

The catalyst was probably the suspicion that Chuck was to blame for her father's death, thought Charlotte. She'd probably realized then how little she really cared for him. Charlotte imagined her in a new apartment, playing her piano until the sparkle came back to her eyes.

"What will happen to Fran?"

"She's already talking with a realtor about buying an old farm with her inheritance. It belongs to one of the people who've been growing herbs for her, so she won't have to start out from scratch again with her herb business."

So the Thornhill murder had a happy ending for Fran as well. Maybe Kitty wasn't so far off base with her rose-tinted glasses after all.

Emerging at the rear of Ledge House, she was struck anew by the stunning beauty of the view. The day was crisp, with a clear, high sky and a bold sun. The outer islands glittered like emeralds. Everything looked neat and clean, as if Mother Nature had donned her finest in celebration of the solution of the murder. Charlotte felt in a celebratory mood as well: she was delighted that she would be working again—she was addicted to the feeling of accomplishment that comes at the end of a good day's work—but she had discovered that acting wasn't the only route to that sweet feeling: helping to restore order to this minute world of pure perfection had its satisfactions, too.

At the top of the Ledges they stopped to rest in the rustic gazebo overlooking the channel. As they sat down in one of the weathered cedar chairs Charlotte noticed the line from *Paradise Lost* that was carved on the lintel: "A happy, rural seat of various views," and thought with pleasure of the world-weary tourists who would replenish their spirits here. Maine's environmentalists criticized outsiders for taking from the State more than they gave. But what they failed to realize was that the currency of Maine life would only retain its value if it were circulated by people with new blood and new ideas. Like the gulls that fed on both herring and shish kebab, the people of Maine would have to adapt if they were to survive.

Thornhill had sensed this. However much his vision had been corrupted by his cupidity and his arrogance, he had built the Ledges in the spirit of working hand in hand with nature for the benefit of mankind. The environmentalists' backward-looking notion of nature as a temple inviolate was contradictory to the progressive ideal in which he'd built his beautiful garden. The stone-paved terraces to which he had devoted thirty years of toil—each stone hewn from the native pink granite and set carefully into place—were a monument to excellence, to the values that this man who had loved mayflowers had tried and failed to uphold. She was sure that Marion would see to it that this was the spirit in which the development would be built.

She thought of Kitty and Stan. Despite the fact that they had fought the development, she expected that a scaled-down development would suit them just fine. They would still have their minute world of pure perfection, but they would no longer be marooned on it like house sparrows on a boat at sea. It would lose something of its mystery: there would no longer be that sense of Gilleys hurtling down the centuries. But what it lost in mystery, it would gain in comfort. Their island would become a suburb—no more waiting for the tide to turn to drive into town. They would have other couples to play bridge with. Stan would even have his own golf course. Fran had seen it in the coals: "Stay in your present house," she had said. "It will bring you good luck."

Under her arm, she carried Daria's painting of the Ledges, the painting that Stan had showed her in his studio. Daria had given it to her as a momento. For Daria it was an unpleasant reminder of her near-fatal night on the channel, but for Charlotte it was a reminder of the values expressed by the Ledges. She could see the masons already at work on the stone monument to Thornhill on a terrace below. That he had built the Ledges was expiation enough in her mind for his sins. And now their beauty would no longer be "buried and hid from the sight of common men," to use the words from *Der Gart*, but freely available to enrich and ennoble the lives of those who experienced it.

"Miss Graham?" said Tracey.

"Charlotte," she said, correcting him for the twelfth time.

"I just wanted to thank you on behalf of the town of Bridge Harbor for your help. We never could have solved this case without you."

Aw shucks, it was nothing, thought Charlotte, picturing herself shuffling her feet in embarrassment. That was how Tracey made her feel, only with him the humble country boy bit was for real. She settled for a polite "You're welcome" and thanked him for requesting her assistance.

"There's one favor I'd like to ask, Miss Graham—Charlotte," he said.

"What's that?"

Pulling a small notebook out of his breast pocket, he tore off a sheet of lined paper and passed it over to her, his mild blue eyes dancing under the visor of his Red Sox cap. "May I please have your autograph, ma'am?"

"Aw shucks," said Charlotte with a wide smile, signing the paper in her large, bold scrawl.